The Tempest

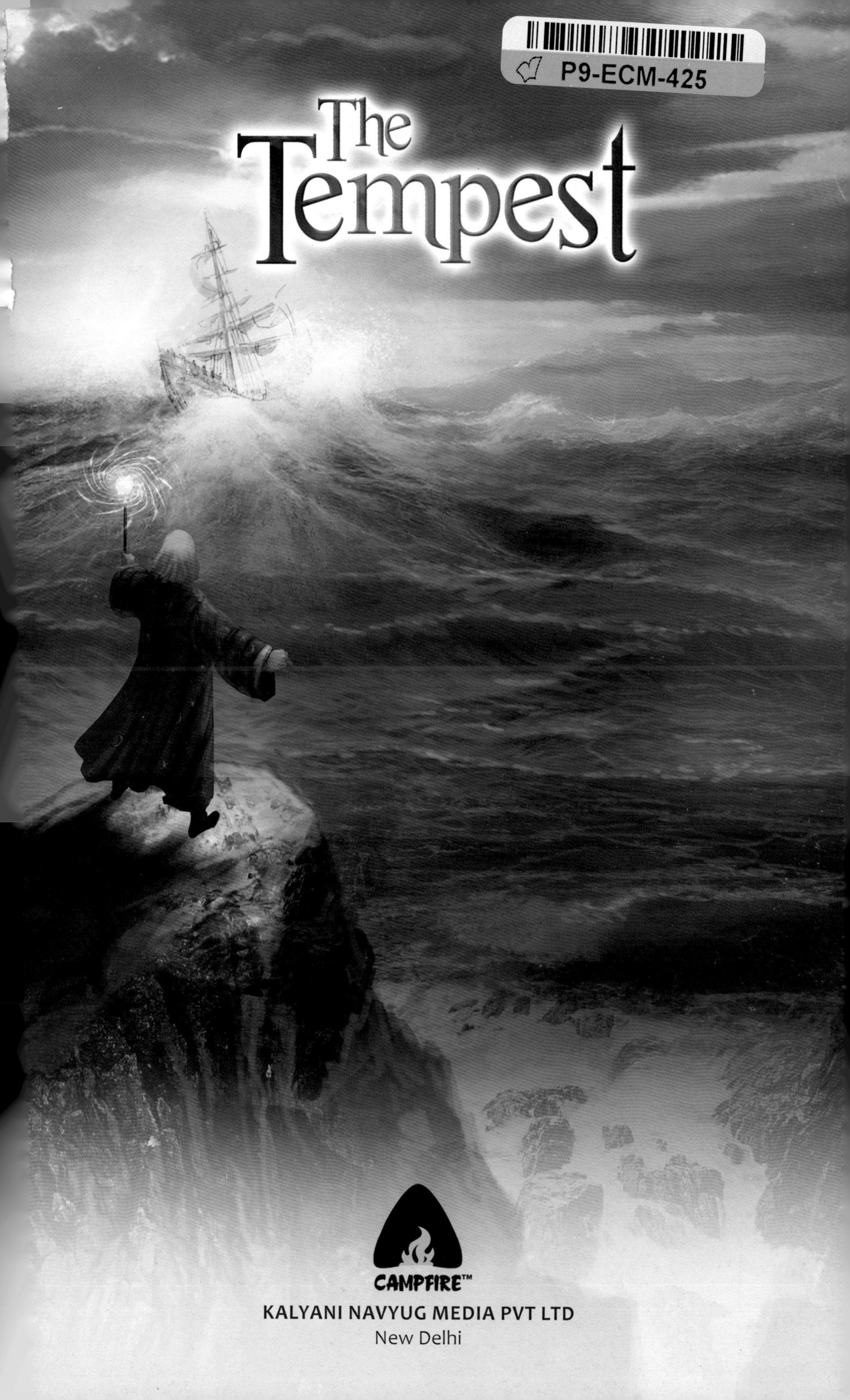

CAMPFIRE™
KALYANI NAVYUG MEDIA PVT LTD
New Delhi

The Tempest

Sitting around the Campfire, telling the story, were:

WORDSMITH **MAX POPOV**
ILLUSTRATORS **MANIKANDAN & AMIT TAYAL**
COLORIST **VINOD S. PILLAI**
LETTERER **BHAVNATH CHOUDHARY**
EDITOR **ADITI RAY**
PRODUCTION CONTROLLER **VISHAL SHARMA**

COVER ART
ILLUSTRATION **AMIT TAYAL**
COLOR & DESIGN **JAYAKRISHNAN K. P.**

CAMPFIRE™

www.campfire.co.in

Published by Kalyani Navyug Media Pvt. Ltd.
101 C, Shiv House, Hari Nagar Ashram, New Delhi 110014
India
ISBN: 978-81-907515-3-7
Copyright © 2012 Kalyani Navyug Media Pvt. Ltd.
Printed in India at Galaxy Offset

About the Author

Famously known as 'The Bard of Avon', William Shakespeare was born in Stratford-upon-Avon, most probably on April 23, 1564. We say probably because till date, nobody has conclusive evidence for Shakespeare's date of birth.

His father, John Shakespeare, was a successful local businessman and his mother, Mary Arden, was the daughter of a wealthy landowner. In 1582, an eighteen-year-old William married an older woman named Anne Hathaway. Soon, they had their first daughter, Susanna and later, two other children. William's only son, Hamnet, died at the tender age of eleven.

Translated into innumerable languages across the globe, Shakespeare's plays and sonnets are undoubtedly the most studied writings in the English language. A playwright of rare genius, he excelled in tragedies, comedies, and histories. Skillfully combining entertainment with unmatched poetry, some of his most famous plays are *Othello*, *Macbeth*, *A Midsummer Night's Dream*, *Romeo and Juliet*, and *The Merchant of Venice*, among many others.

Shakespeare was also an actor. In 1599, he became one of the partners in the new Globe Theatre in London and a part owner of his own theater company called The Chamberlain's Men—a group of remarkable actors who were also business partners and close friends of Shakespeare. When Queen Elizabeth died in 1603 and was succeeded by her cousin King James of Scotland, The Chamberlain's Men was renamed The King's Men.

Shakespeare died in 1616. The characters he created and the stories he told have held the interest of people for the past 400 years! Till date, his plays are performed all over the world and have been turned into movies, comics, cartoons, operas, and musicals.

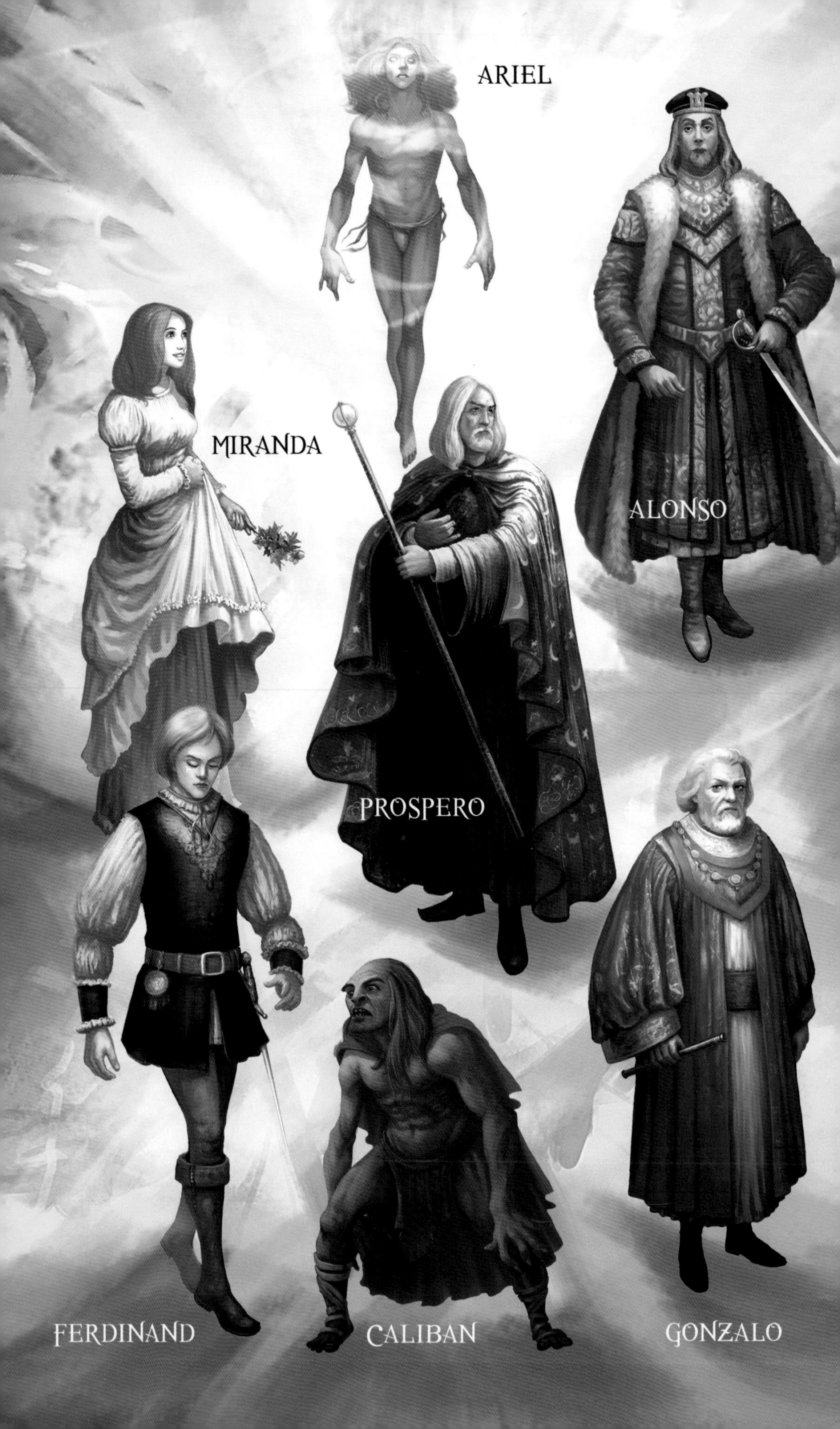
ARIEL
MIRANDA
ALONSO
PROSPERO
FERDINAND
CALIBAN
GONZALO

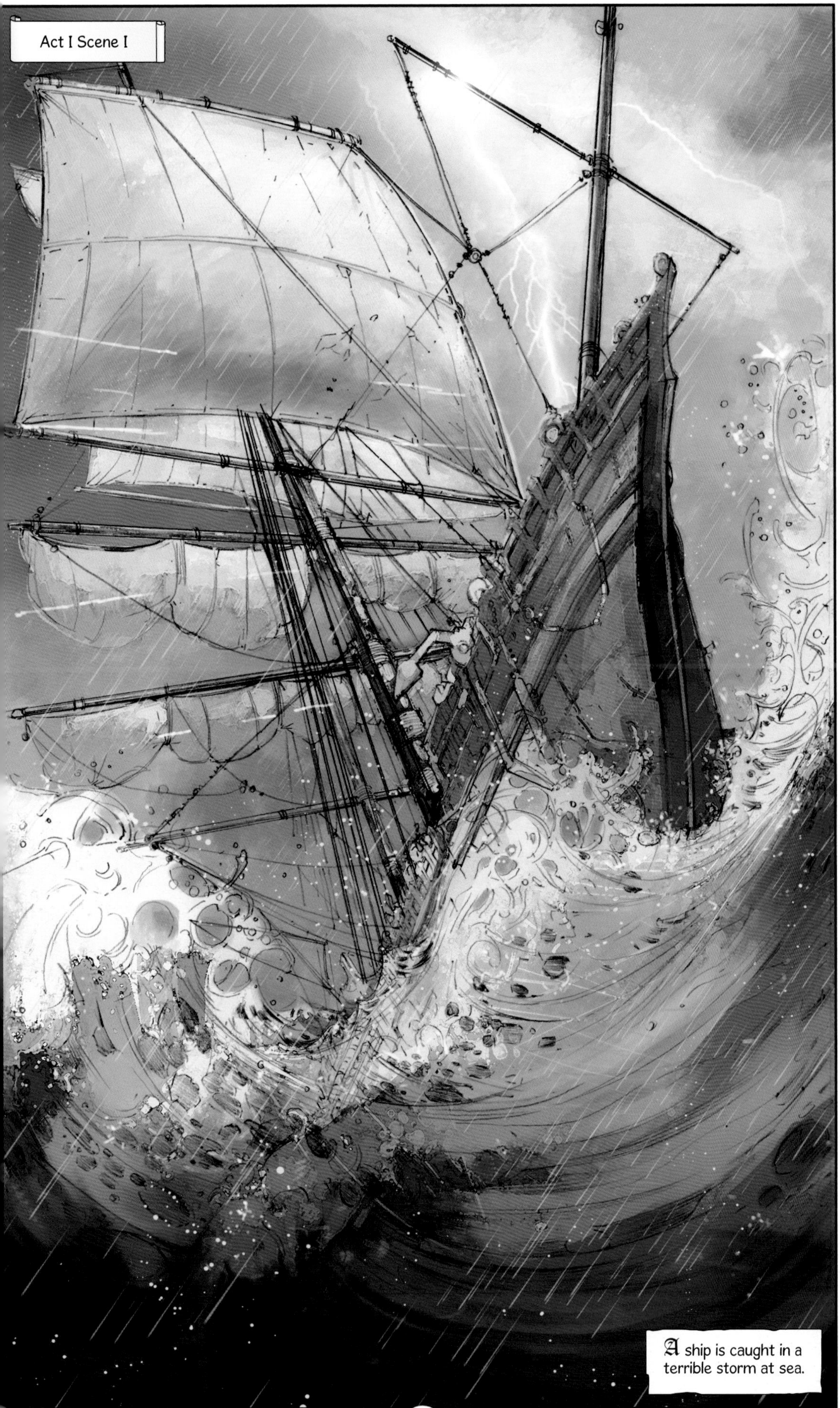
Act I Scene I
A ship is caught in a terrible storm at sea.

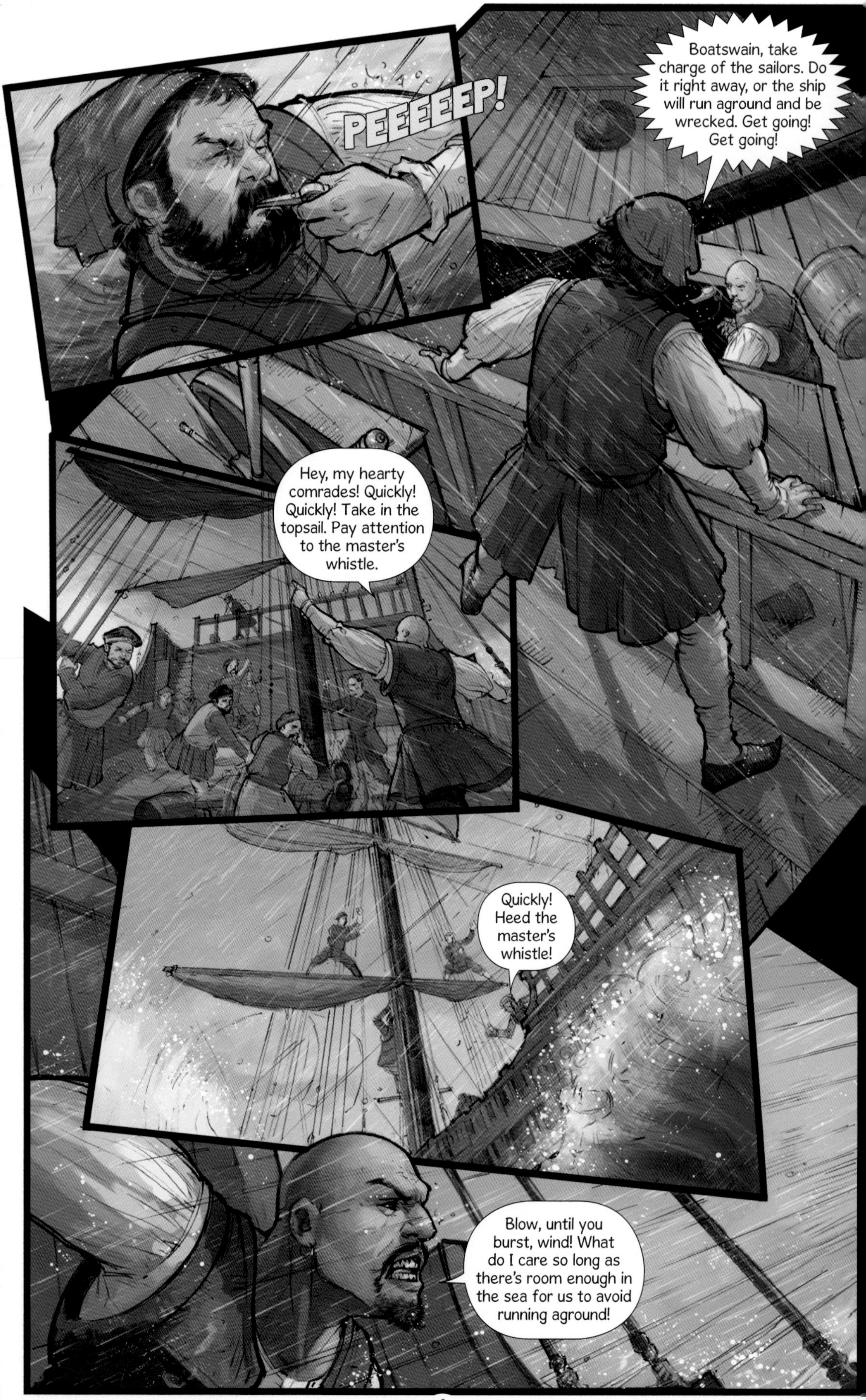
PEEEEEP!
Boatswain, take charge of the sailors. Do it right away, or the ship will run aground and be wrecked. Get going! Get going!
Hey, my hearty comrades! Quickly! Quickly! Take in the topsail. Pay attention to the master's whistle.
Quickly! Heed the master's whistle!
Blow, until you burst, wind! What do I care so long as there's room enough in the sea for us to avoid running aground!

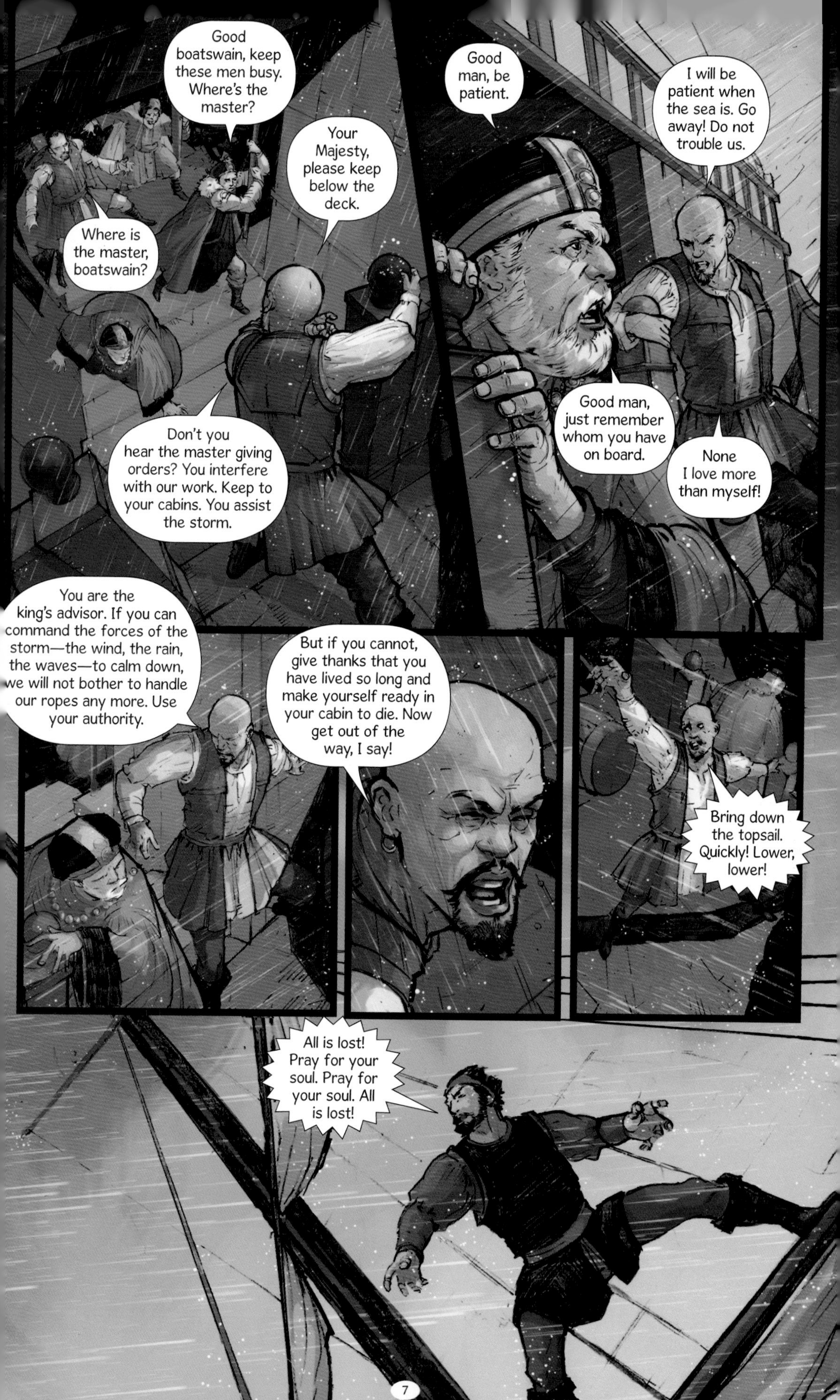
Good boatswain, keep these men busy. Where's the master?
Where is the master, boatswain?
Your Majesty, please keep below the deck.
Don't you hear the master giving orders? You interfere with our work. Keep to your cabins. You assist the storm.
Good man, be patient.
I will be patient when the sea is. Go away! Do not trouble us.
Good man, just remember whom you have on board.
None I love more than myself!
You are the king's advisor. If you can command the forces of the storm—the wind, the rain, the waves—to calm down, we will not bother to handle our ropes any more. Use your authority.
But if you cannot, give thanks that you have lived so long and make yourself ready in your cabin to die. Now get out of the way, I say!
Bring down the topsail. Quickly! Lower, lower!
All is lost! Pray for your soul. Pray for your soul. All is lost!

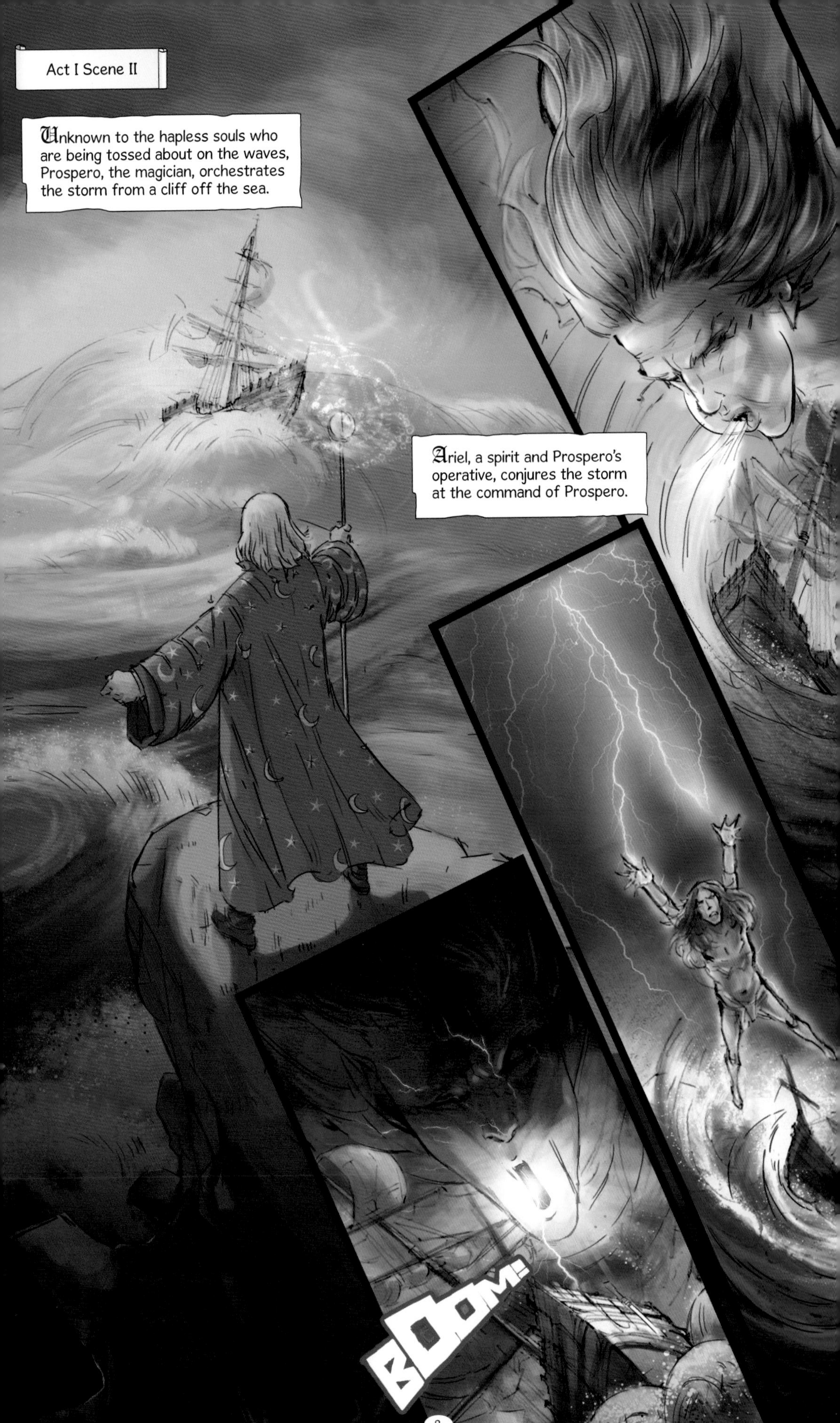
Act I Scene II
Unknown to the hapless souls who are being tossed about on the waves, Prospero, the magician, orchestrates the storm from a cliff off the sea.
Ariel, a spirit and Prospero's operative, conjures the storm at the command of Prospero.
BOOM!

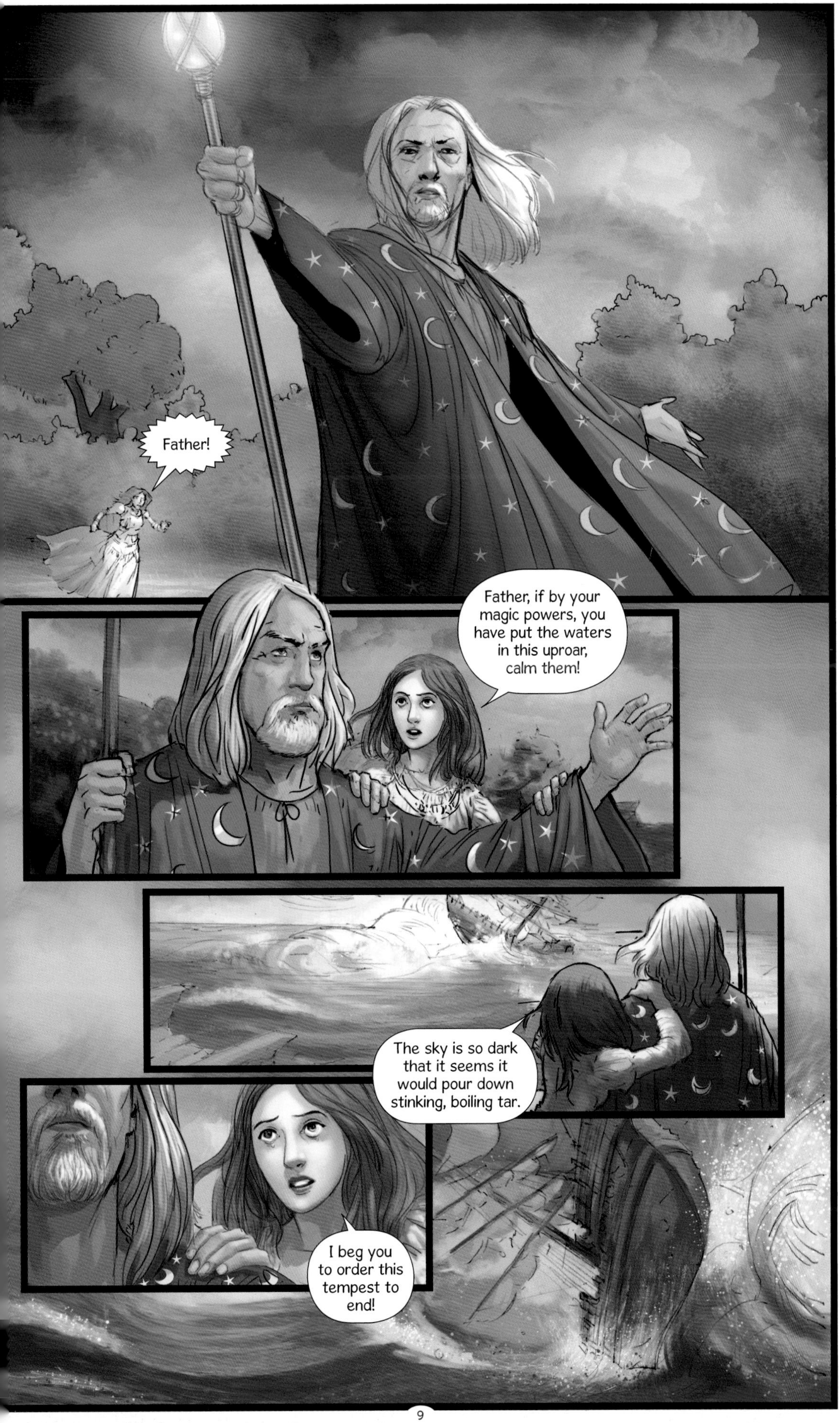
Father!
Father, if by your magic powers, you have put the waters in this uproar, calm them!
The sky is so dark that it seems it would pour down stinking, boiling tar.
I beg you to order this tempest to end!

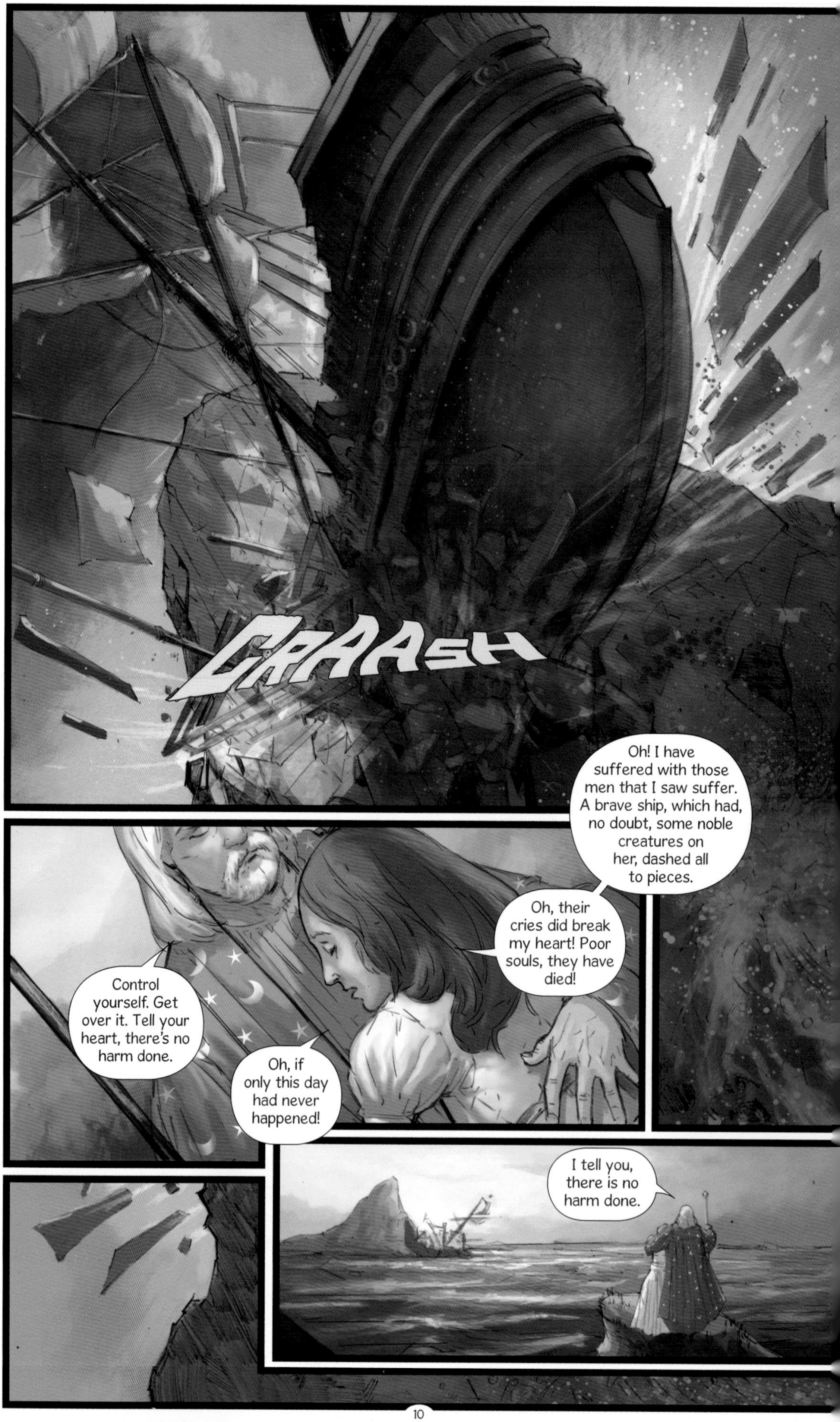
CRAASH
Oh! I have suffered with those men that I saw suffer. A brave ship, which had, no doubt, some noble creatures on her, dashed all to pieces.
Oh, their cries did break my heart! Poor souls, they have died!
Control yourself. Get over it. Tell your heart, there's no harm done.
Oh, if only this day had never happened!
I tell you, there is no harm done.

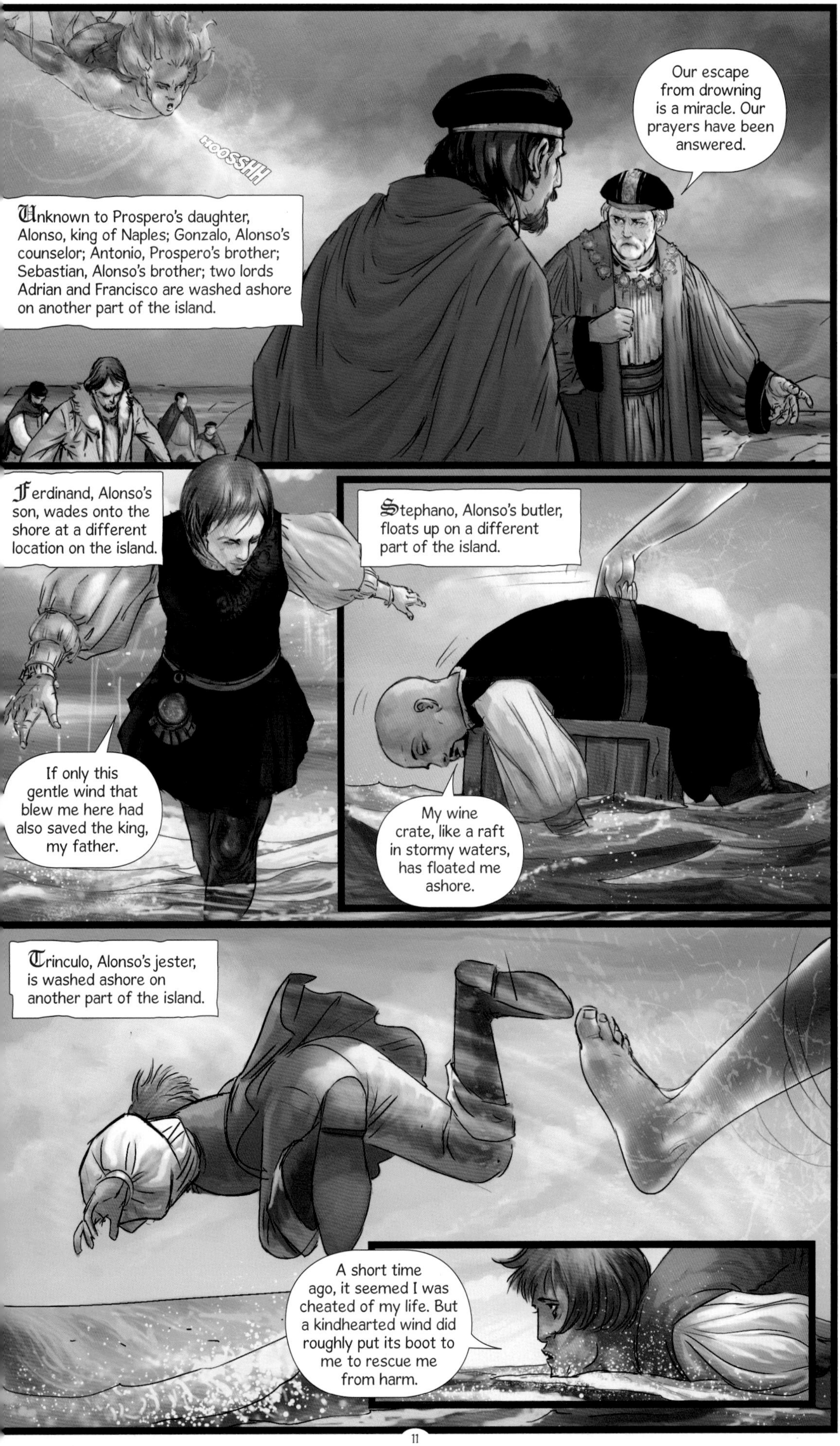
Unknown to Prospero's daughter, Alonso, king of Naples; Gonzalo, Alonso's counselor; Antonio, Prospero's brother; Sebastian, Alonso's brother; two lords Adrian and Francisco are washed ashore on another part of the island.
Our escape from drowning is a miracle. Our prayers have been answered.
Ferdinand, Alonso's son, wades onto the shore at a different location on the island.
If only this gentle wind that blew me here had also saved the king, my father.
Stephano, Alonso's butler, floats up on a different part of the island.
My wine crate, like a raft in stormy waters, has floated me ashore.
Trinculo, Alonso's jester, is washed ashore on another part of the island.
A short time ago, it seemed I was cheated of my life. But a kindhearted wind did roughly put its boot to me to rescue me from harm.

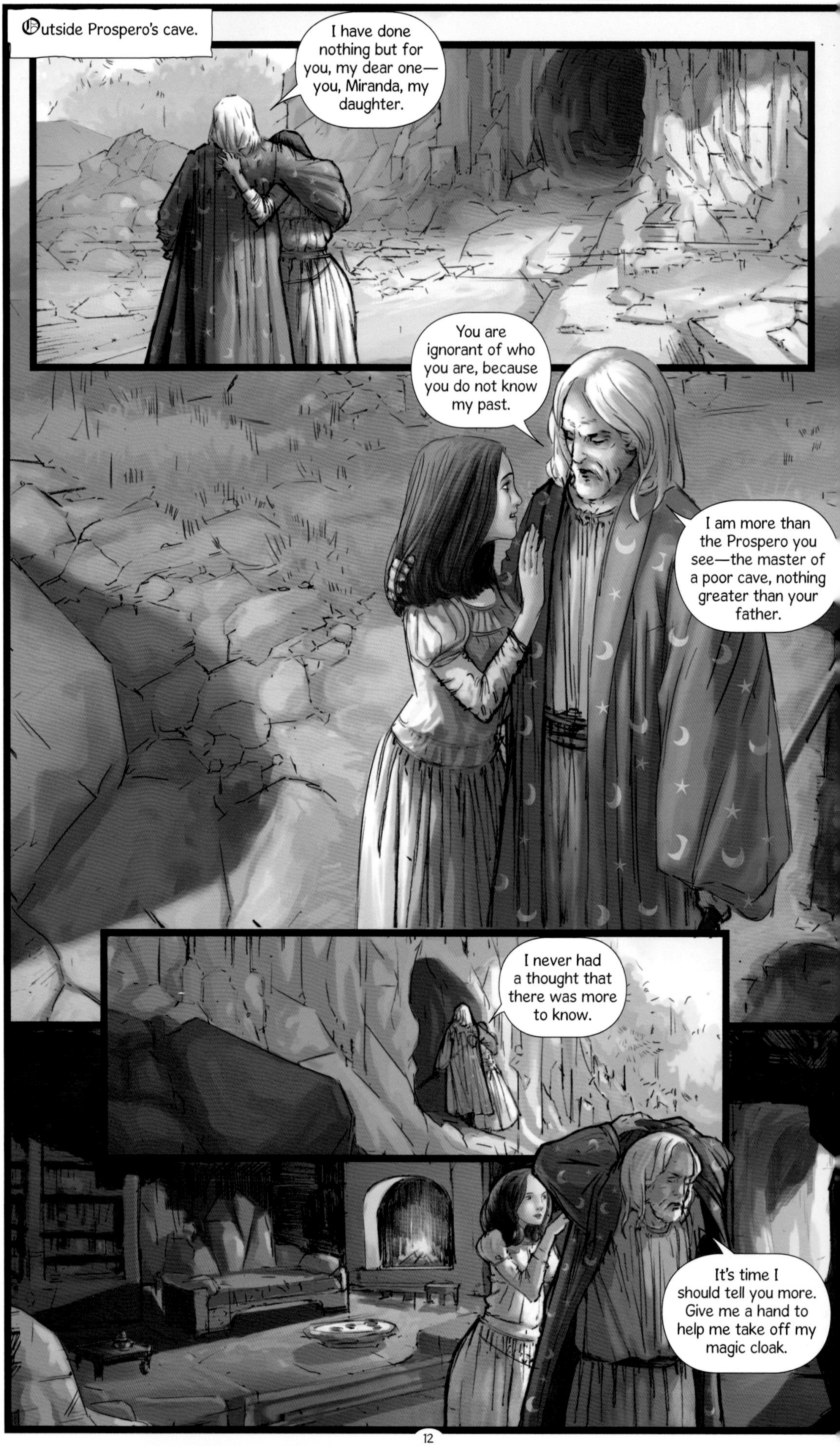
Outside Prospero's cave.
I have done nothing but for you, my dear one—you, Miranda, my daughter.
You are ignorant of who you are, because you do not know my past.
I am more than the Prospero you see—the master of a poor cave, nothing greater than your father.
I never had a thought that there was more to know.
It's time I should tell you more. Give me a hand to help me take off my magic cloak.

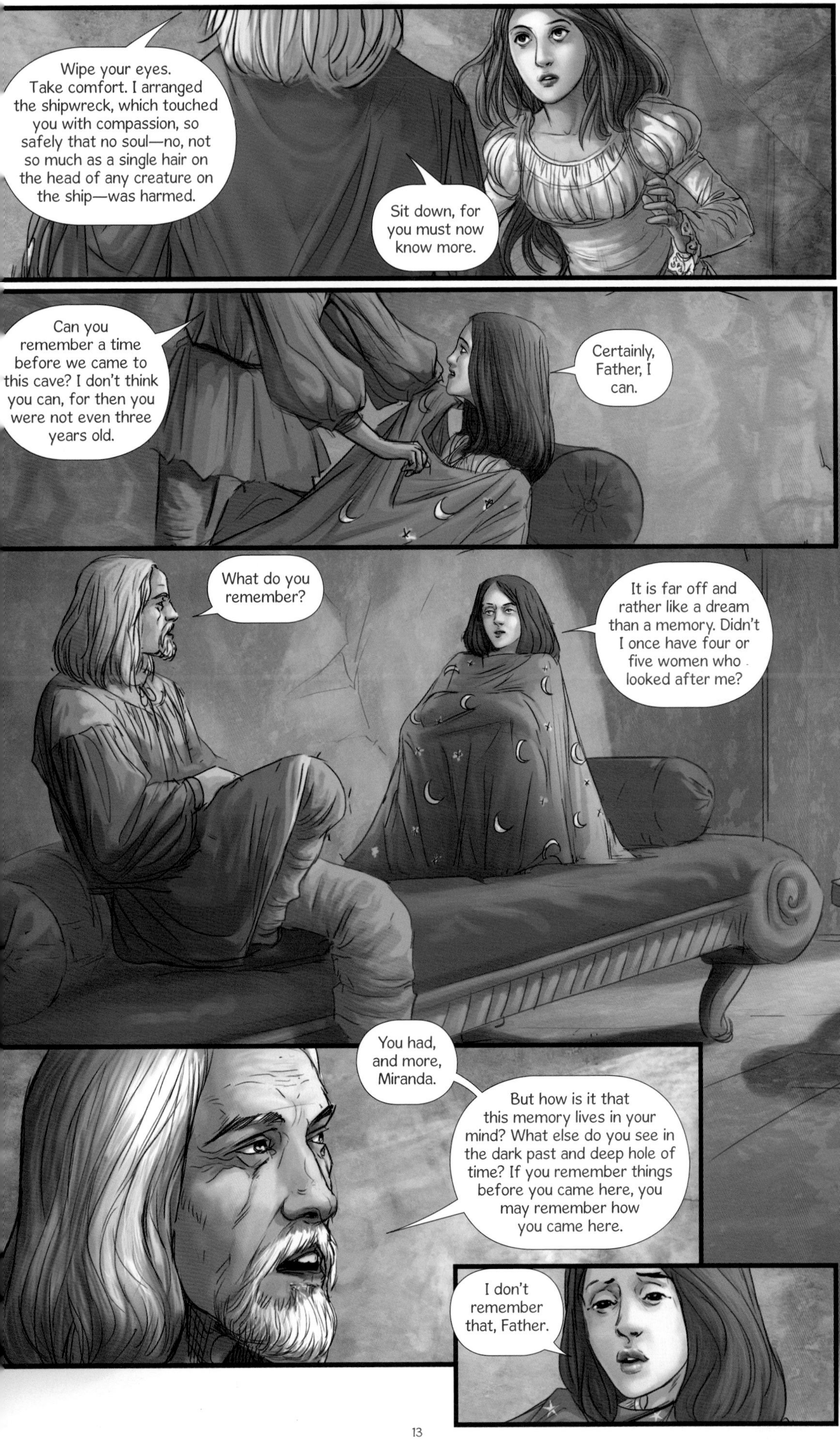
Wipe your eyes. Take comfort. I arranged the shipwreck, which touched you with compassion, so safely that no soul—no, not so much as a single hair on the head of any creature on the ship—was harmed.
Sit down, for you must now know more.
Can you remember a time before we came to this cave? I don't think you can, for then you were not even three years old.
Certainly, Father, I can.
What do you remember?
It is far off and rather like a dream than a memory. Didn't I once have four or five women who looked after me?
You had, and more, Miranda.
But how is it that this memory lives in your mind? What else do you see in the dark past and deep hole of time? If you remember things before you came here, you may remember how you came here.
I don't remember that, Father.

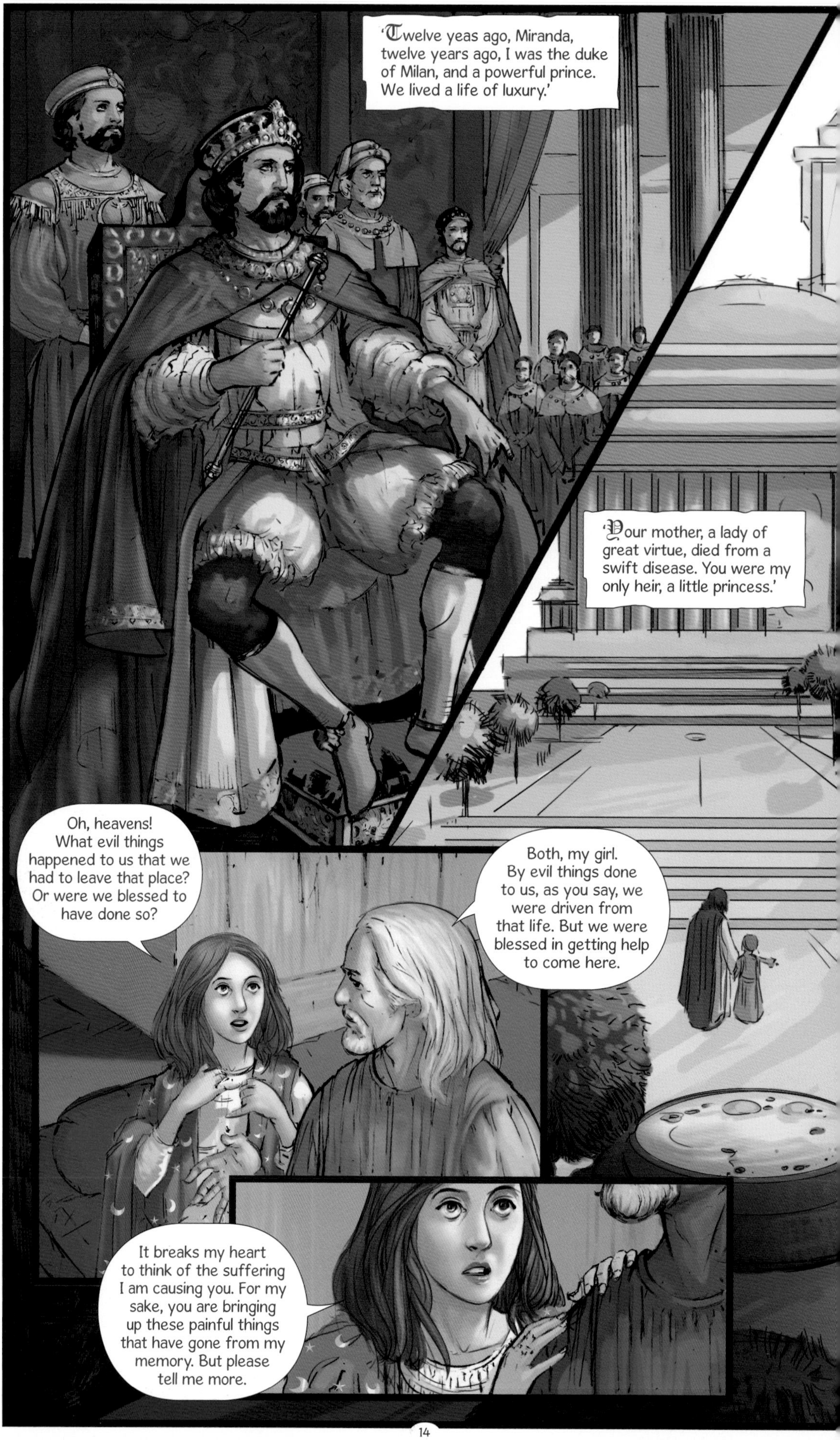
'Twelve yeas ago, Miranda, twelve years ago, I was the duke of Milan, and a powerful prince. We lived a life of luxury.'
'Your mother, a lady of great virtue, died from a swift disease. You were my only heir, a little princess.'
Oh, heavens! What evil things happened to us that we had to leave that place? Or were we blessed to have done so?
Both, my girl. By evil things done to us, as you say, we were driven from that life. But we were blessed in getting help to come here.
It breaks my heart to think of the suffering I am causing you. For my sake, you are bringing up these painful things that have gone from my memory. But please tell me more.

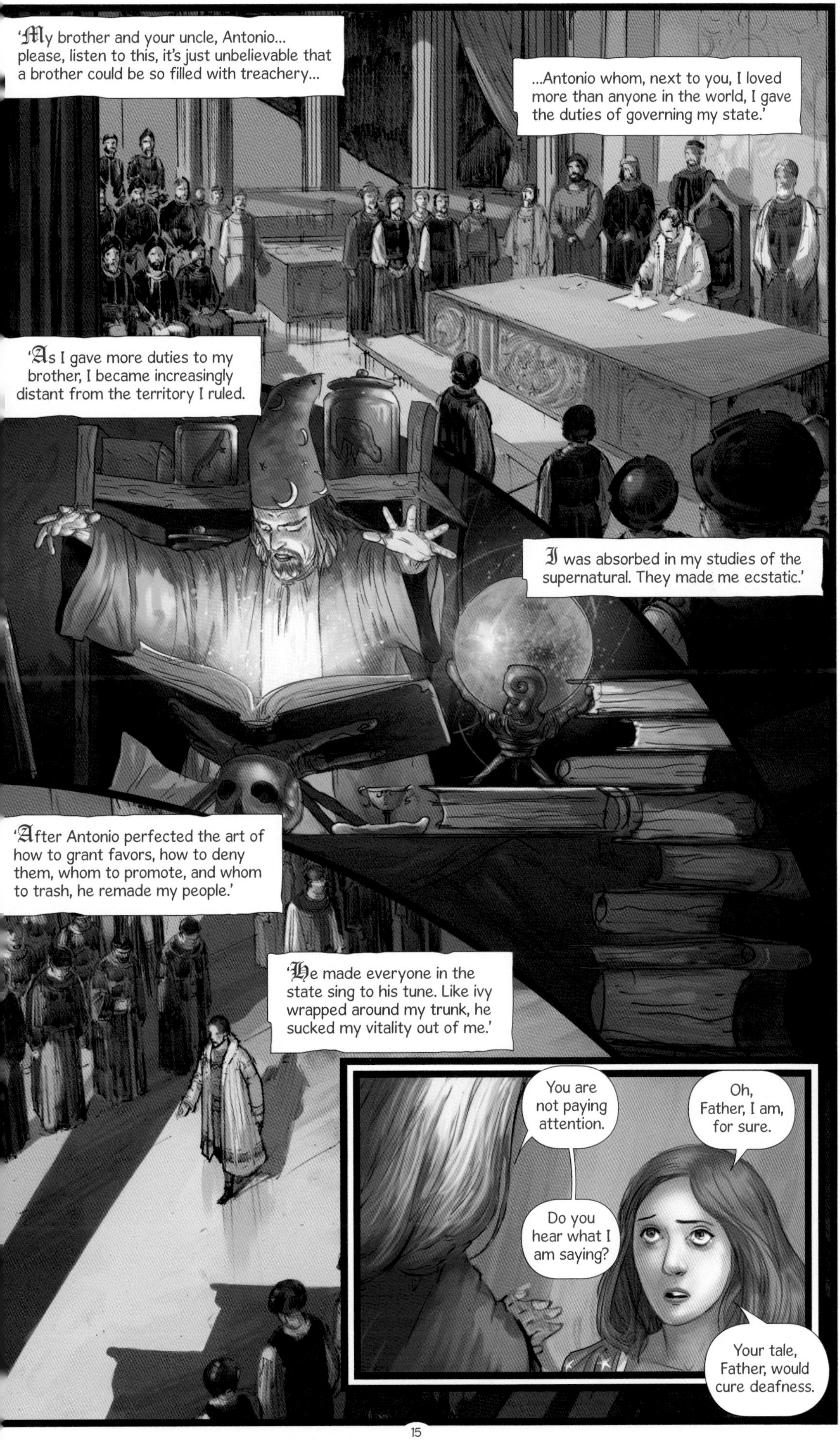
'My brother and your uncle, Antonio... please, listen to this, it's just unbelievable that a brother could be so filled with treachery...
...Antonio whom, next to you, I loved more than anyone in the world, I gave the duties of governing my state.'
'As I gave more duties to my brother, I became increasingly distant from the territory I ruled.
I was absorbed in my studies of the supernatural. They made me ecstatic.'
'After Antonio perfected the art of how to grant favors, how to deny them, whom to promote, and whom to trash, he remade my people.'
'He made everyone in the state sing to his tune. Like ivy wrapped around my trunk, he sucked my vitality out of me.'
You are not paying attention.
Do you hear what I am saying?
Oh, Father, I am, for sure.
Your tale, Father, would cure deafness.

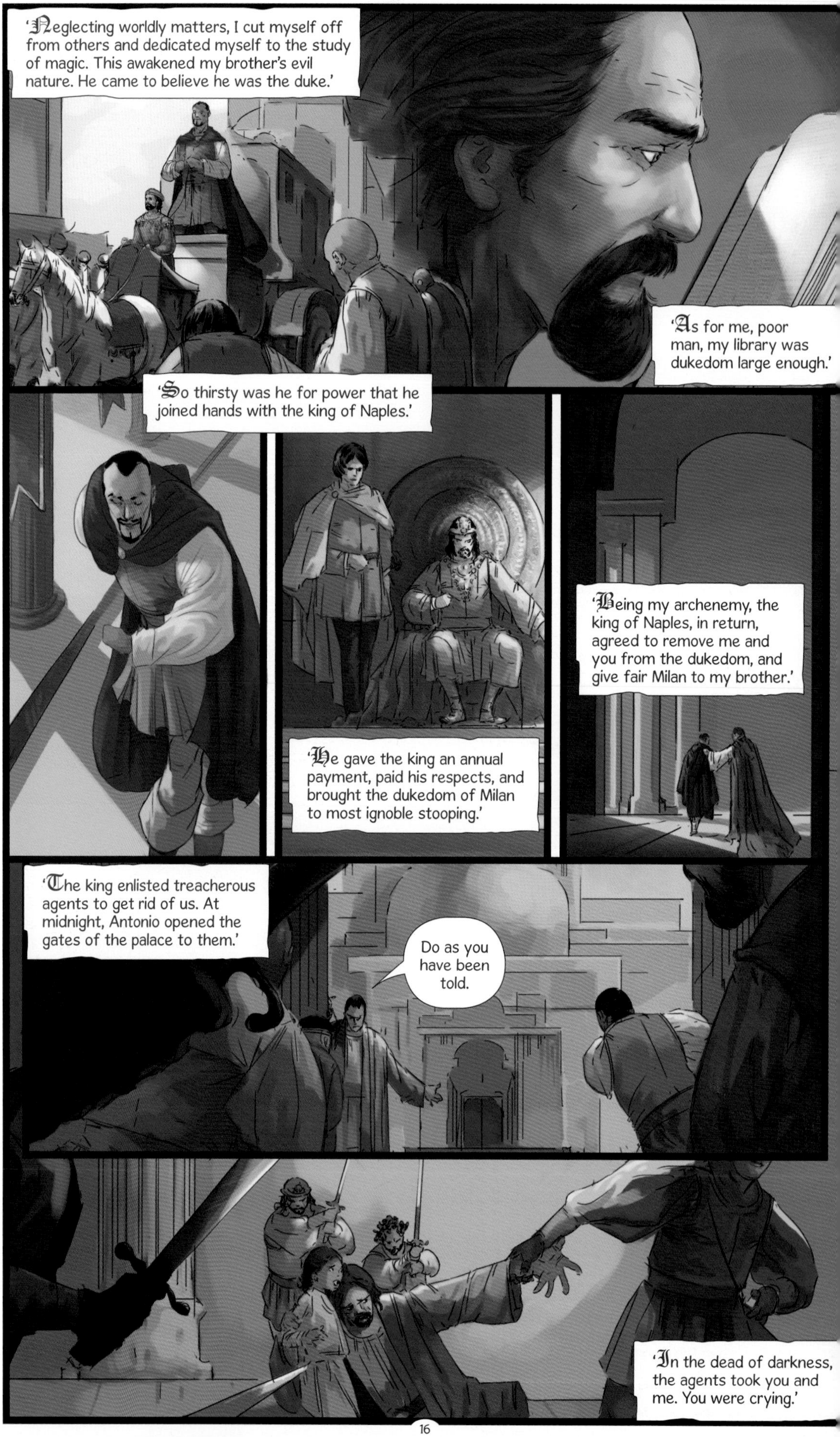

'Neglecting worldly matters, I cut myself off from others and dedicated myself to the study of magic. This awakened my brother's evil nature. He came to believe he was the duke.'
'As for me, poor man, my library was dukedom large enough.'
'So thirsty was he for power that he joined hands with the king of Naples.'
'He gave the king an annual payment, paid his respects, and brought the dukedom of Milan to most ignoble stooping.'
'Being my archenemy, the king of Naples, in return, agreed to remove me and you from the dukedom, and give fair Milan to my brother.'
'The king enlisted treacherous agents to get rid of us. At midnight, Antonio opened the gates of the palace to them.'
Do as you have been told.
'In the dead of darkness, the agents took you and me. You were crying.'

Why didn't they kill us that very hour?

They dared not, for the love that my people had for me. They had to disguise their bloody business. They had to paint a pretty picture.

'So they hurried us to a boat, and took us several kilometers out to sea.

There they prepared a rotten carcass of a boat, with no ropes, sails, or masts.

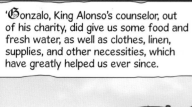

Even the rats instinctively quit that boat.'

'They left us in that boat to cry to the sea that roared back at us.'

Oh, what trouble was I to you then.

Oh, a little angel you were that kept me going. Your smile was filled with strength from heaven, which gave me courage to carry on.

How did we survive?

'Gonzalo, King Alonso's counselor, out of his charity, did give us some food and fresh water, as well as clothes, linen, supplies, and other necessities, which have greatly helped us ever since.

Knowing I loved my books, he provided me from my own library books that I prized above my dukedom.'

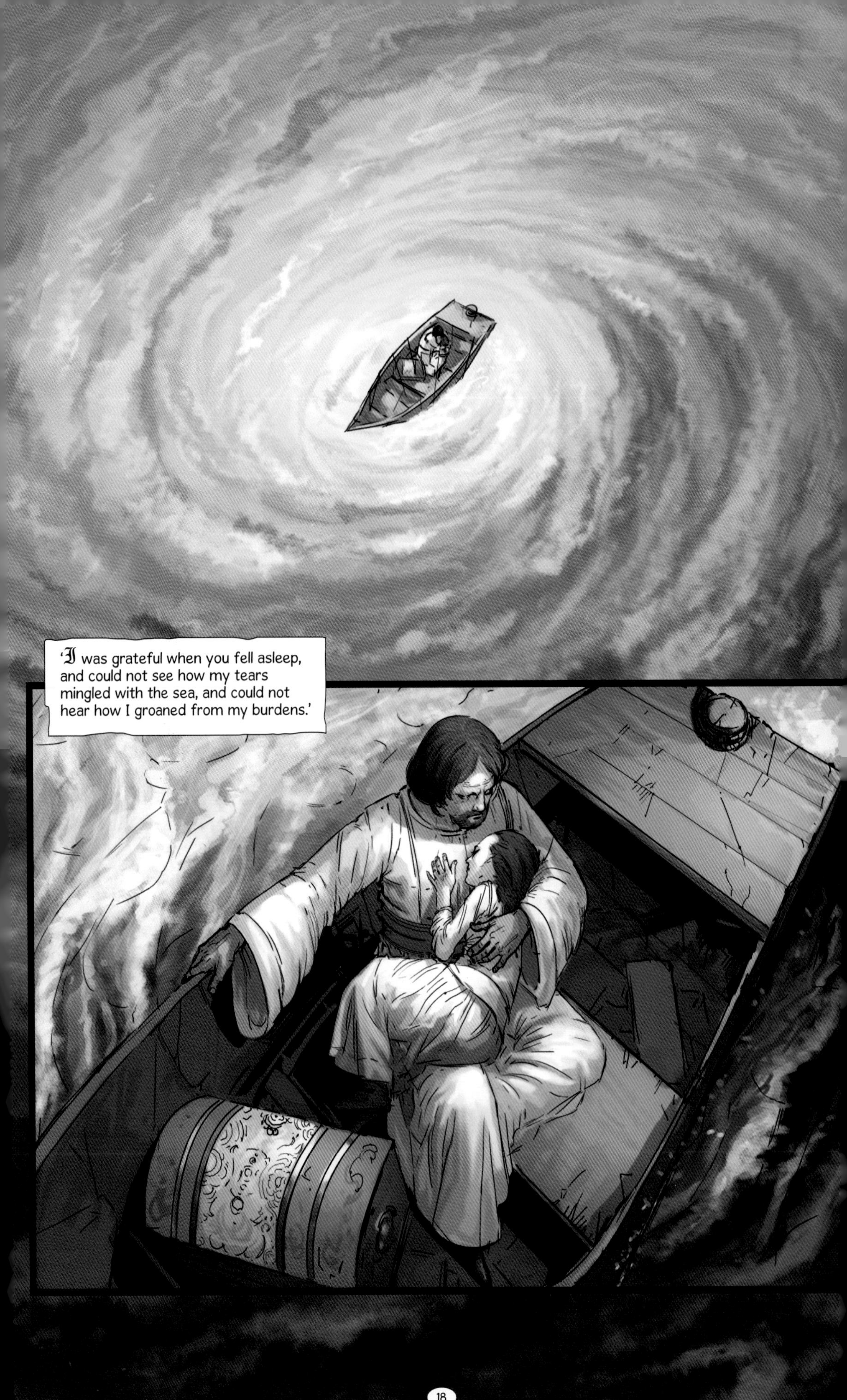
'I was grateful when you fell asleep, and could not see how my tears mingled with the sea, and could not hear how I groaned from my burdens.'

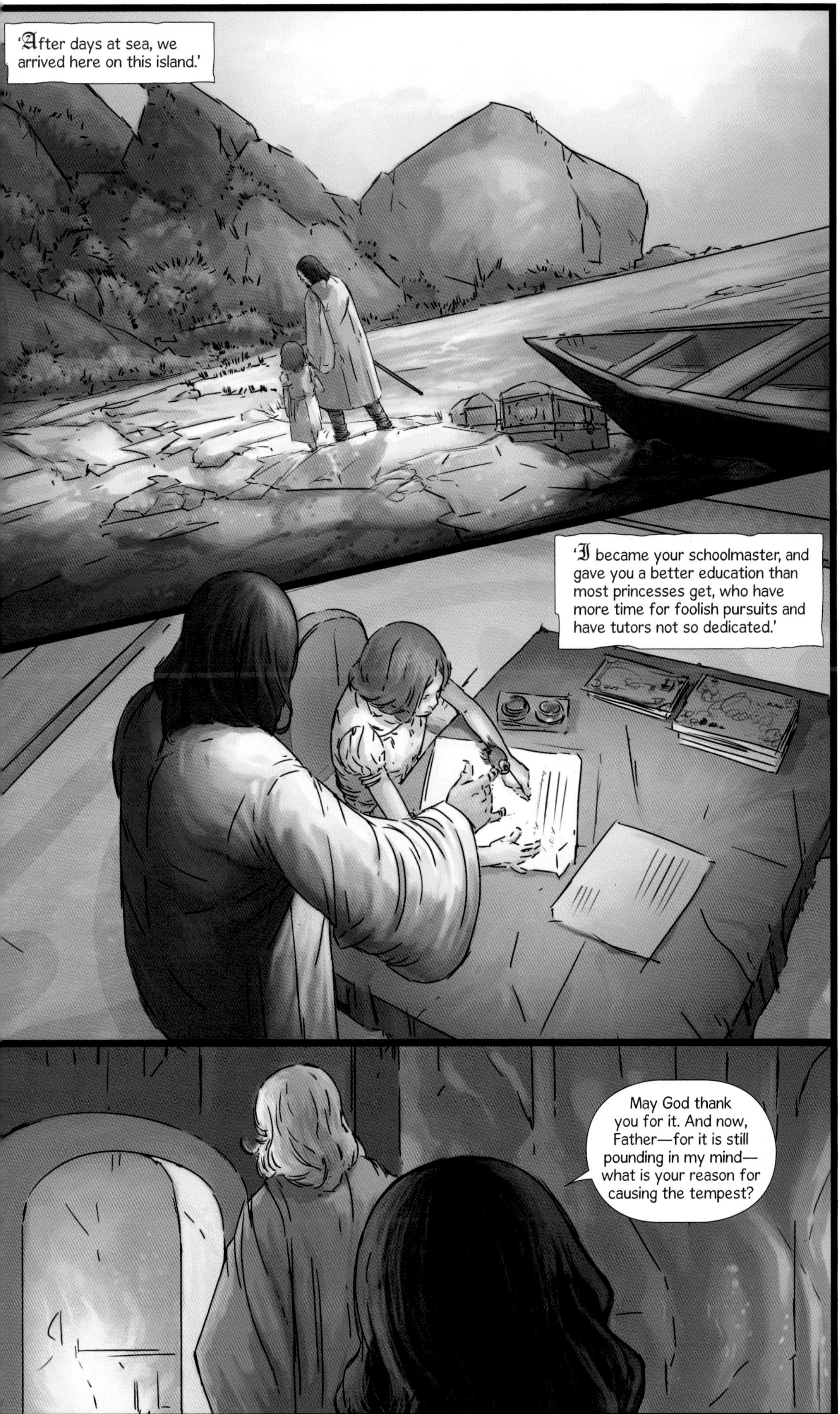
'After days at sea, we arrived here on this island.'
'I became your schoolmaster, and gave you a better education than most princesses get, who have more time for foolish pursuits and have tutors not so dedicated.'
May God thank you for it. And now, Father—for it is still pounding in my mind—what is your reason for causing the tempest?

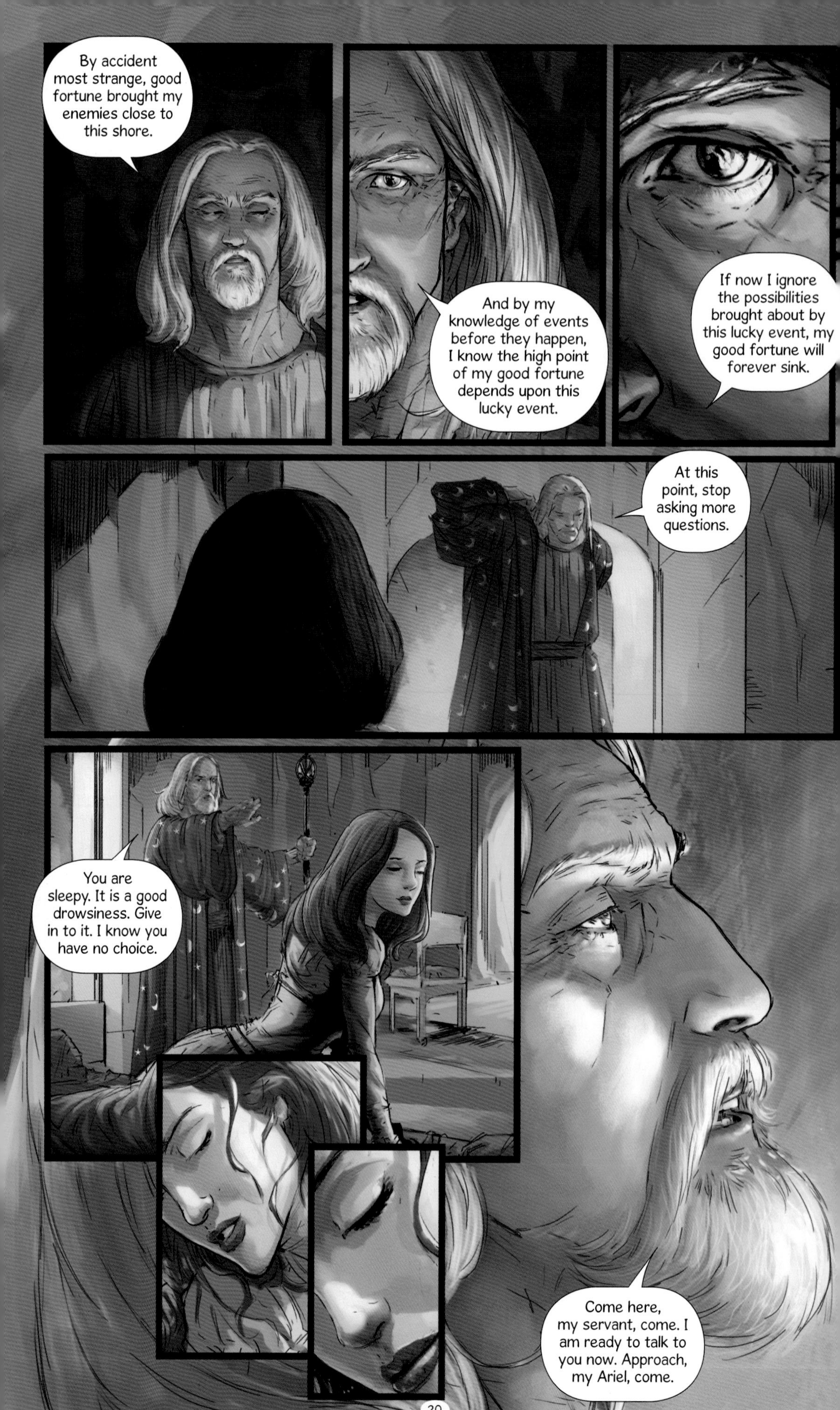
By accident most strange, good fortune brought my enemies close to this shore.
And by my knowledge of events before they happen, I know the high point of my good fortune depends upon this lucky event.
If now I ignore the possibilities brought about by this lucky event, my good fortune will forever sink.
At this point, stop asking more questions.
You are sleepy. It is a good drowsiness. Give in to it. I know you have no choice.
Come here, my servant, come. I am ready to talk to you now. Approach, my Ariel, come.

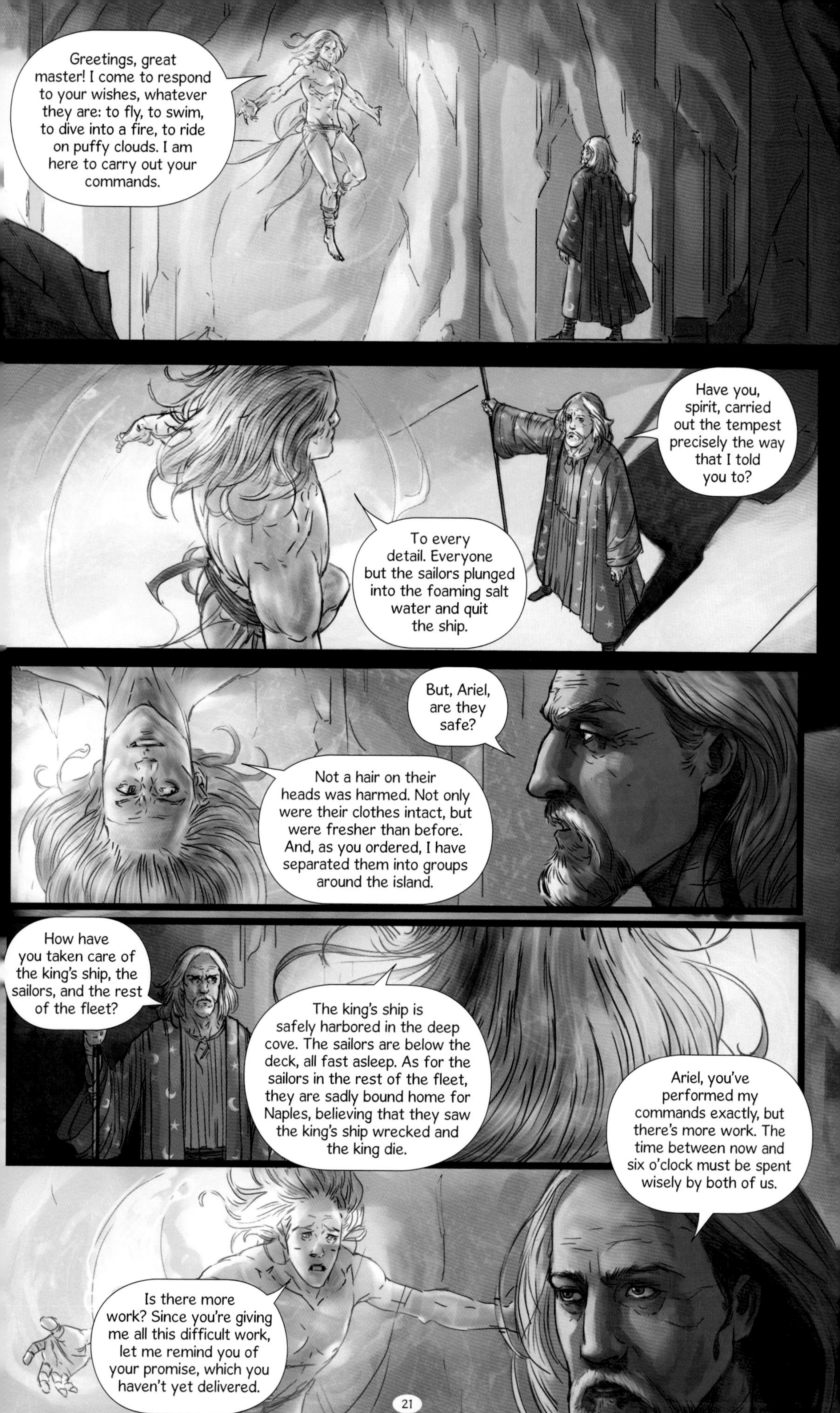

Greetings, great master! I come to respond to your wishes, whatever they are: to fly, to swim, to dive into a fire, to ride on puffy clouds. I am here to carry out your commands.
Have you, spirit, carried out the tempest precisely the way that I told you to?
To every detail. Everyone but the sailors plunged into the foaming salt water and quit the ship.
But, Ariel, are they safe?
Not a hair on their heads was harmed. Not only were their clothes intact, but were fresher than before. And, as you ordered, I have separated them into groups around the island.
How have you taken care of the king's ship, the sailors, and the rest of the fleet?
The king's ship is safely harbored in the deep cove. The sailors are below the deck, all fast asleep. As for the sailors in the rest of the fleet, they are sadly bound home for Naples, believing that they saw the king's ship wrecked and the king die.
Ariel, you've performed my commands exactly, but there's more work. The time between now and six o'clock must be spent wisely by both of us.
Is there more work? Since you're giving me all this difficult work, let me remind you of your promise, which you haven't yet delivered.

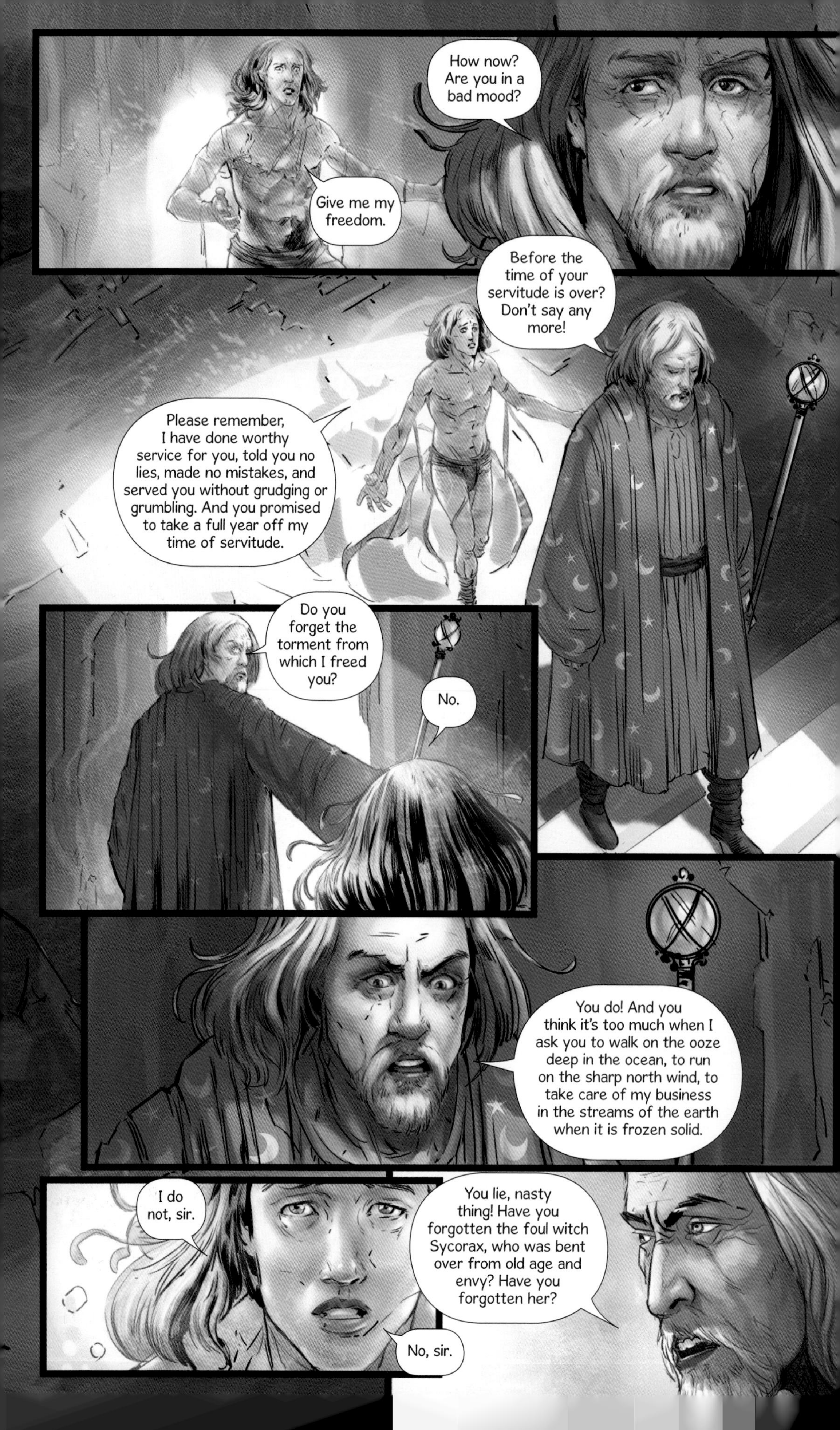
How now? Are you in a bad mood?
Give me my freedom.
Before the time of your servitude is over? Don't say any more!
Please remember, I have done worthy service for you, told you no lies, made no mistakes, and served you without grudging or grumbling. And you promised to take a full year off my time of servitude.
Do you forget the torment from which I freed you?
No.
You do! And you think it's too much when I ask you to walk on the ooze deep in the ocean, to run on the sharp north wind, to take care of my business in the streams of the earth when it is frozen solid.
I do not, sir.
You lie, nasty thing! Have you forgotten the foul witch Sycorax, who was bent over from old age and envy? Have you forgotten her?
No, sir.

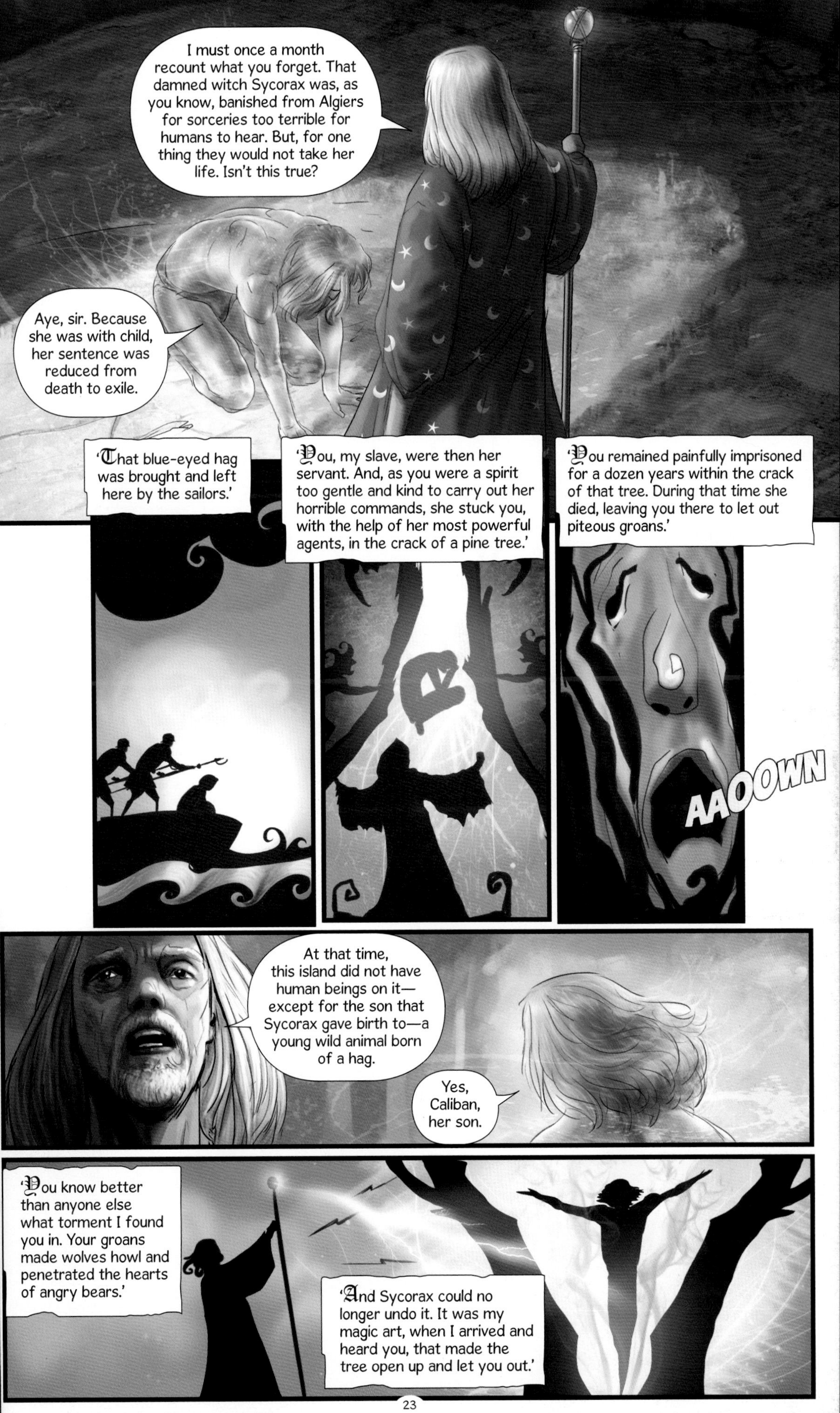
I must once a month recount what you forget. That damned witch Sycorax was, as you know, banished from Algiers for sorceries too terrible for humans to hear. But, for one thing they would not take her life. Isn't this true?
Aye, sir. Because she was with child, her sentence was reduced from death to exile.
'That blue-eyed hag was brought and left here by the sailors.'
'You, my slave, were then her servant. And, as you were a spirit too gentle and kind to carry out her horrible commands, she stuck you, with the help of her most powerful agents, in the crack of a pine tree.'
'You remained painfully imprisoned for a dozen years within the crack of that tree. During that time she died, leaving you there to let out piteous groans.'
AAOOWN
At that time, this island did not have human beings on it—except for the son that Sycorax gave birth to—a young wild animal born of a hag.
Yes, Caliban, her son.
'You know better than anyone else what torment I found you in. Your groans made wolves howl and penetrated the hearts of angry bears.'
'And Sycorax could no longer undo it. It was my magic art, when I arrived and heard you, that made the tree open up and let you out.'

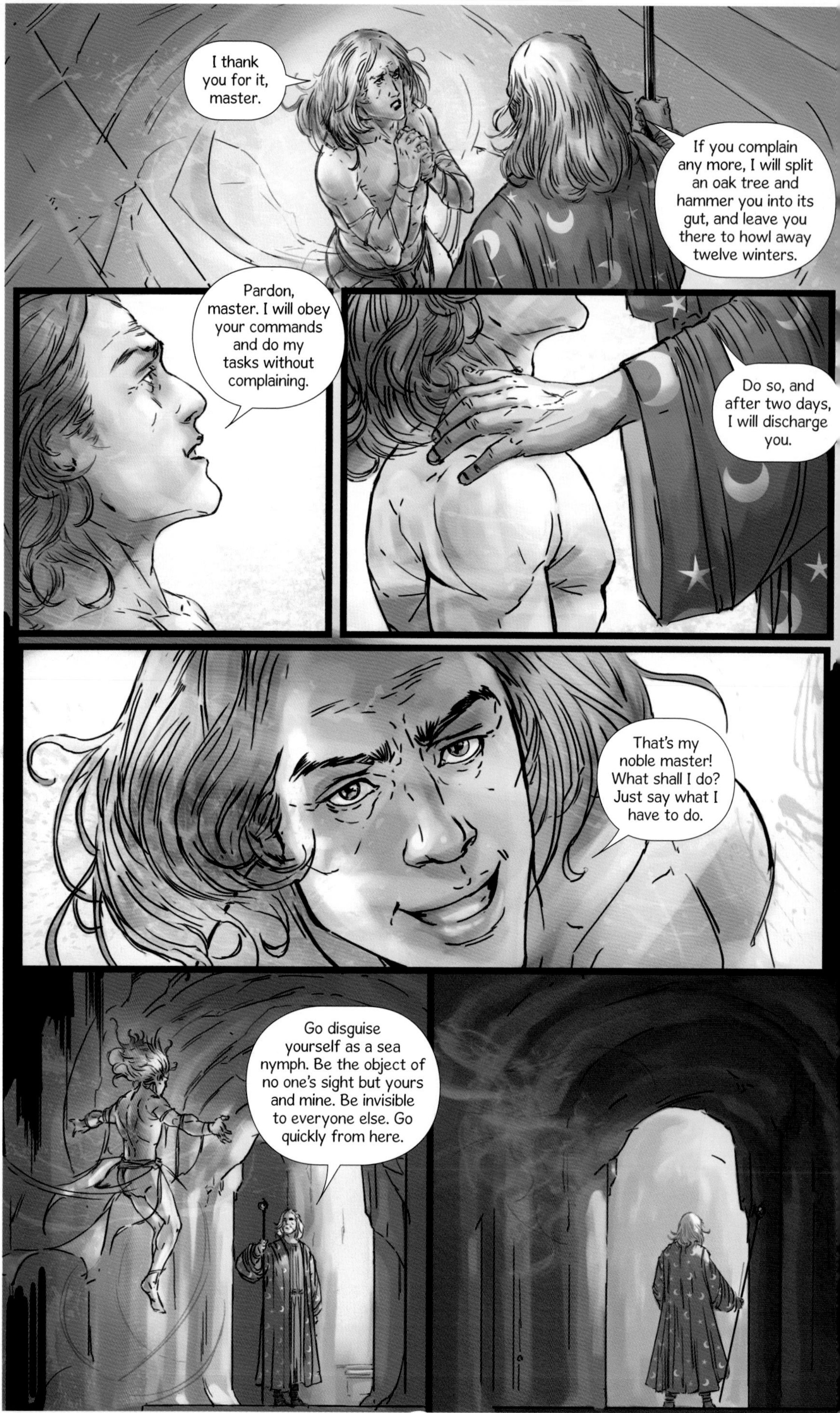
I thank you for it, master.
If you complain any more, I will split an oak tree and hammer you into its gut, and leave you there to howl away twelve winters.
Pardon, master. I will obey your commands and do my tasks without complaining.
Do so, and after two days, I will discharge you.
That's my noble master! What shall I do? Just say what I have to do.
Go disguise yourself as a sea nymph. Be the object of no one's sight but yours and mine. Be invisible to everyone else. Go quickly from here.

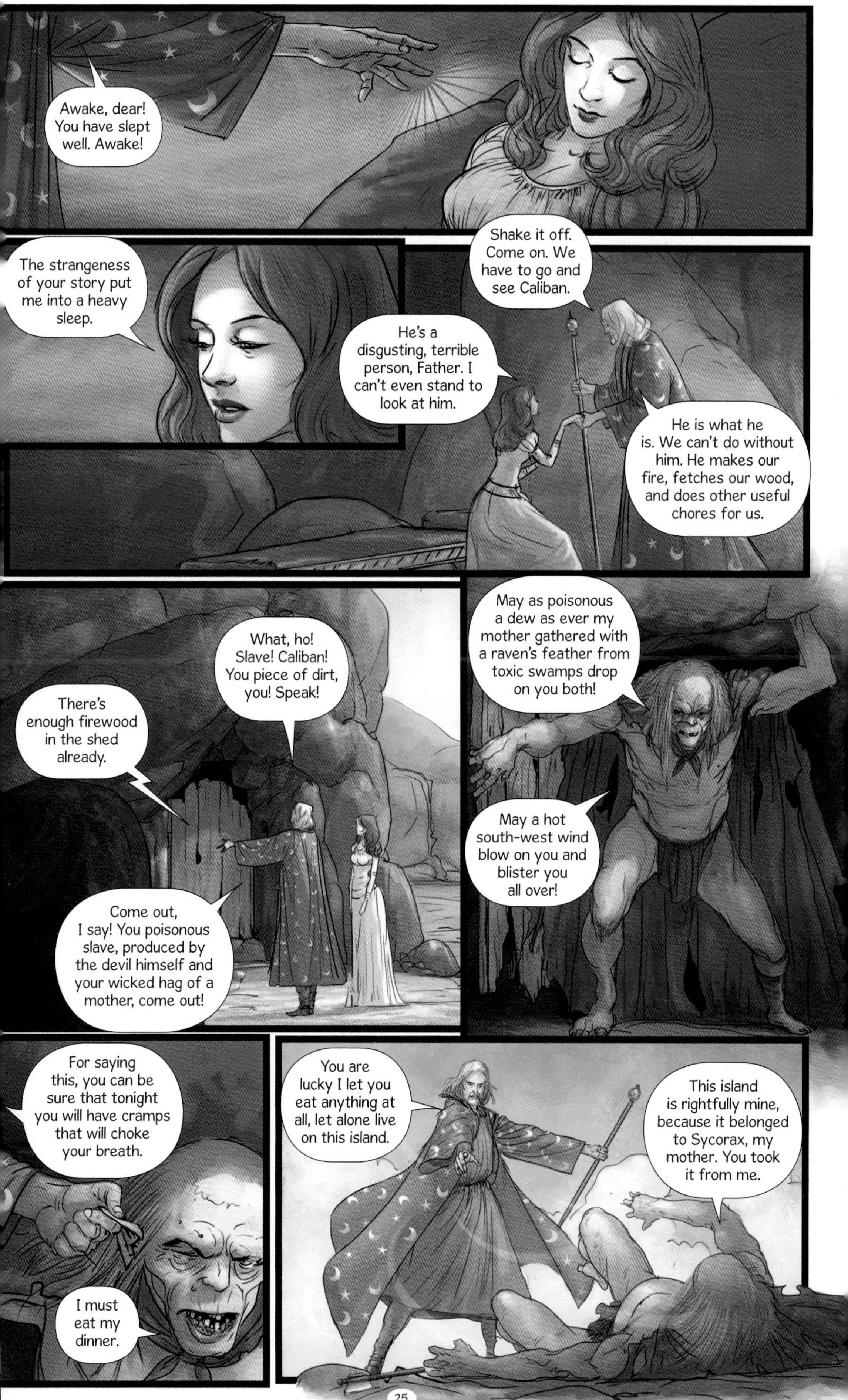
Awake, dear! You have slept well. Awake!
The strangeness of your story put me into a heavy sleep.
Shake it off. Come on. We have to go and see Caliban.
He's a disgusting, terrible person, Father. I can't even stand to look at him.
He is what he is. We can't do without him. He makes our fire, fetches our wood, and does other useful chores for us.
What, ho! Slave! Caliban! You piece of dirt, you! Speak!
There's enough firewood in the shed already.
Come out, I say! You poisonous slave, produced by the devil himself and your wicked hag of a mother, come out!
May as poisonous a dew as ever my mother gathered with a raven's feather from toxic swamps drop on you both!
May a hot south-west wind blow on you and blister you all over!
For saying this, you can be sure that tonight you will have cramps that will choke your breath.
I must eat my dinner.
You are lucky I let you eat anything at all, let alone live on this island.
This island is rightfully mine, because it belonged to Sycorax, my mother. You took it from me.

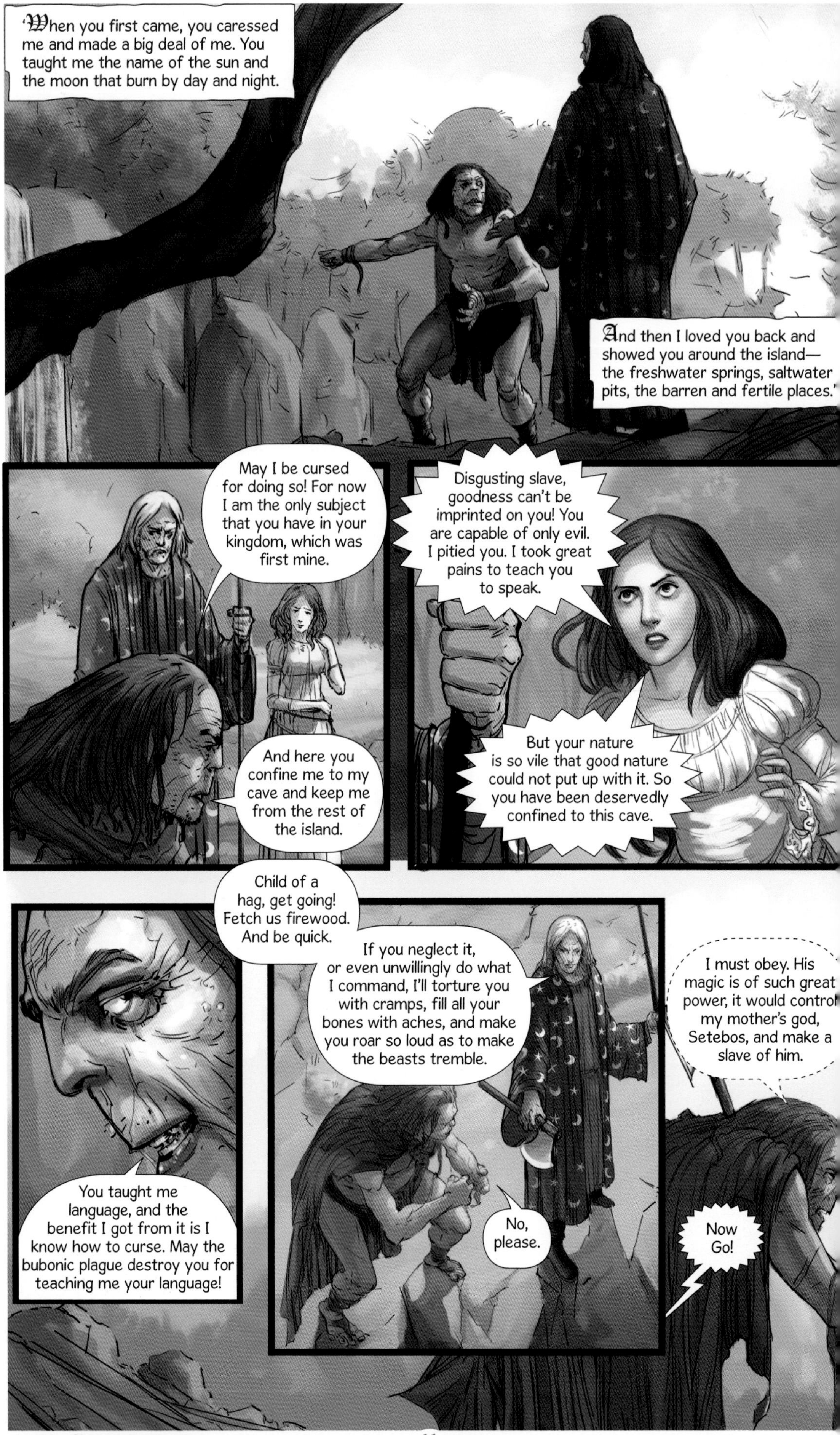
'When you first came, you caressed me and made a big deal of me. You taught me the name of the sun and the moon that burn by day and night.
And then I loved you back and showed you around the island—the freshwater springs, saltwater pits, the barren and fertile places.'
May I be cursed for doing so! For now I am the only subject that you have in your kingdom, which was first mine.
And here you confine me to my cave and keep me from the rest of the island.
Disgusting slave, goodness can't be imprinted on you! You are capable of only evil. I pitied you. I took great pains to teach you to speak.
But your nature is so vile that good nature could not put up with it. So you have been deservedly confined to this cave.
You taught me language, and the benefit I got from it is I know how to curse. May the bubonic plague destroy you for teaching me your language!
Child of a hag, get going! Fetch us firewood. And be quick.
If you neglect it, or even unwillingly do what I command, I'll torture you with cramps, fill all your bones with aches, and make you roar so loud as to make the beasts tremble.
No, please.
I must obey. His magic is of such great power, it would control my mother's god, Setebos, and make a slave of him.
Now Go!

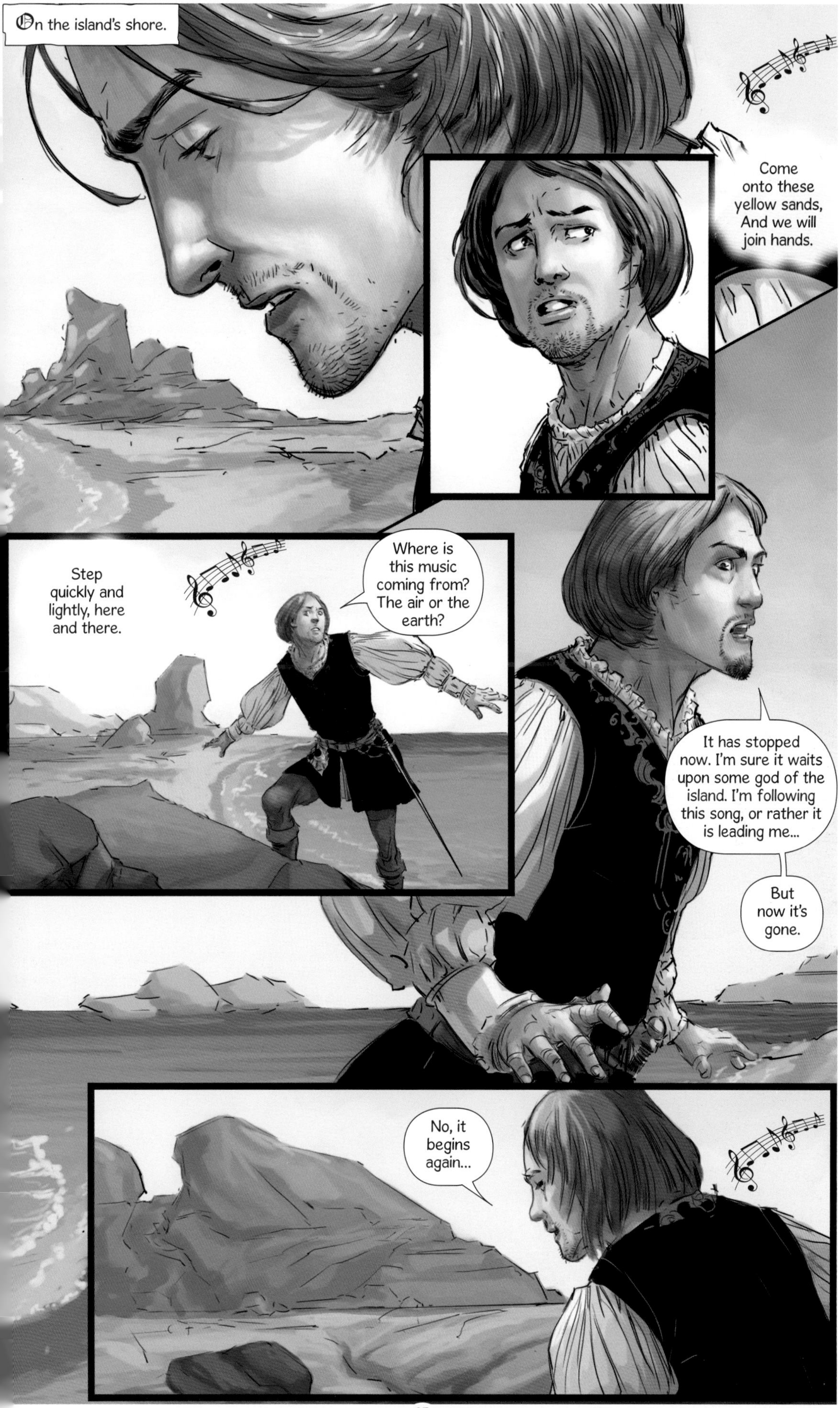
On the island's shore.
Come onto these yellow sands, And we will join hands.
Step quickly and lightly, here and there.
Where is this music coming from? The air or the earth?
It has stopped now. I'm sure it waits upon some god of the island. I'm following this song, or rather it is leading me...
But now it's gone.
No, it begins again...

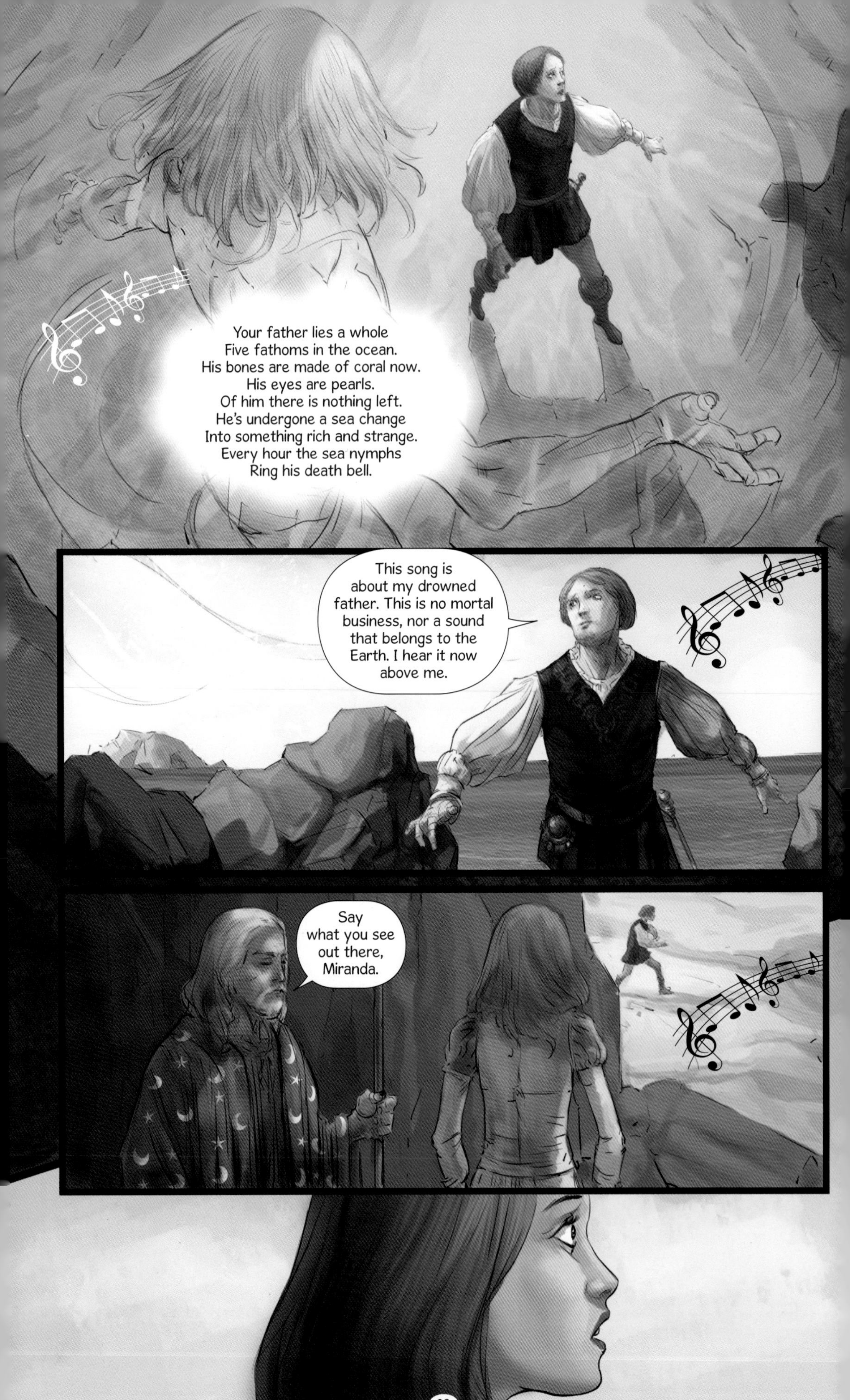
Your father lies a whole
Five fathoms in the ocean.
His bones are made of coral now.
His eyes are pearls.
Of him there is nothing left.
He's undergone a sea change
Into something rich and strange.
Every hour the sea nymphs
Ring his death bell.
This song is about my drowned father. This is no mortal business, nor a sound that belongs to the Earth. I hear it now above me.
Say what you see out there, Miranda.

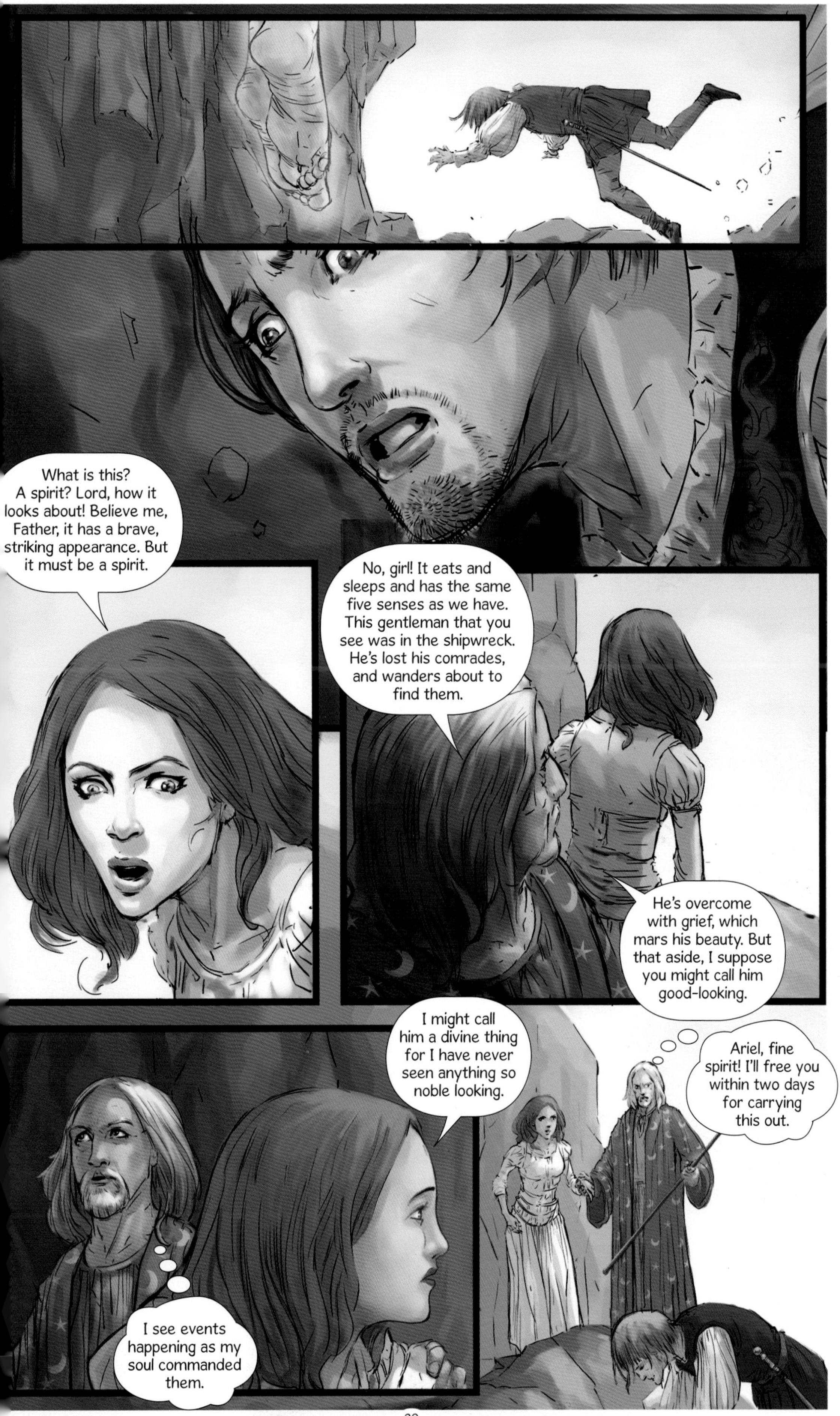
What is this? A spirit? Lord, how it looks about! Believe me, Father, it has a brave, striking appearance. But it must be a spirit.
No, girl! It eats and sleeps and has the same five senses as we have. This gentleman that you see was in the shipwreck. He's lost his comrades, and wanders about to find them.
He's overcome with grief, which mars his beauty. But that aside, I suppose you might call him good-looking.
I might call him a divine thing for I have never seen anything so noble looking.
I see events happening as my soul commanded them.
Ariel, fine spirit! I'll free you within two days for carrying this out.

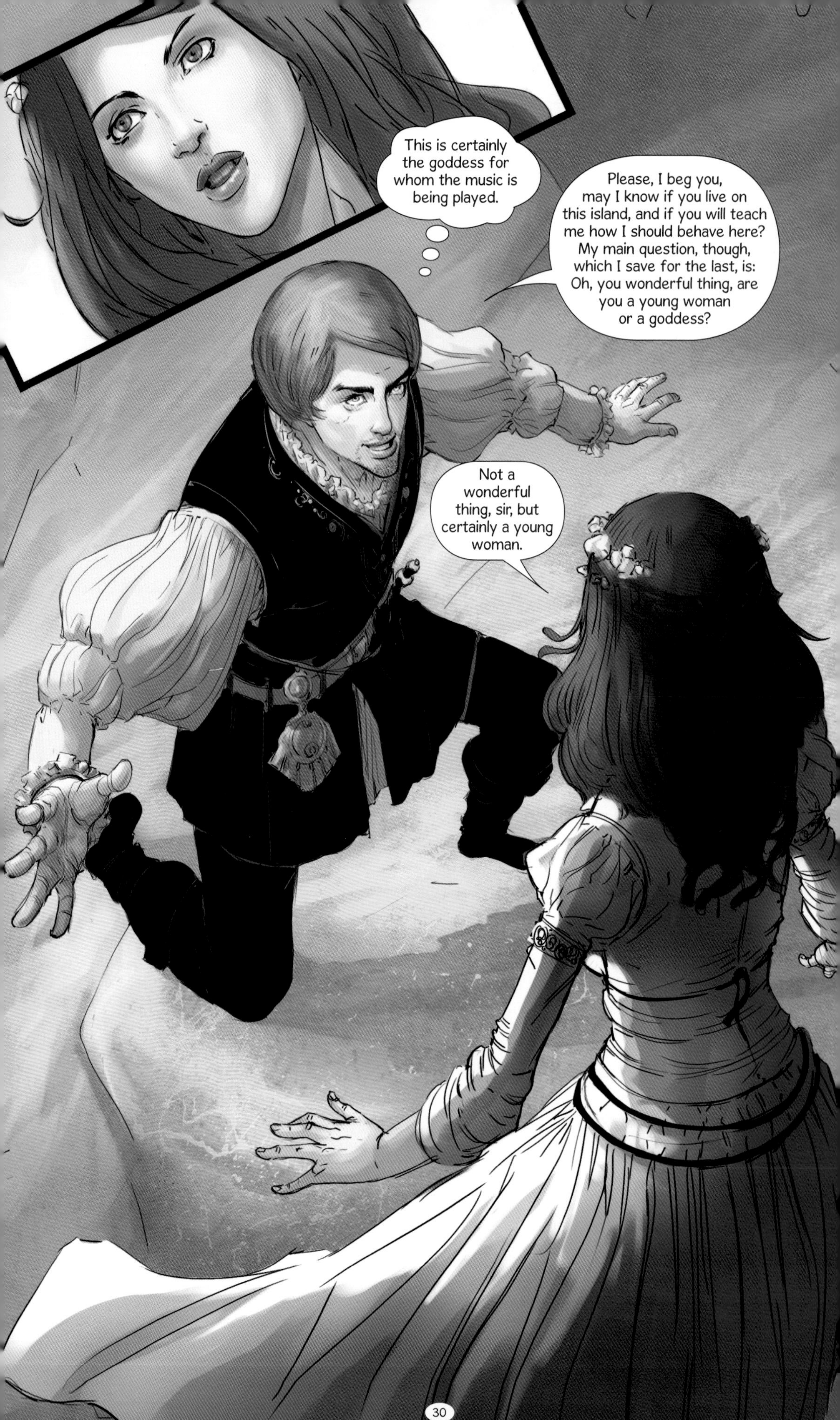
This is certainly the goddess for whom the music is being played.
Please, I beg you, may I know if you live on this island, and if you will teach me how I should behave here? My main question, though, which I save for the last, is: Oh, you wonderful thing, are you a young woman or a goddess?
Not a wonderful thing, sir, but certainly a young woman.

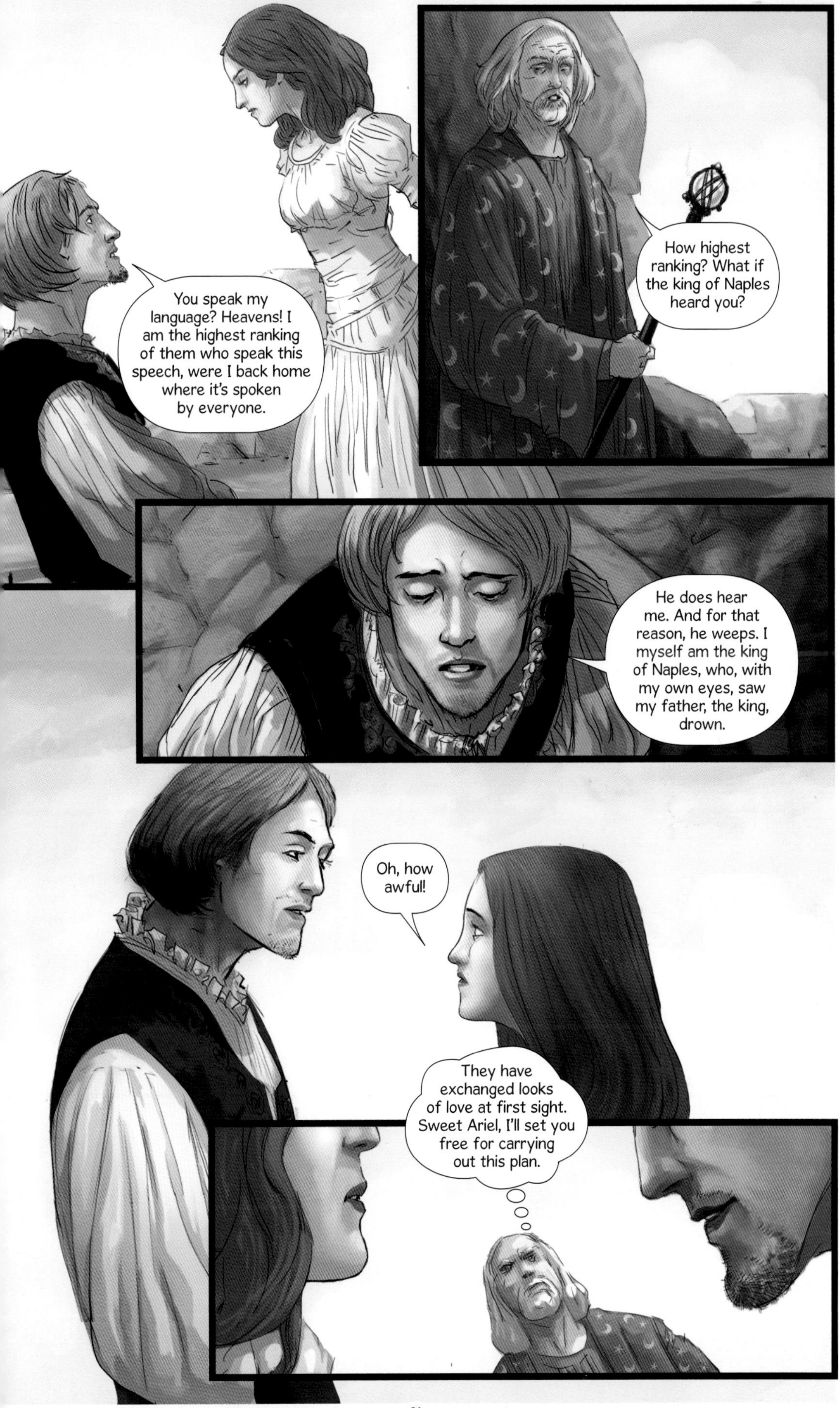

You speak my language? Heavens! I am the highest ranking of them who speak this speech, were I back home where it's spoken by everyone.
How highest ranking? What if the king of Naples heard you?
He does hear me. And for that reason, he weeps. I myself am the king of Naples, who, with my own eyes, saw my father, the king, drown.
Oh, how awful!
They have exchanged looks of love at first sight. Sweet Ariel, I'll set you free for carrying out this plan.

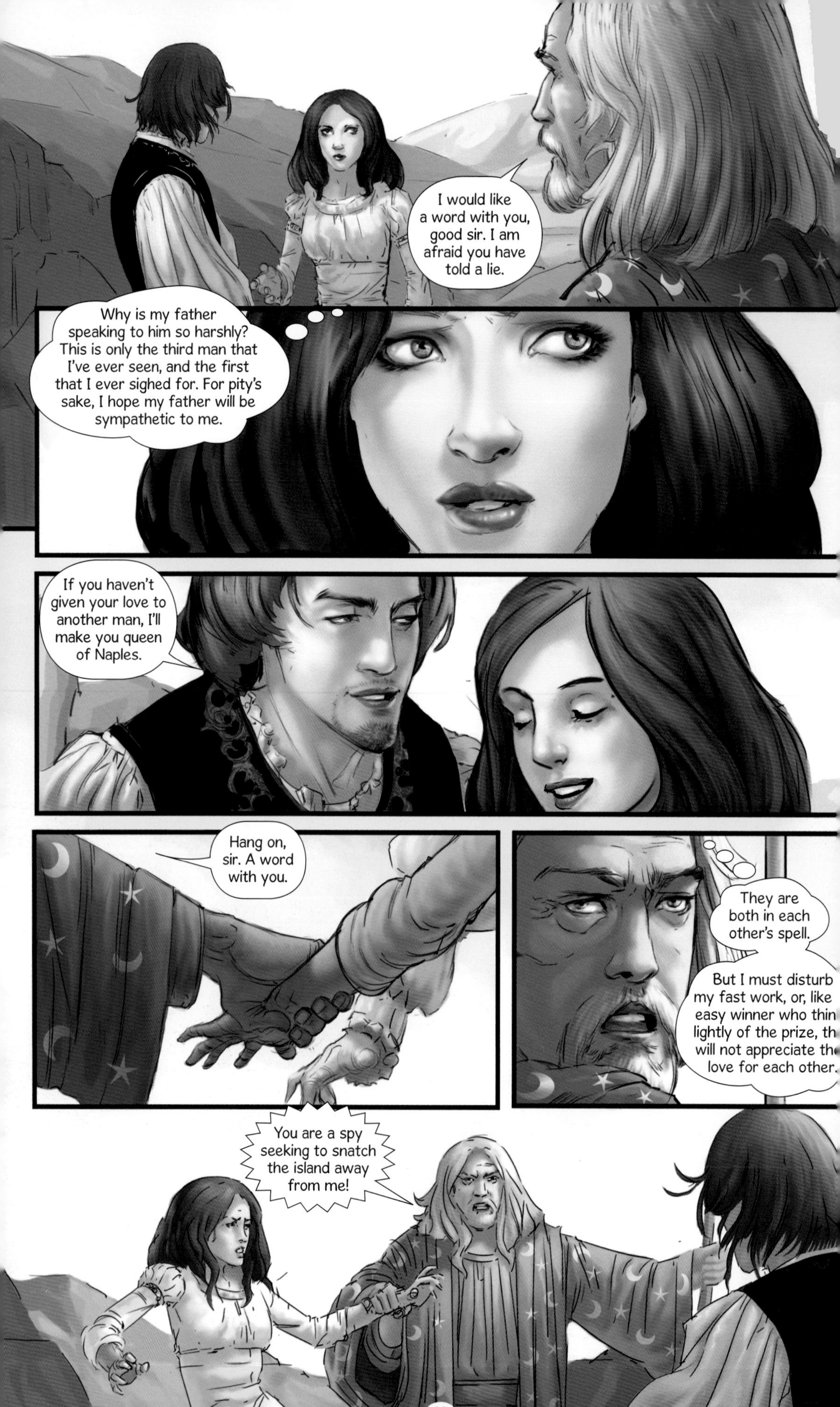
I would like a word with you, good sir. I am afraid you have told a lie.
Why is my father speaking to him so harshly? This is only the third man that I've ever seen, and the first that I ever sighed for. For pity's sake, I hope my father will be sympathetic to me.
If you haven't given your love to another man, I'll make you queen of Naples.
Hang on, sir. A word with you.
They are both in each other's spell.
But I must disturb my fast work, or, like easy winner who thin lightly of the prize, th will not appreciate th love for each other.
You are a spy seeking to snatch the island away from me!

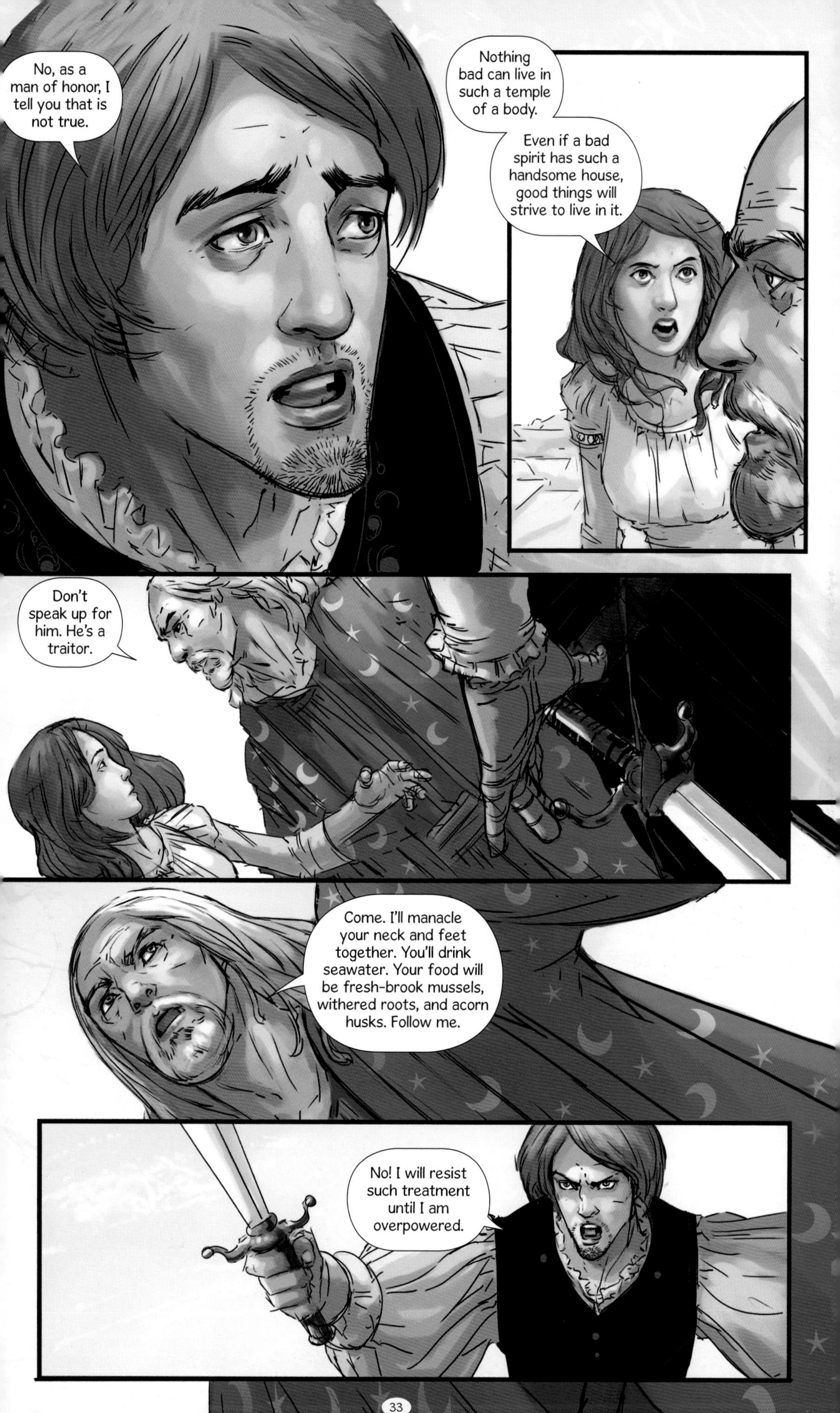
No, as a man of honor, I tell you that is not true.
Nothing bad can live in such a temple of a body.
Even if a bad spirit has such a handsome house, good things will strive to live in it.
Don't speak up for him. He's a traitor.
Come. I'll manacle your neck and feet together. You'll drink seawater. Your food will be fresh-brook mussels, withered roots, and acorn husks. Follow me.
No! I will resist such treatment until I am overpowered.

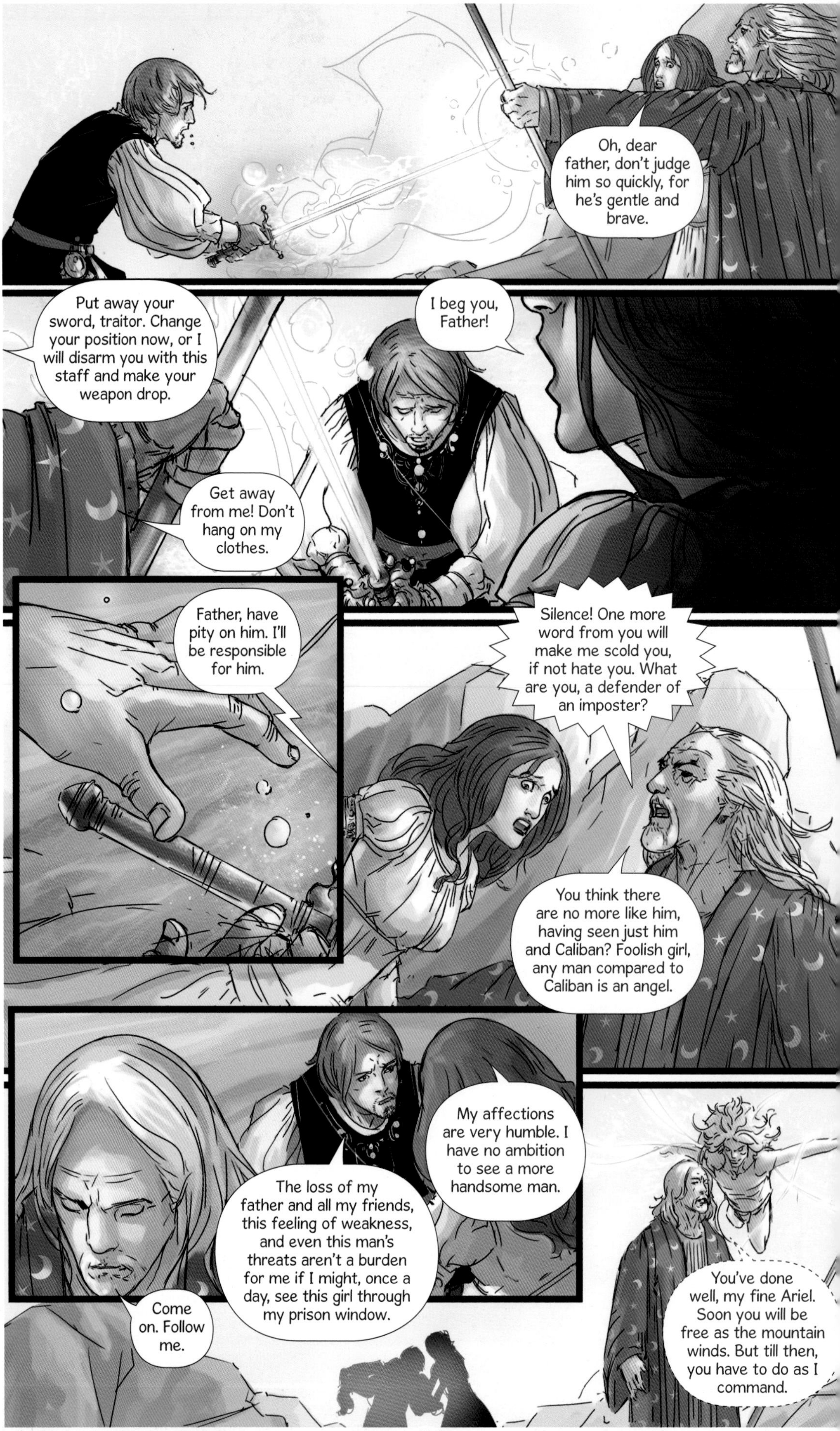
Oh, dear father, don't judge him so quickly, for he's gentle and brave.
Put away your sword, traitor. Change your position now, or I will disarm you with this staff and make your weapon drop.
I beg you, Father!
Get away from me! Don't hang on my clothes.
Father, have pity on him. I'll be responsible for him.
Silence! One more word from you will make me scold you, if not hate you. What are you, a defender of an imposter?
You think there are no more like him, having seen just him and Caliban? Foolish girl, any man compared to Caliban is an angel.
My affections are very humble. I have no ambition to see a more handsome man.
The loss of my father and all my friends, this feeling of weakness, and even this man's threats aren't a burden for me if I might, once a day, see this girl through my prison window.
Come on. Follow me.
You've done well, my fine Ariel. Soon you will be free as the mountain winds. But till then, you have to do as I command.

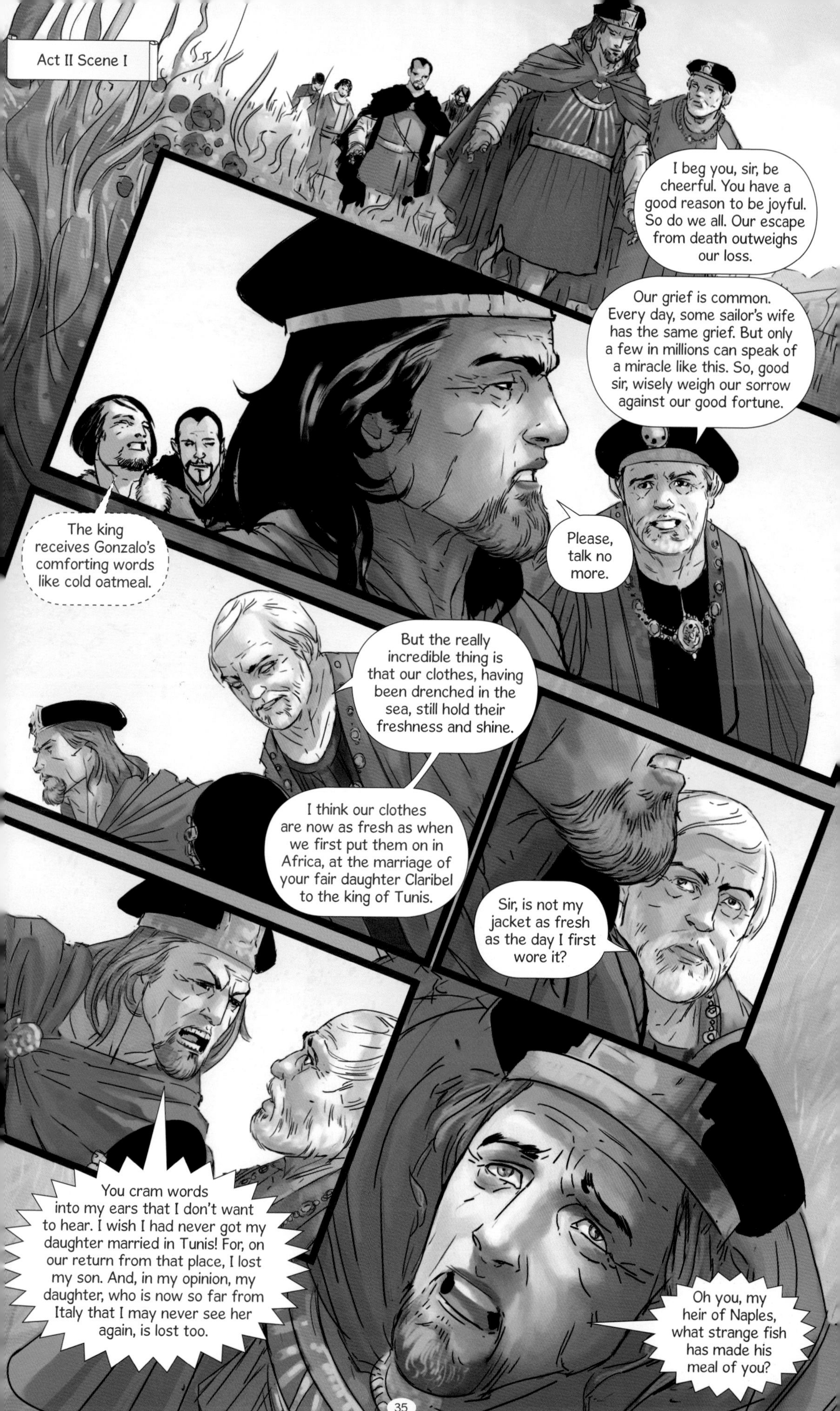
Act II Scene I
I beg you, sir, be cheerful. You have a good reason to be joyful. So do we all. Our escape from death outweighs our loss.
Our grief is common. Every day, some sailor's wife has the same grief. But only a few in millions can speak of a miracle like this. So, good sir, wisely weigh our sorrow against our good fortune.
The king receives Gonzalo's comforting words like cold oatmeal.
Please, talk no more.
But the really incredible thing is that our clothes, having been drenched in the sea, still hold their freshness and shine.
I think our clothes are now as fresh as when we first put them on in Africa, at the marriage of your fair daughter Claribel to the king of Tunis.
Sir, is not my jacket as fresh as the day I first wore it?
You cram words into my ears that I don't want to hear. I wish I had never got my daughter married in Tunis! For, on our return from that place, I lost my son. And, in my opinion, my daughter, who is now so far from Italy that I may never see her again, is lost too.
Oh you, my heir of Naples, what strange fish has made his meal of you?

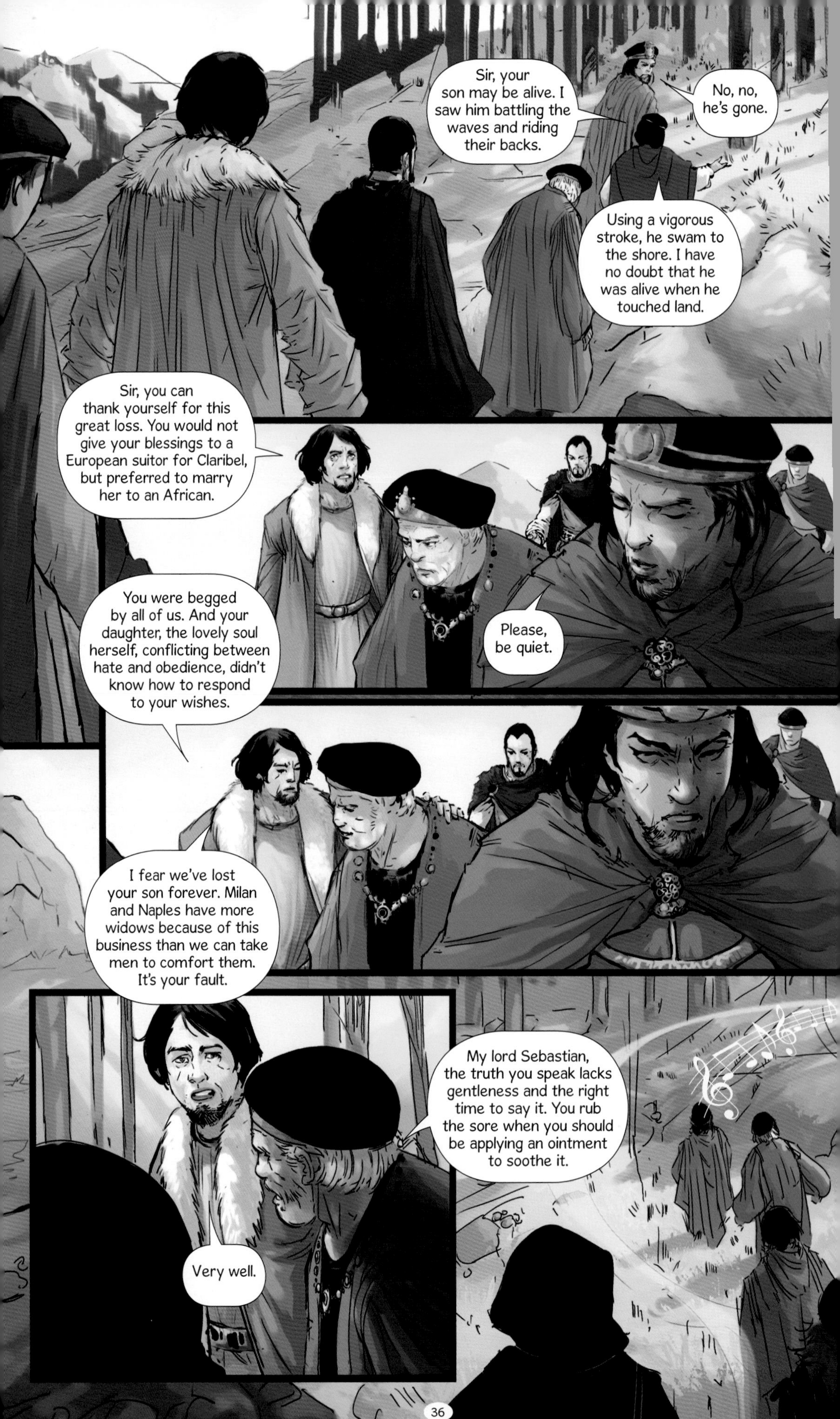
Sir, your son may be alive. I saw him battling the waves and riding their backs.
No, no, he's gone.
Using a vigorous stroke, he swam to the shore. I have no doubt that he was alive when he touched land.
Sir, you can thank yourself for this great loss. You would not give your blessings to a European suitor for Claribel, but preferred to marry her to an African.
You were begged by all of us. And your daughter, the lovely soul herself, conflicting between hate and obedience, didn't know how to respond to your wishes.
Please, be quiet.
I fear we've lost your son forever. Milan and Naples have more widows because of this business than we can take men to comfort them. It's your fault.
Very well.
My lord Sebastian, the truth you speak lacks gentleness and the right time to say it. You rub the sore when you should be applying an ointment to soothe it.

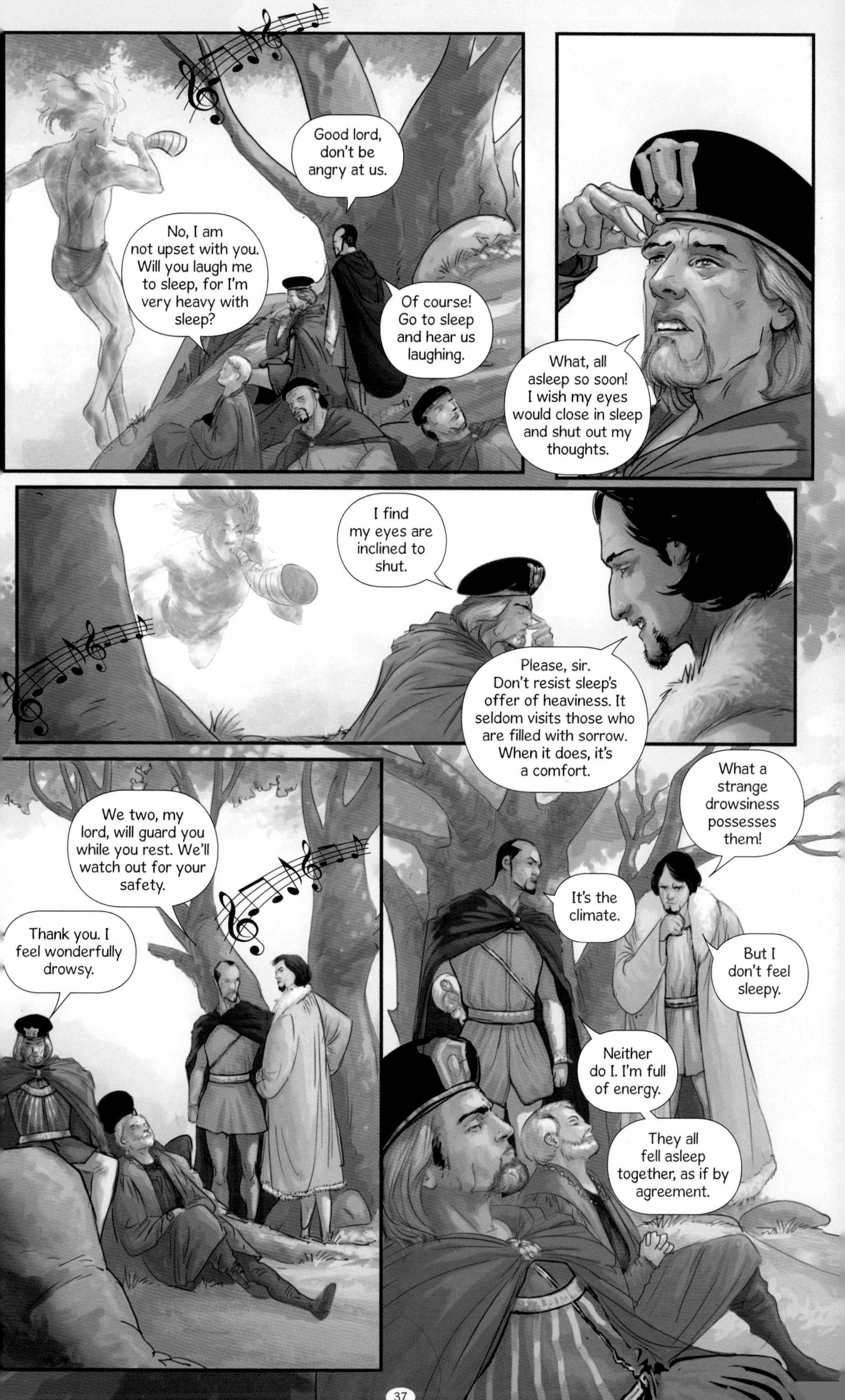
Good lord, don't be angry at us.
No, I am not upset with you. Will you laugh me to sleep, for I'm very heavy with sleep?
Of course! Go to sleep and hear us laughing.
What, all asleep so soon! I wish my eyes would close in sleep and shut out my thoughts.
I find my eyes are inclined to shut.
Please, sir. Don't resist sleep's offer of heaviness. It seldom visits those who are filled with sorrow. When it does, it's a comfort.
We two, my lord, will guard you while you rest. We'll watch out for your safety.
Thank you. I feel wonderfully drowsy.
What a strange drowsiness possesses them!
It's the climate.
But I don't feel sleepy.
Neither do I. I'm full of energy.
They all fell asleep together, as if by agreement.

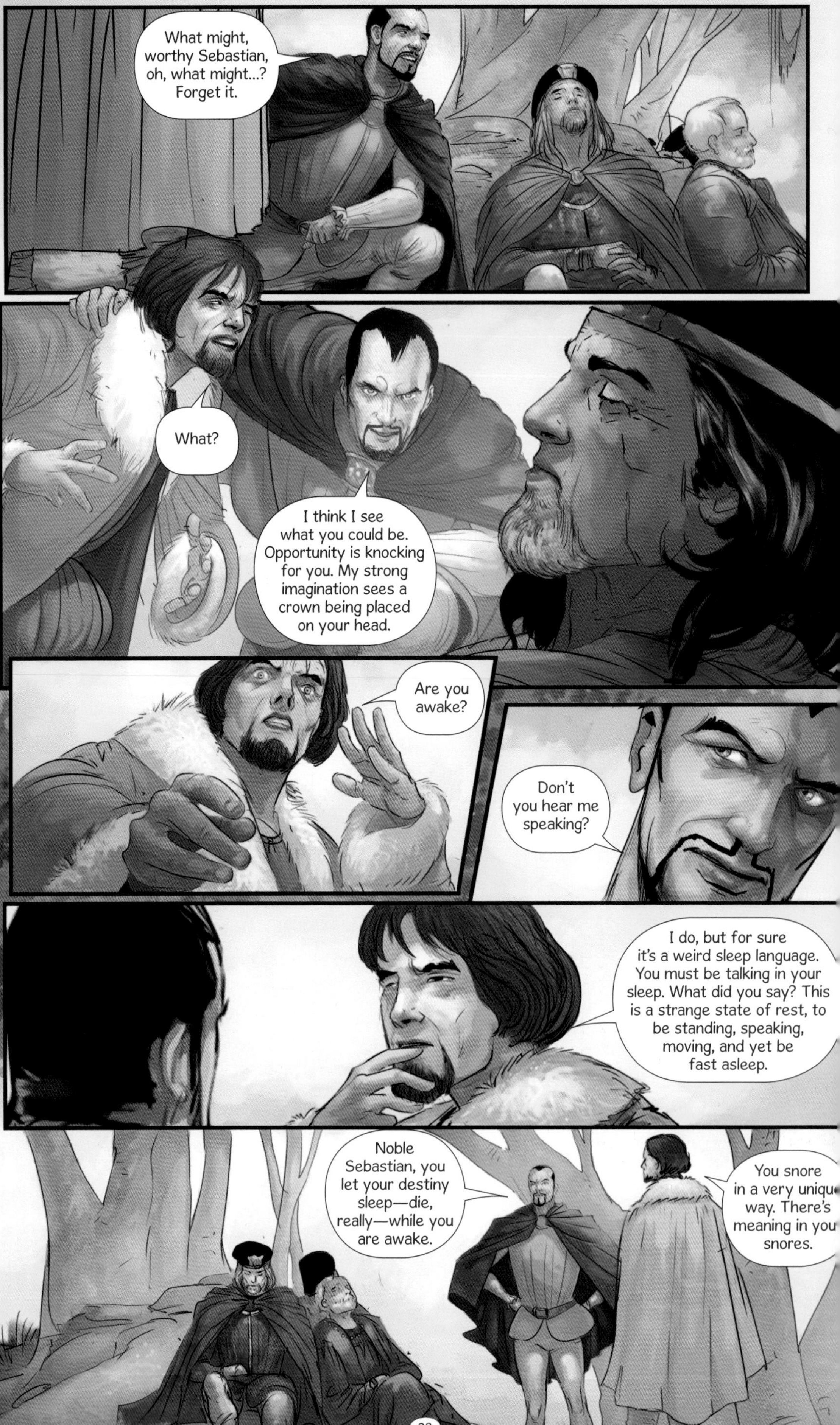
What might, worthy Sebastian, oh, what might...? Forget it.
What?
I think I see what you could be. Opportunity is knocking for you. My strong imagination sees a crown being placed on your head.
Are you awake?
Don't you hear me speaking?
I do, but for sure it's a weird sleep language. You must be talking in your sleep. What did you say? This is a strange state of rest, to be standing, speaking, moving, and yet be fast asleep.
Noble Sebastian, you let your destiny sleep—die, really—while you are awake.
You snore in a very uniqu way. There's meaning in you snores.

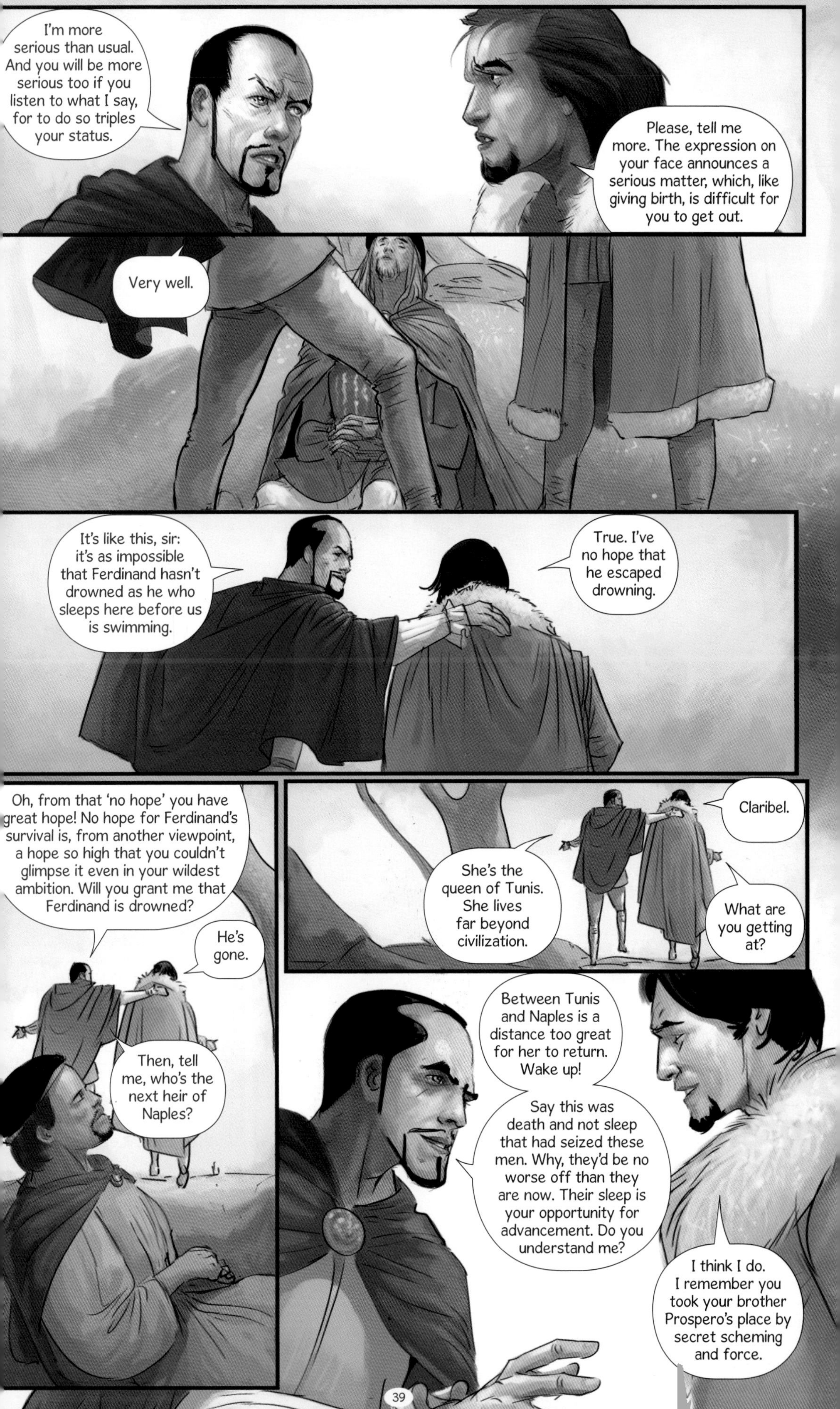
I'm more serious than usual. And you will be more serious too if you listen to what I say, for to do so triples your status.
Please, tell me more. The expression on your face announces a serious matter, which, like giving birth, is difficult for you to get out.
Very well.
It's like this, sir: it's as impossible that Ferdinand hasn't drowned as he who sleeps here before us is swimming.
True. I've no hope that he escaped drowning.
Oh, from that 'no hope' you have great hope! No hope for Ferdinand's survival is, from another viewpoint, a hope so high that you couldn't glimpse it even in your wildest ambition. Will you grant me that Ferdinand is drowned?
He's gone.
Then, tell me, who's the next heir of Naples?
Claribel.
She's the queen of Tunis. She lives far beyond civilization.
What are you getting at?
Between Tunis and Naples is a distance too great for her to return. Wake up!
Say this was death and not sleep that had seized these men. Why, they'd be no worse off than they are now. Their sleep is your opportunity for advancement. Do you understand me?
I think I do. I remember you took your brother Prospero's place by secret scheming and force.

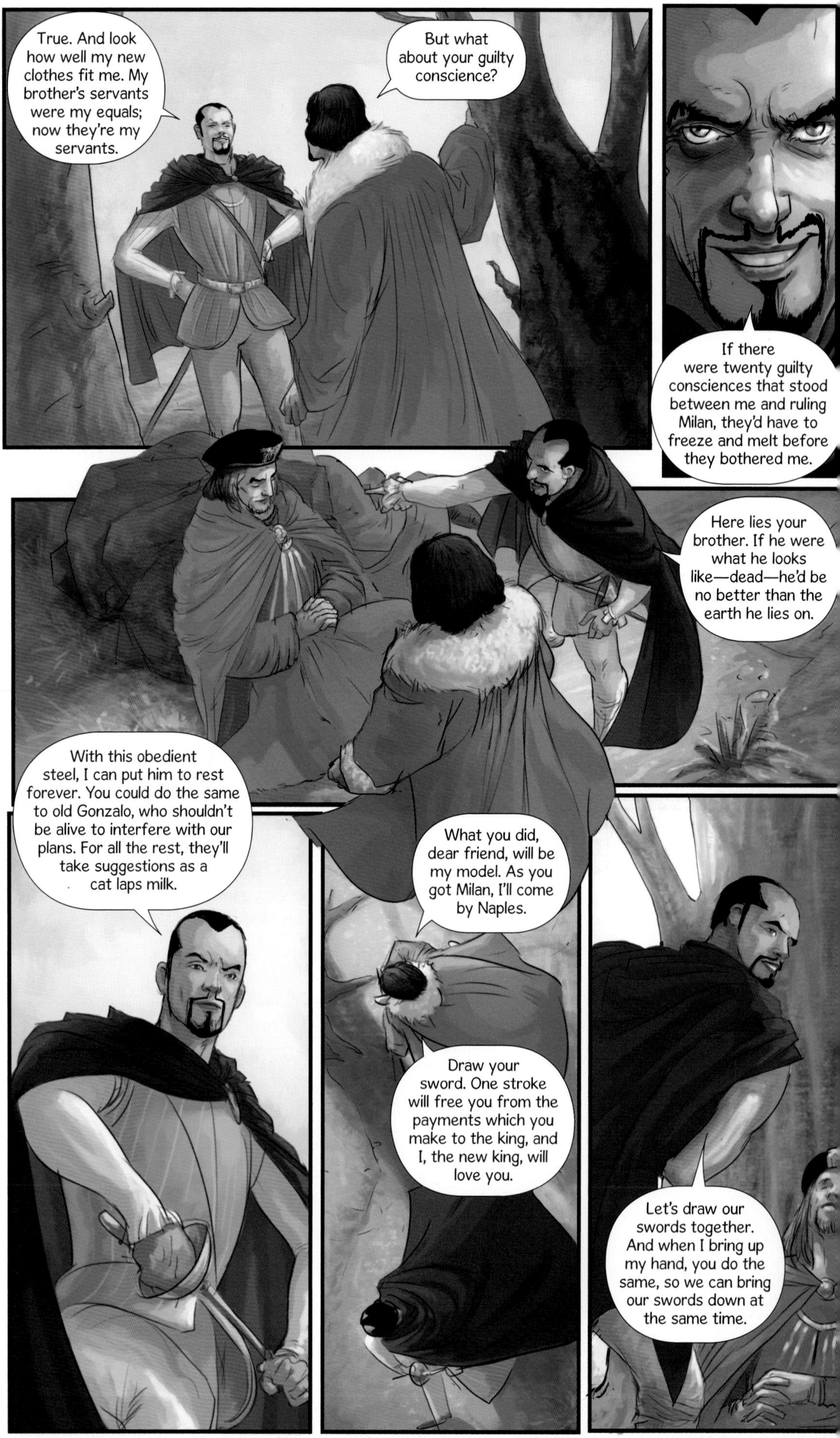
True. And look how well my new clothes fit me. My brother's servants were my equals; now they're my servants.
But what about your guilty conscience?
If there were twenty guilty consciences that stood between me and ruling Milan, they'd have to freeze and melt before they bothered me.
Here lies your brother. If he were what he looks like—dead—he'd be no better than the earth he lies on.
With this obedient steel, I can put him to rest forever. You could do the same to old Gonzalo, who shouldn't be alive to interfere with our plans. For all the rest, they'll take suggestions as a cat laps milk.
What you did, dear friend, will be my model. As you got Milan, I'll come by Naples.
Draw your sword. One stroke will free you from the payments which you make to the king, and I, the new king, will love you.
Let's draw our swords together. And when I bring up my hand, you do the same, so we can bring our swords down at the same time.

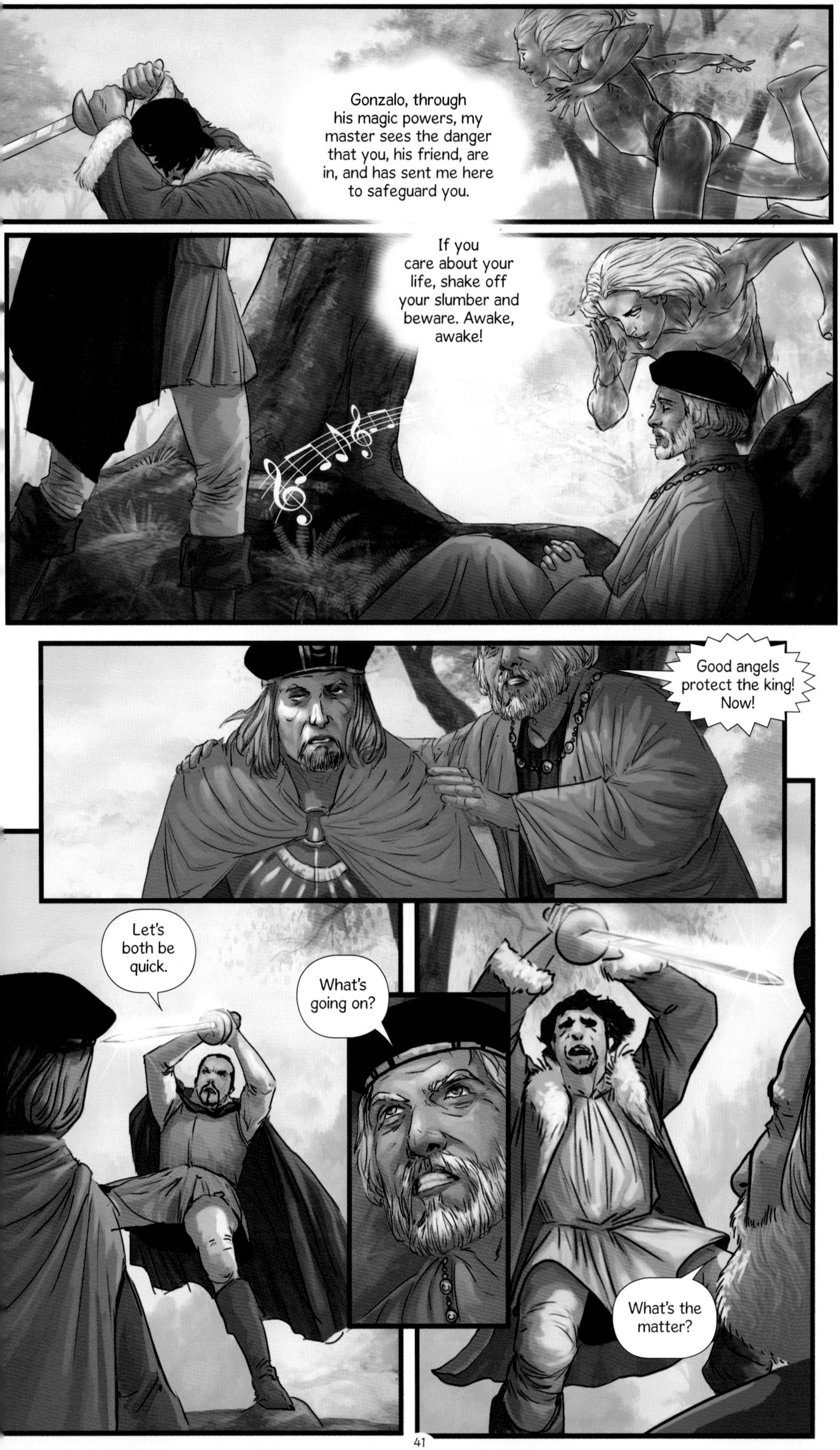
Gonzalo, through his magic powers, my master sees the danger that you, his friend, are in, and has sent me here to safeguard you.
If you care about your life, shake off your slumber and beware. Awake, awake!
Good angels protect the king! Now!
Let's both be quick.
What's going on?
What's the matter?

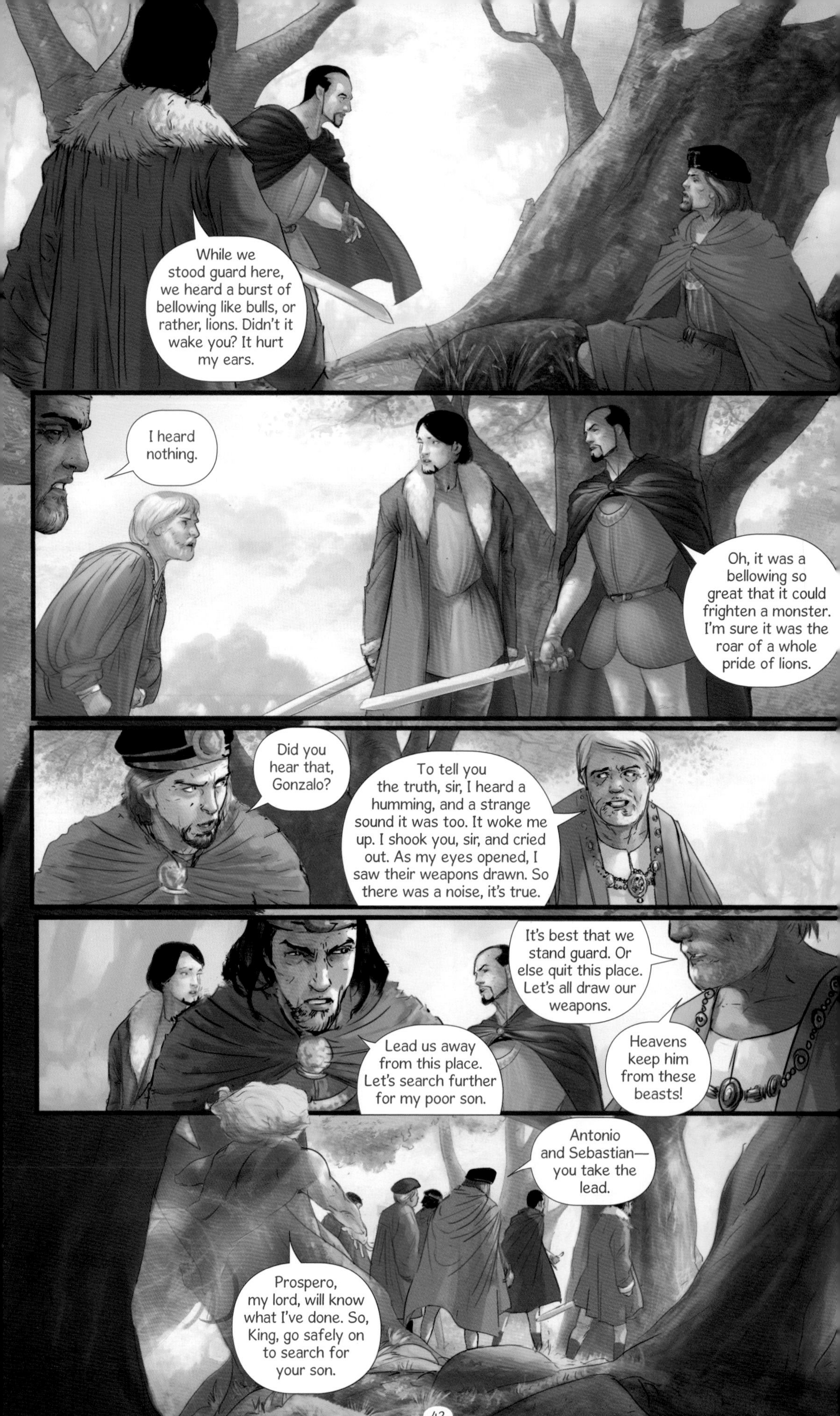
While we stood guard here, we heard a burst of bellowing like bulls, or rather, lions. Didn't it wake you? It hurt my ears.
I heard nothing.
Oh, it was a bellowing so great that it could frighten a monster. I'm sure it was the roar of a whole pride of lions.
Did you hear that, Gonzalo?
To tell you the truth, sir, I heard a humming, and a strange sound it was too. It woke me up. I shook you, sir, and cried out. As my eyes opened, I saw their weapons drawn. So there was a noise, it's true.
It's best that we stand guard. Or else quit this place. Let's all draw our weapons.
Lead us away from this place. Let's search further for my poor son.
Heavens keep him from these beasts!
Antonio and Sebastian—you take the lead.
Prospero, my lord, will know what I've done. So, King, go safely on to search for your son.

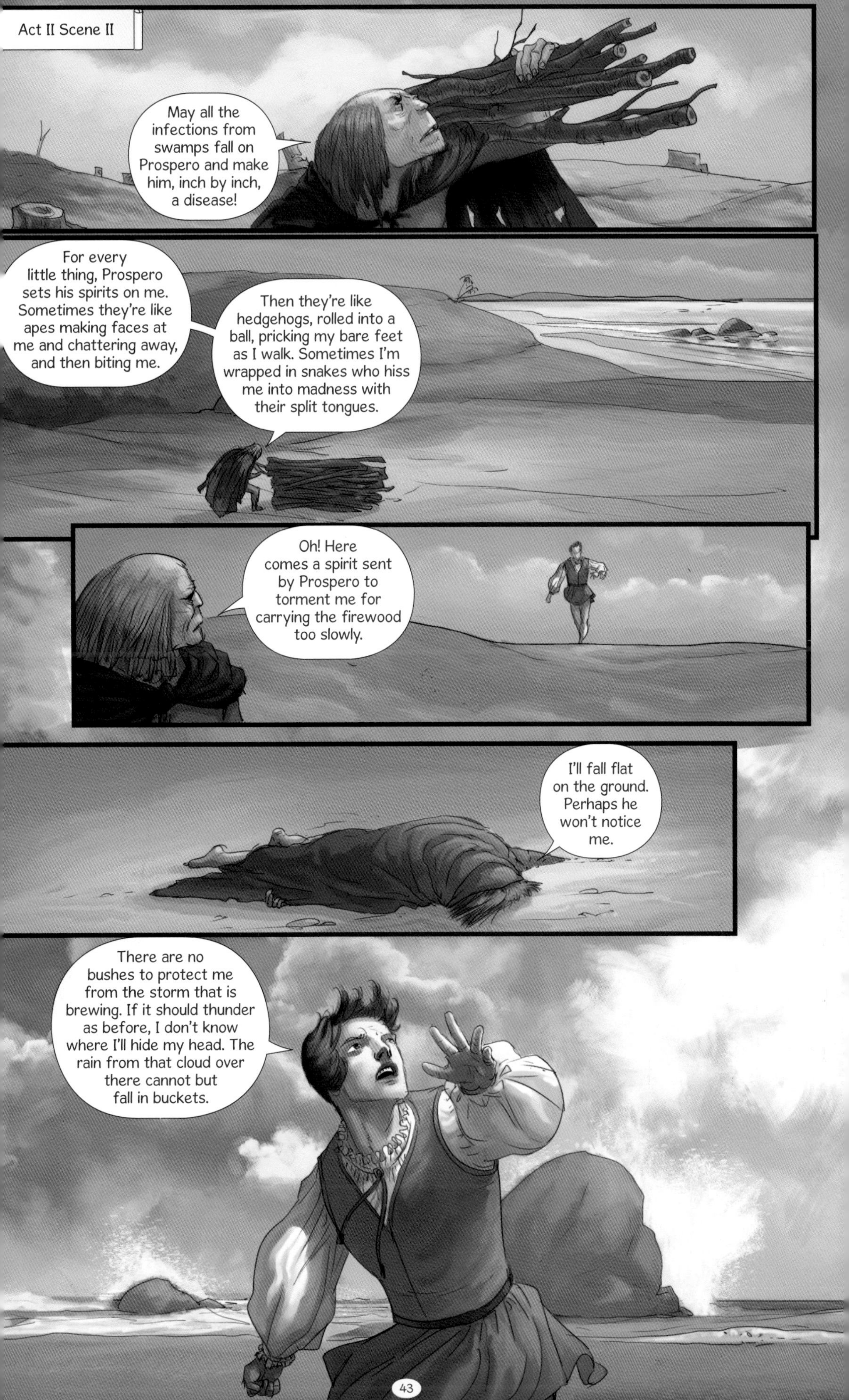
Act II Scene II
May all the infections from swamps fall on Prospero and make him, inch by inch, a disease!
For every little thing, Prospero sets his spirits on me. Sometimes they're like apes making faces at me and chattering away, and then biting me.
Then they're like hedgehogs, rolled into a ball, pricking my bare feet as I walk. Sometimes I'm wrapped in snakes who hiss me into madness with their split tongues.
Oh! Here comes a spirit sent by Prospero to torment me for carrying the firewood too slowly.
I'll fall flat on the ground. Perhaps he won't notice me.
There are no bushes to protect me from the storm that is brewing. If it should thunder as before, I don't know where I'll hide my head. The rain from that cloud over there cannot but fall in buckets.

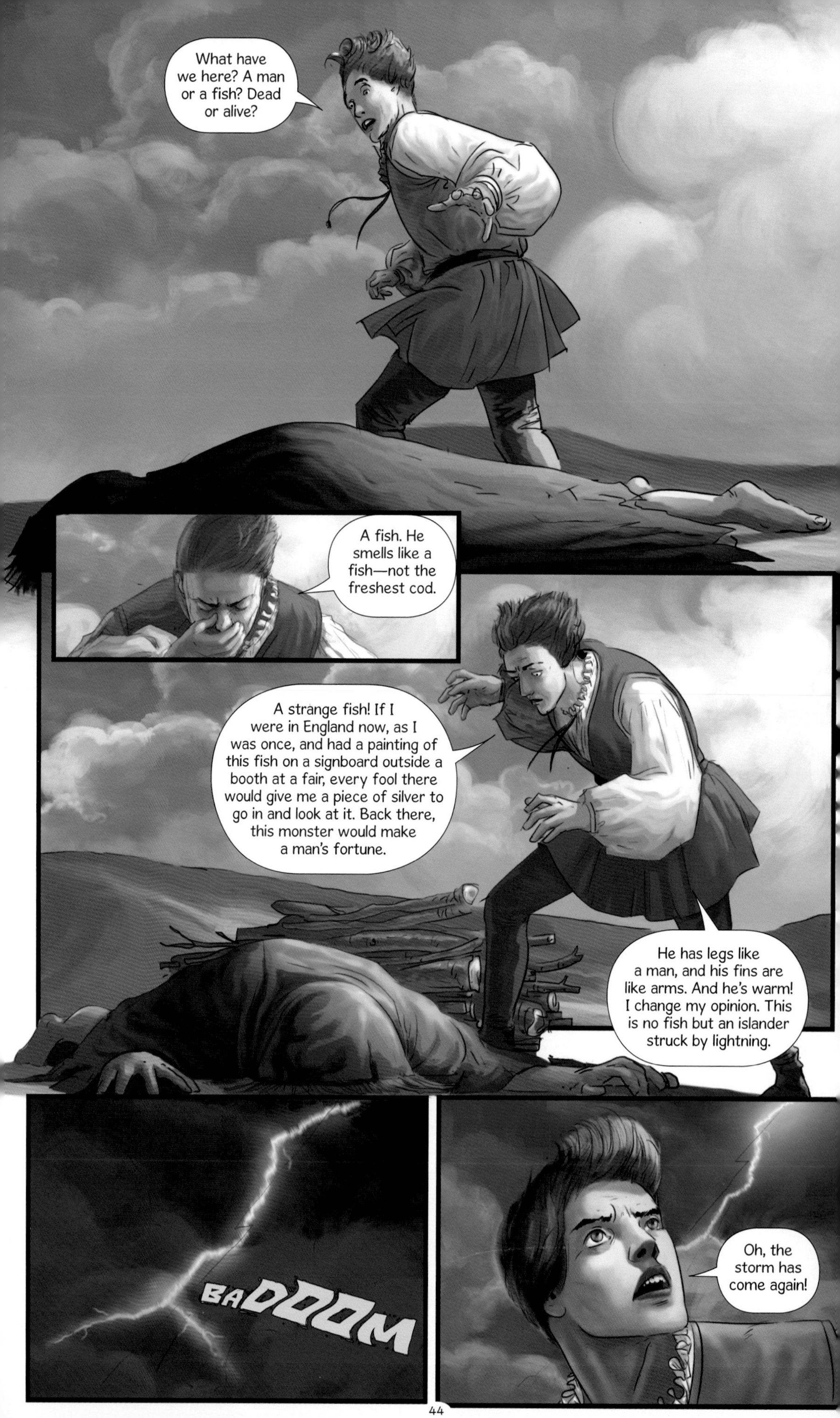
What have we here? A man or a fish? Dead or alive?
A fish. He smells like a fish—not the freshest cod.
A strange fish! If I were in England now, as I was once, and had a painting of this fish on a signboard outside a booth at a fair, every fool there would give me a piece of silver to go in and look at it. Back there, this monster would make a man's fortune.
He has legs like a man, and his fins are like arms. And he's warm! I change my opinion. This is no fish but an islander struck by lightning.
BADOOM
Oh, the storm has come again!

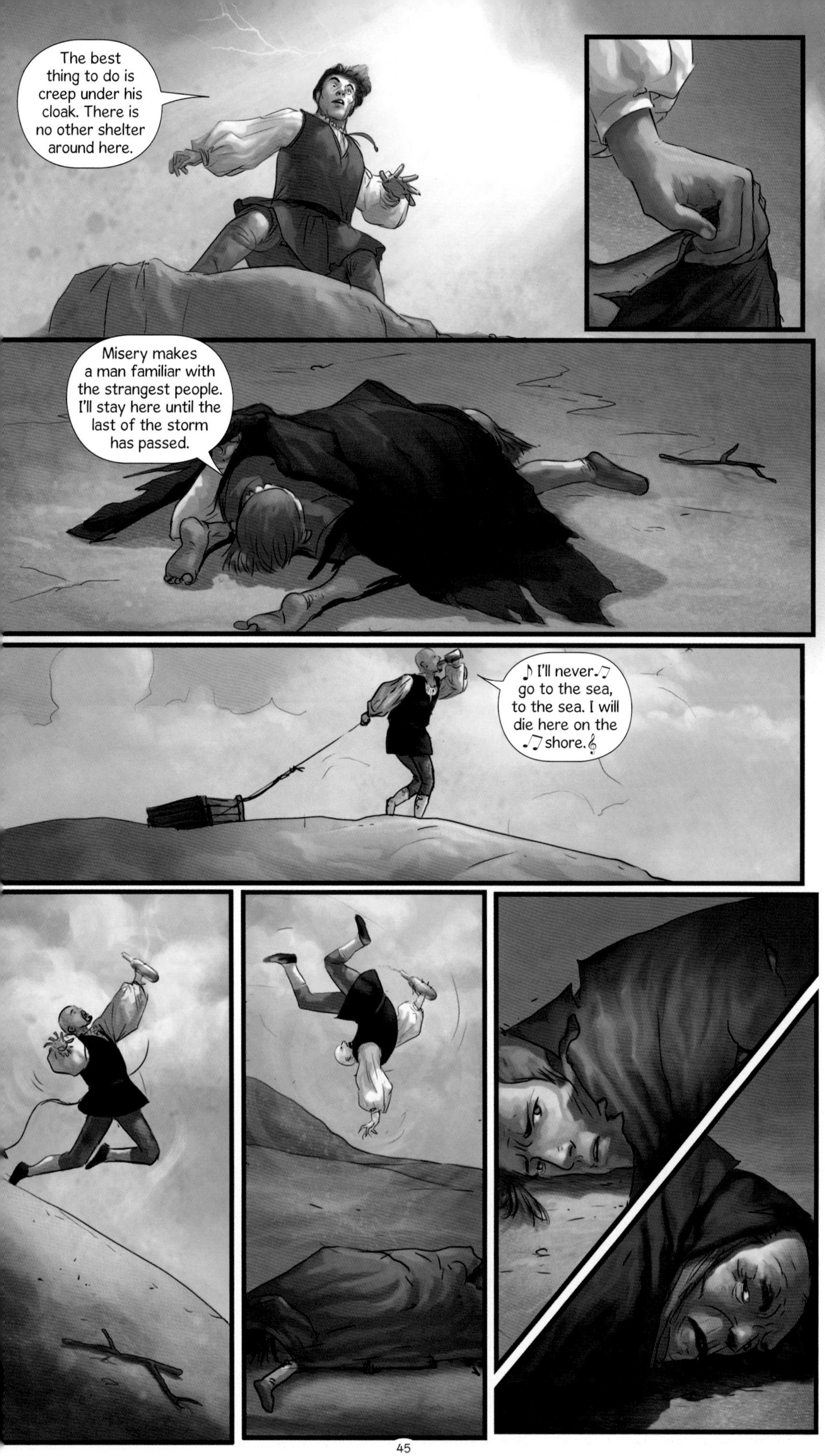
The best thing to do is creep under his cloak. There is no other shelter around here.
Misery makes a man familiar with the strangest people. I'll stay here until the last of the storm has passed.
♪ I'll never ♫ go to the sea, to the sea. I will die here on the ♫ shore. 𝄞

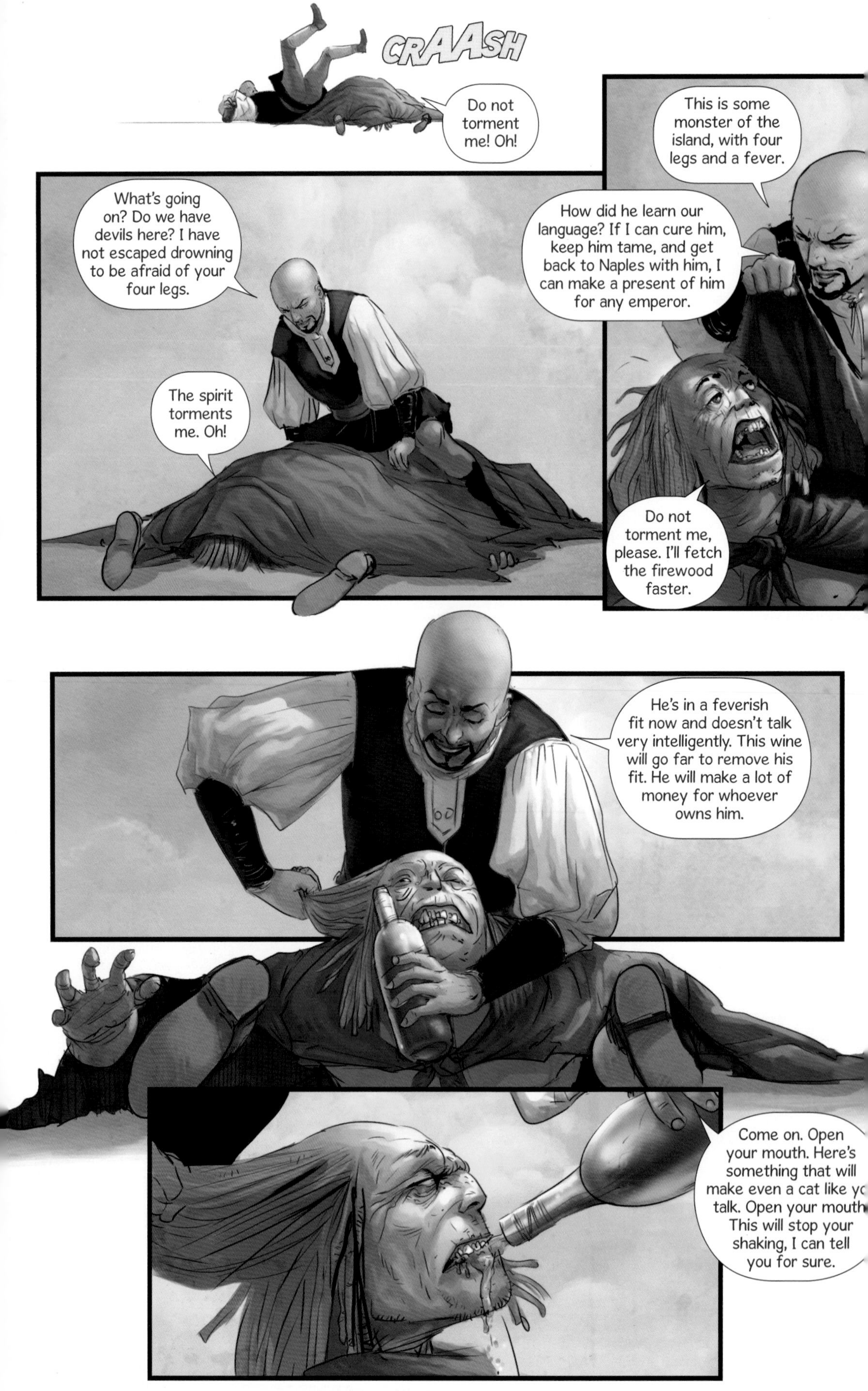
CRAASH
Do not torment me! Oh!
What's going on? Do we have devils here? I have not escaped drowning to be afraid of your four legs.
The spirit torments me. Oh!
This is some monster of the island, with four legs and a fever.
How did he learn our language? If I can cure him, keep him tame, and get back to Naples with him, I can make a present of him for any emperor.
Do not torment me, please. I'll fetch the firewood faster.
He's in a feverish fit now and doesn't talk very intelligently. This wine will go far to remove his fit. He will make a lot of money for whoever owns him.
Come on. Open your mouth. Here's something that will make even a cat like yo talk. Open your mouth This will stop your shaking, I can tell you for sure.

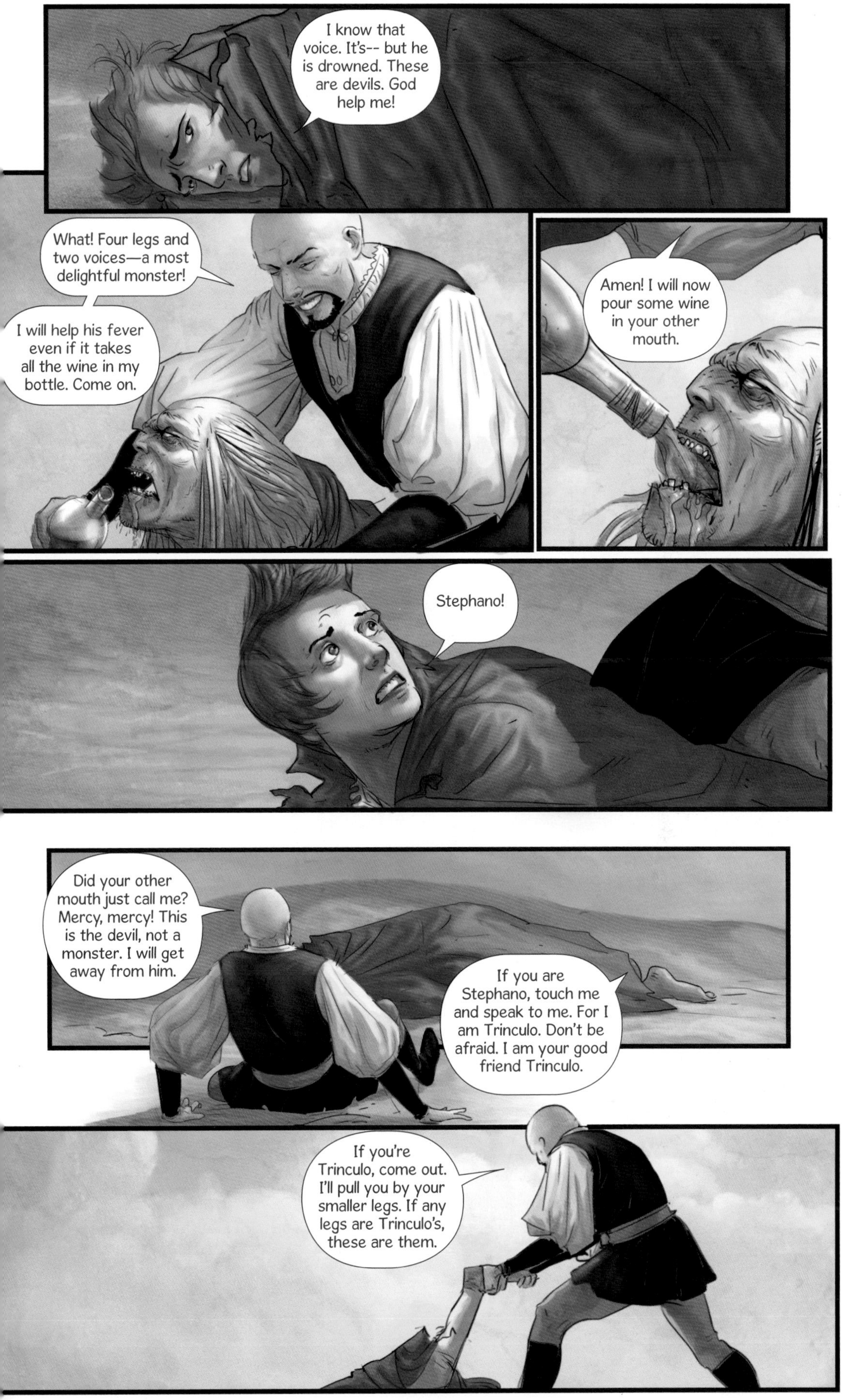
I know that voice. It's-- but he is drowned. These are devils. God help me!
What! Four legs and two voices—a most delightful monster!
I will help his fever even if it takes all the wine in my bottle. Come on.
Amen! I will now pour some wine in your other mouth.
Stephano!
Did your other mouth just call me? Mercy, mercy! This is the devil, not a monster. I will get away from him.
If you are Stephano, touch me and speak to me. For I am Trinculo. Don't be afraid. I am your good friend Trinculo.
If you're Trinculo, come out. I'll pull you by your smaller legs. If any legs are Trinculo's, these are them.

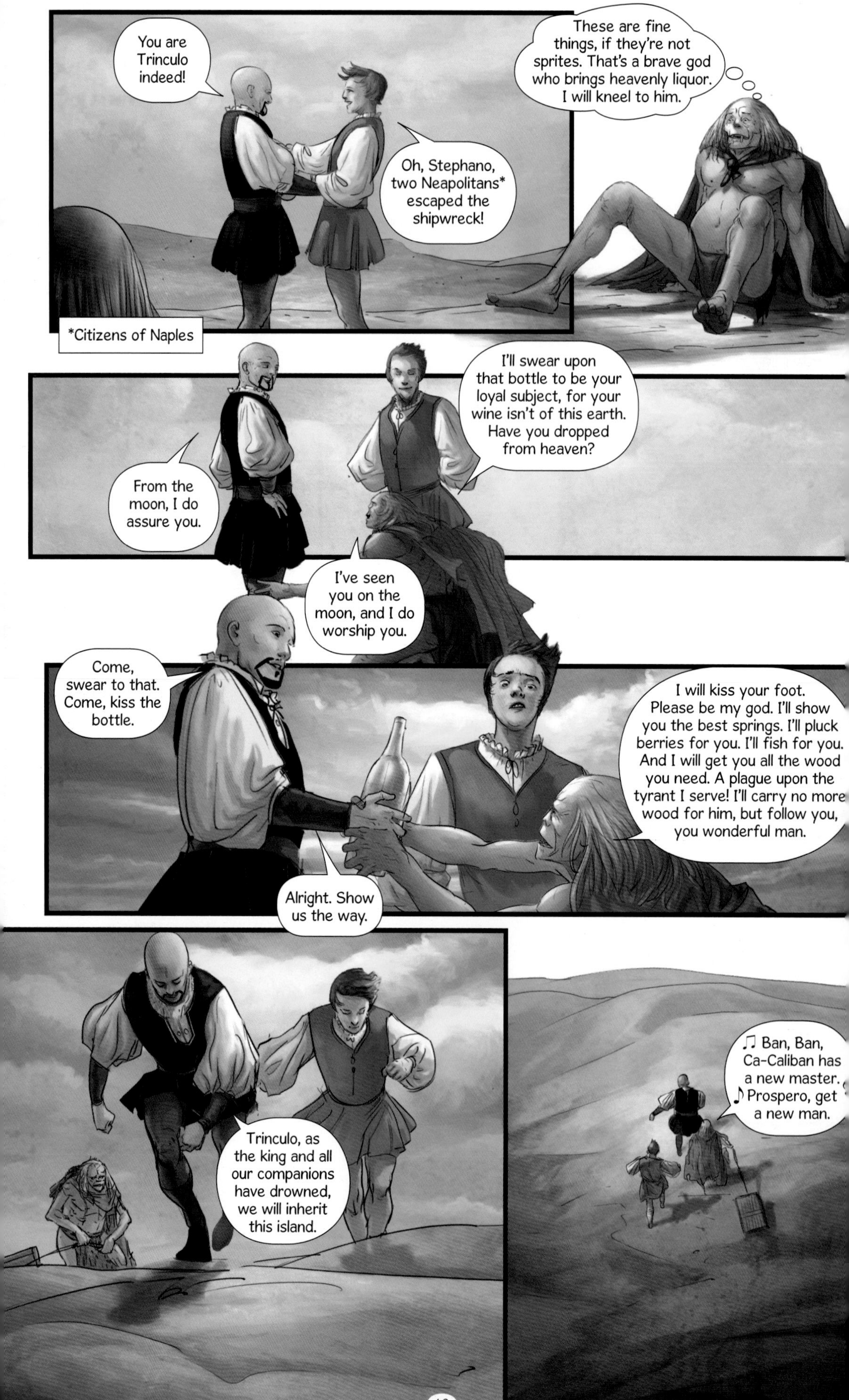
You are Trinculo indeed!
Oh, Stephano, two Neapolitans* escaped the shipwreck!
These are fine things, if they're not sprites. That's a brave god who brings heavenly liquor. I will kneel to him.
*Citizens of Naples
I'll swear upon that bottle to be your loyal subject, for your wine isn't of this earth. Have you dropped from heaven?
From the moon, I do assure you.
I've seen you on the moon, and I do worship you.
Come, swear to that. Come, kiss the bottle.
I will kiss your foot. Please be my god. I'll show you the best springs. I'll pluck berries for you. I'll fish for you. And I will get you all the wood you need. A plague upon the tyrant I serve! I'll carry no more wood for him, but follow you, you wonderful man.
Alright. Show us the way.
Trinculo, as the king and all our companions have drowned, we will inherit this island.
♫ Ban, Ban, Ca-Caliban has a new master. ♪ Prospero, get a new man.

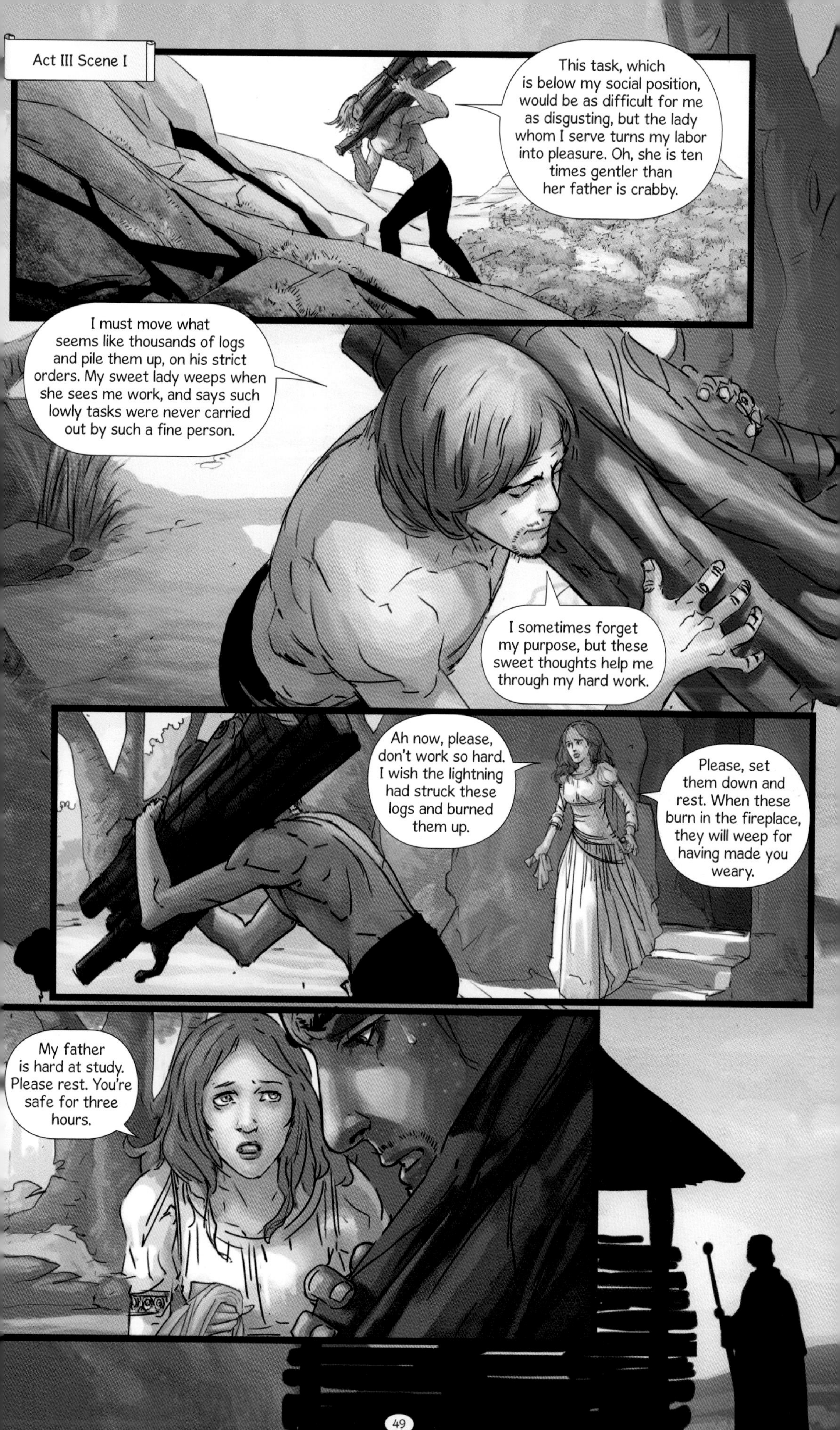
Act III Scene I
This task, which is below my social position, would be as difficult for me as disgusting, but the lady whom I serve turns my labor into pleasure. Oh, she is ten times gentler than her father is crabby.
I must move what seems like thousands of logs and pile them up, on his strict orders. My sweet lady weeps when she sees me work, and says such lowly tasks were never carried out by such a fine person.
I sometimes forget my purpose, but these sweet thoughts help me through my hard work.
Ah now, please, don't work so hard. I wish the lightning had struck these logs and burned them up.
Please, set them down and rest. When these burn in the fireplace, they will weep for having made you weary.
My father is hard at study. Please rest. You're safe for three hours.

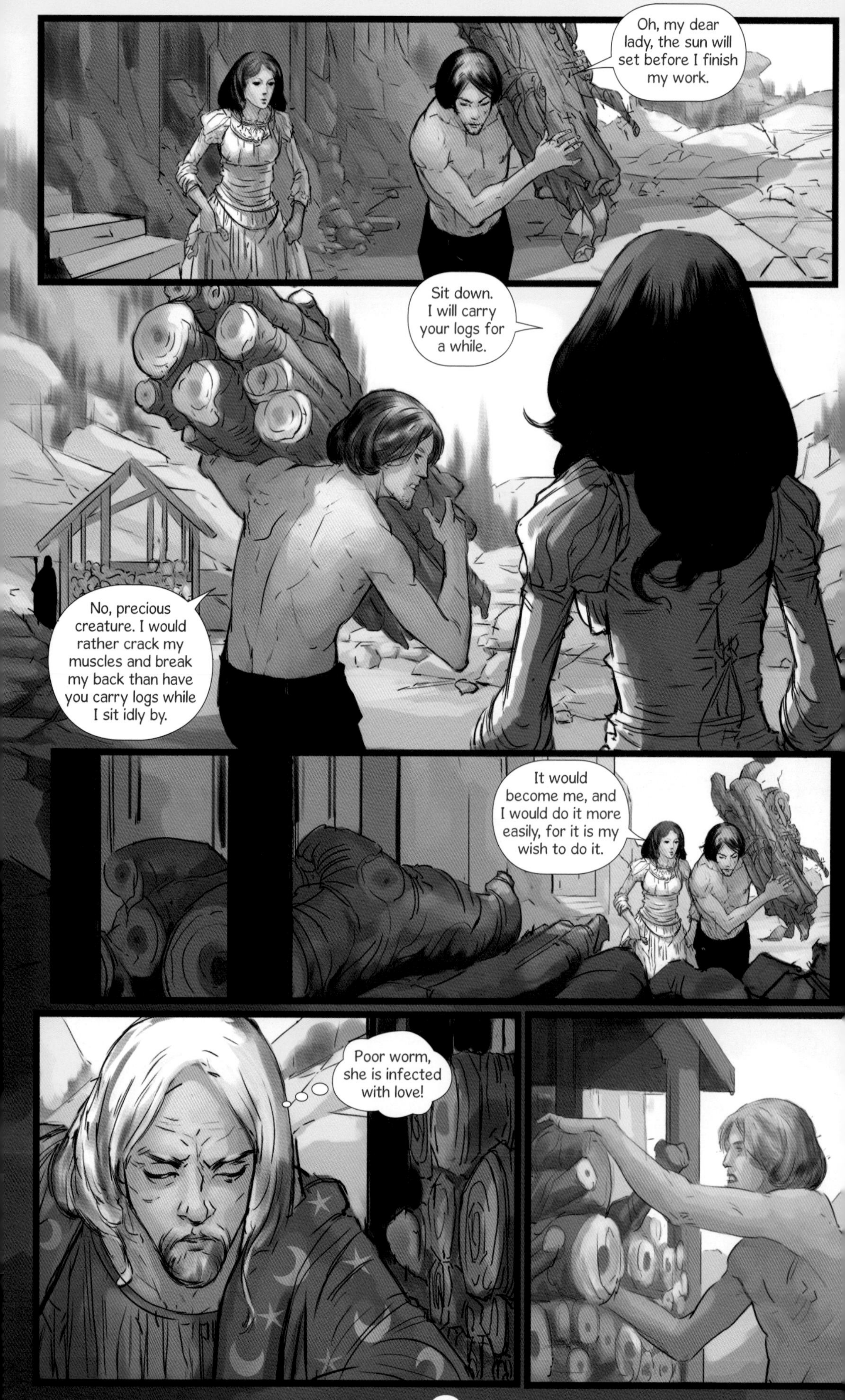
Oh, my dear lady, the sun will set before I finish my work.
Sit down. I will carry your logs for a while.
No, precious creature. I would rather crack my muscles and break my back than have you carry logs while I sit idly by.
It would become me, and I would do it more easily, for it is my wish to do it.
Poor worm, she is infected with love!

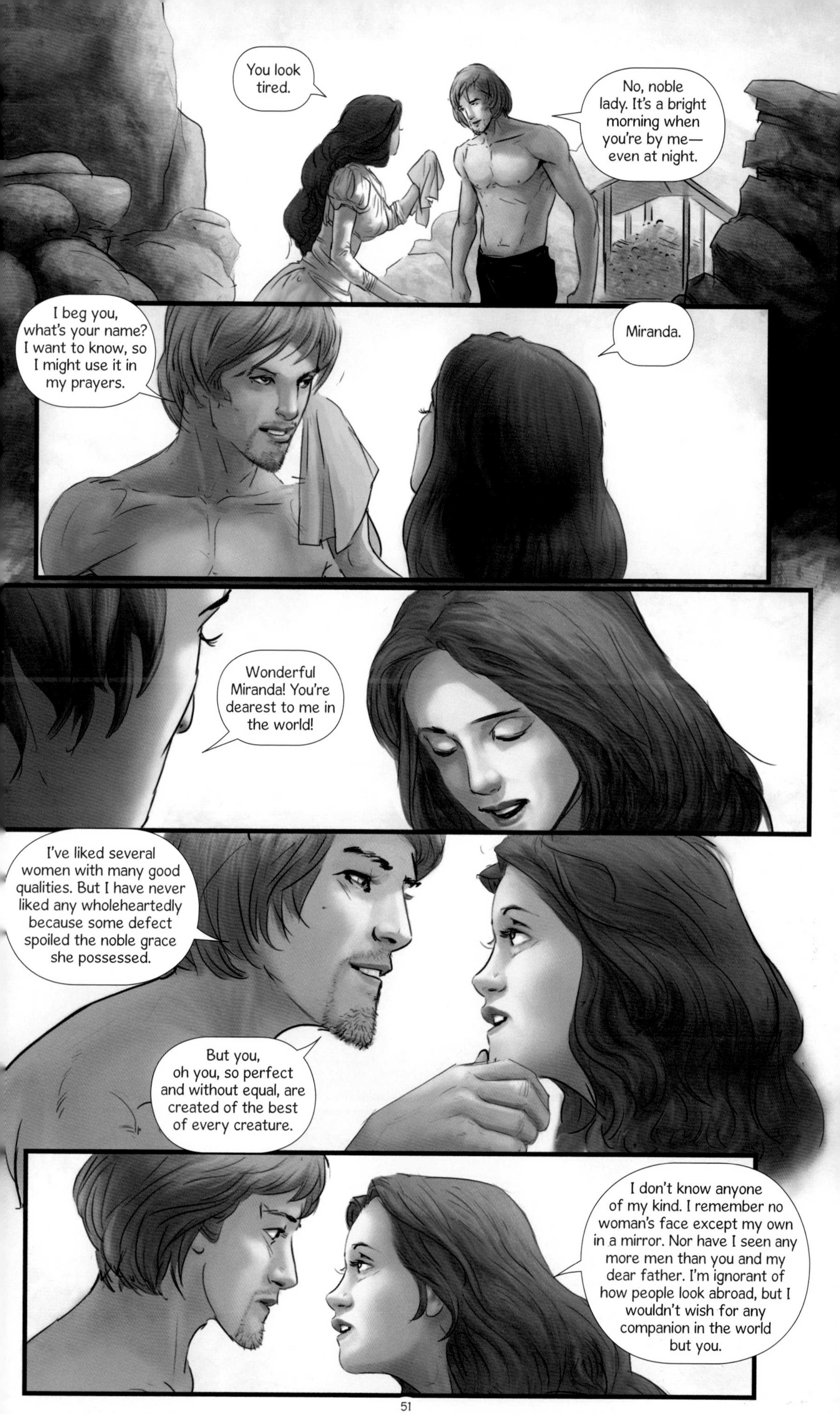
You look tired.
No, noble lady. It's a bright morning when you're by me—even at night.
I beg you, what's your name? I want to know, so I might use it in my prayers.
Miranda.
Wonderful Miranda! You're dearest to me in the world!
I've liked several women with many good qualities. But I have never liked any wholeheartedly because some defect spoiled the noble grace she possessed.
But you, oh you, so perfect and without equal, are created of the best of every creature.
I don't know anyone of my kind. I remember no woman's face except my own in a mirror. Nor have I seen any more men than you and my dear father. I'm ignorant of how people look abroad, but I wouldn't wish for any companion in the world but you.

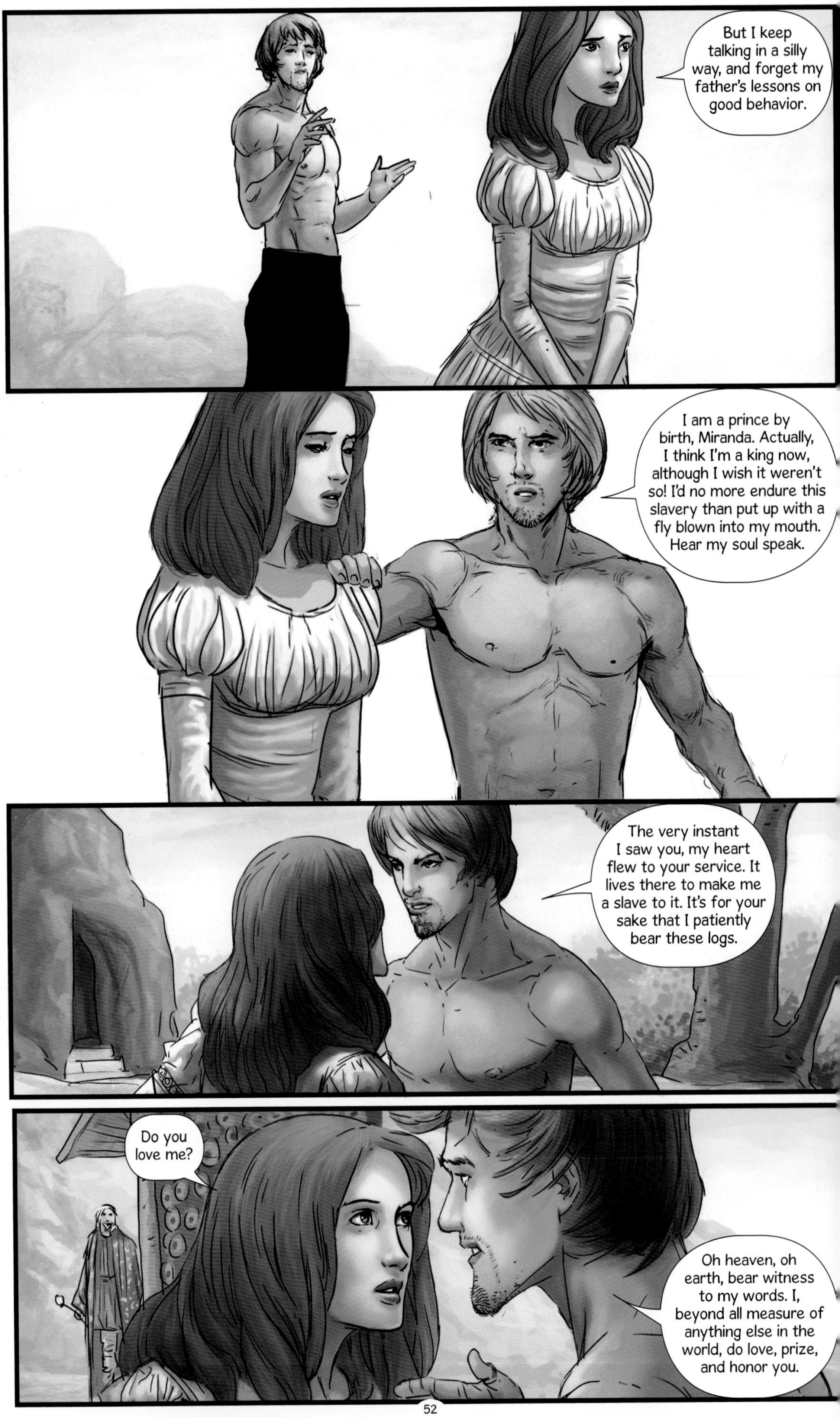
But I keep talking in a silly way, and forget my father's lessons on good behavior.
I am a prince by birth, Miranda. Actually, I think I'm a king now, although I wish it weren't so! I'd no more endure this slavery than put up with a fly blown into my mouth. Hear my soul speak.
The very instant I saw you, my heart flew to your service. It lives there to make me a slave to it. It's for your sake that I patiently bear these logs.
Do you love me?
Oh heaven, oh earth, bear witness to my words. I, beyond all measure of anything else in the world, do love, prize, and honor you.

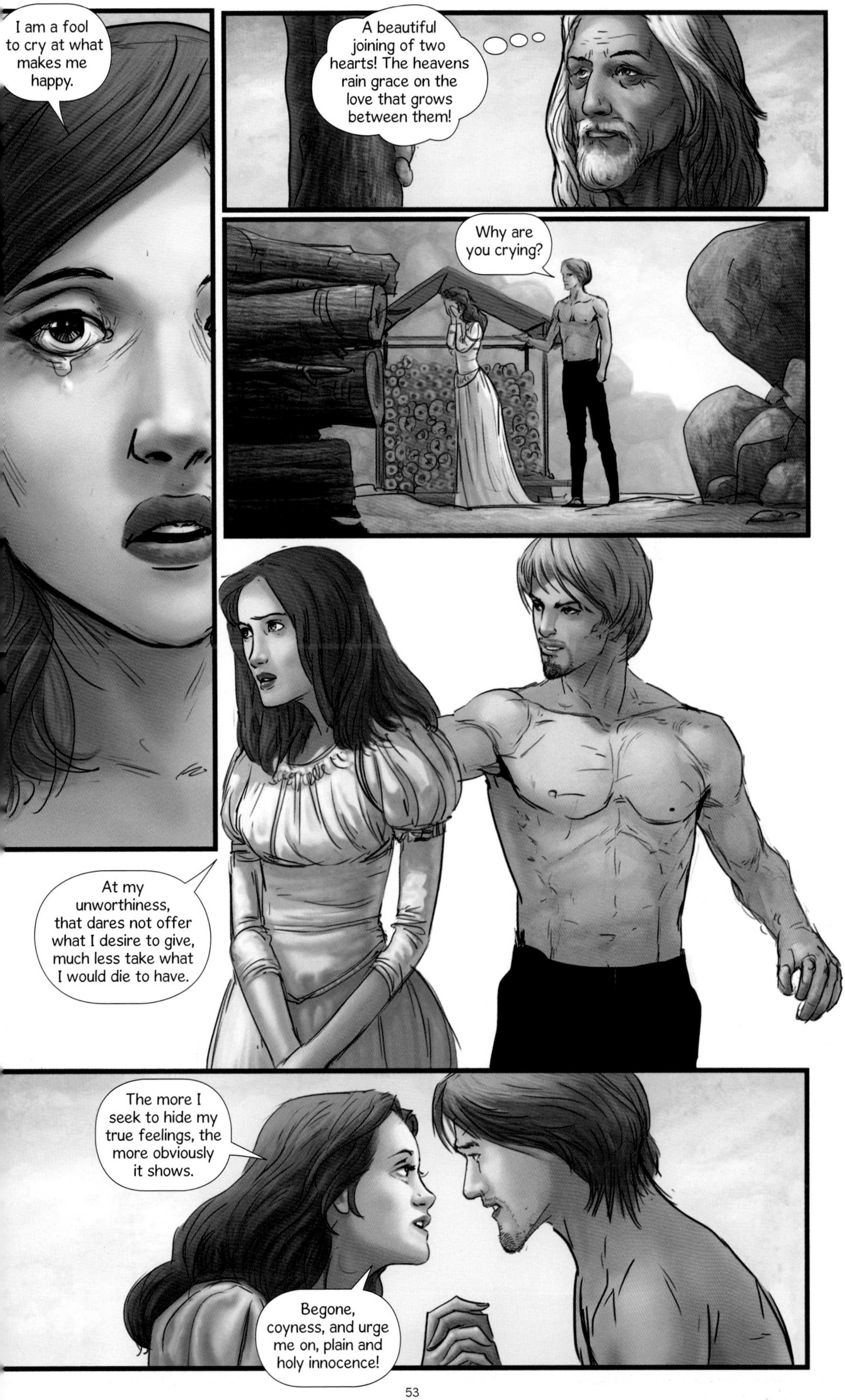

I am a fool to cry at what makes me happy.
A beautiful joining of two hearts! The heavens rain grace on the love that grows between them!
Why are you crying?
At my unworthiness, that dares not offer what I desire to give, much less take what I would die to have.
The more I seek to hide my true feelings, the more obviously it shows.
Begone, coyness, and urge me on, plain and holy innocence!

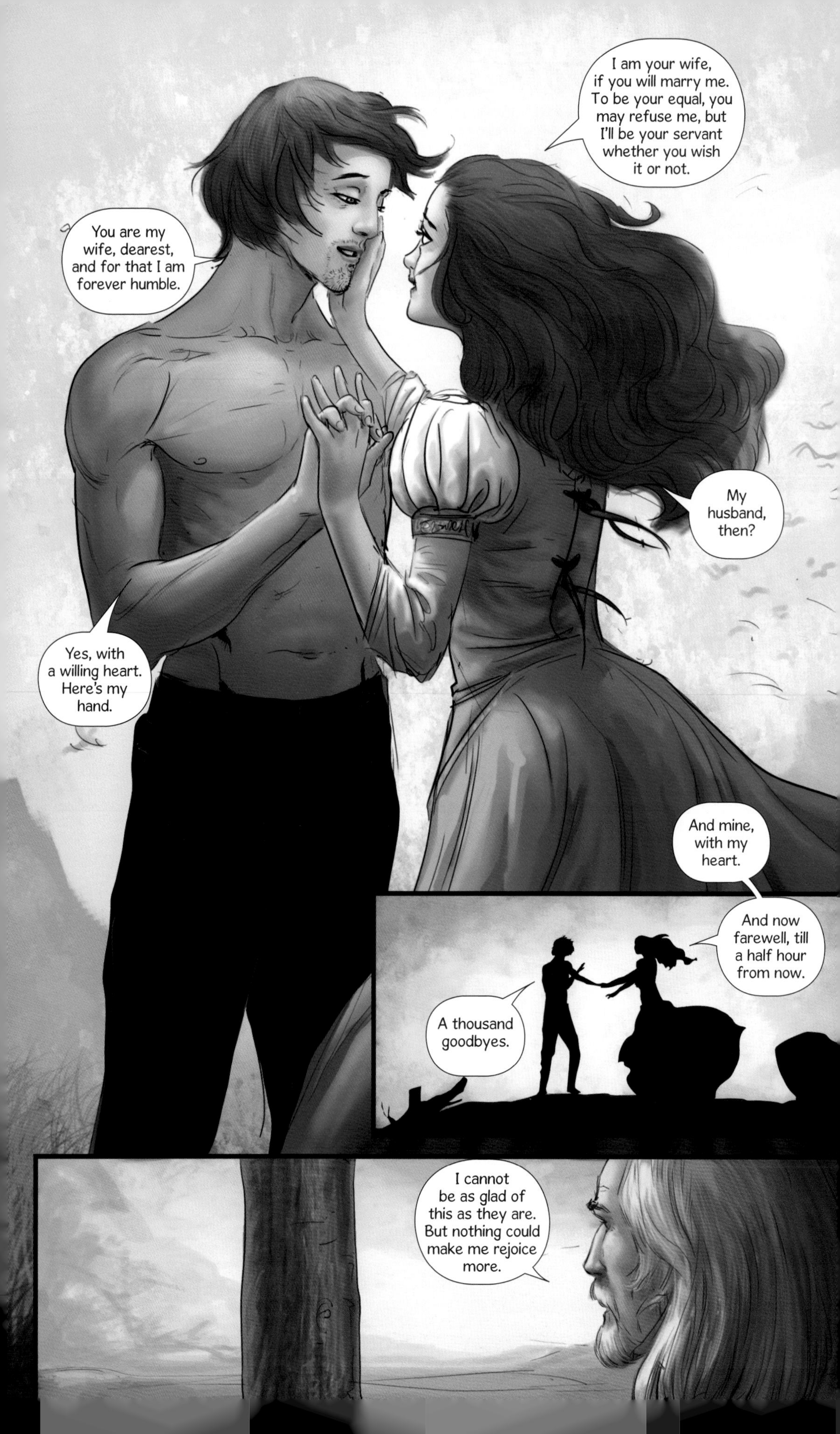
I am your wife, if you will marry me. To be your equal, you may refuse me, but I'll be your servant whether you wish it or not.
You are my wife, dearest, and for that I am forever humble.
My husband, then?
Yes, with a willing heart. Here's my hand.
And mine, with my heart.
And now farewell, till a half hour from now.
A thousand goodbyes.
I cannot be as glad of this as they are. But nothing could make me rejoice more.

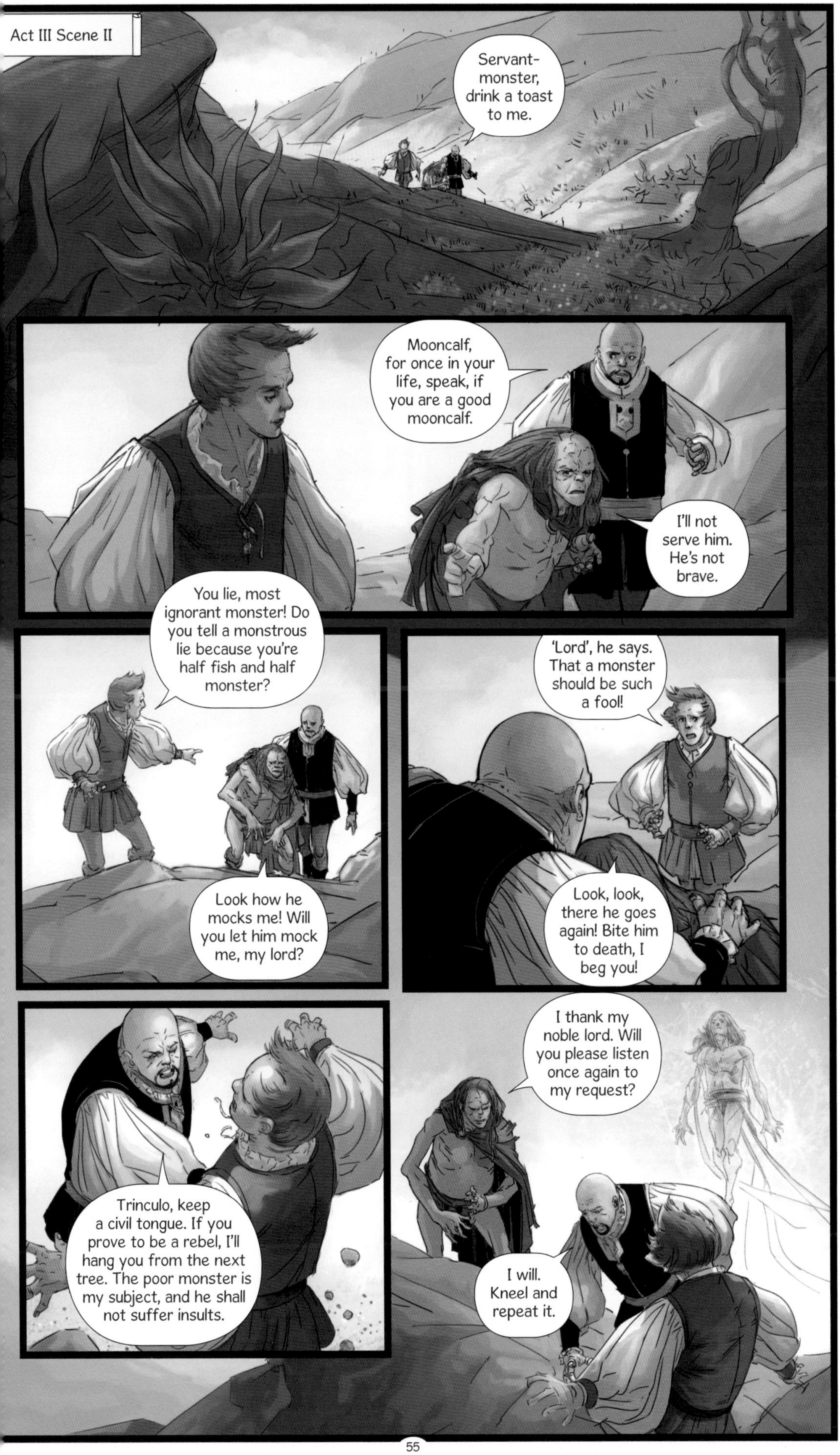
Act III Scene II
Servant-monster, drink a toast to me.
Mooncalf, for once in your life, speak, if you are a good mooncalf.
I'll not serve him. He's not brave.
You lie, most ignorant monster! Do you tell a monstrous lie because you're half fish and half monster?
Look how he mocks me! Will you let him mock me, my lord?
'Lord', he says. That a monster should be such a fool!
Look, look, there he goes again! Bite him to death, I beg you!
Trinculo, keep a civil tongue. If you prove to be a rebel, I'll hang you from the next tree. The poor monster is my subject, and he shall not suffer insults.
I thank my noble lord. Will you please listen once again to my request?
I will. Kneel and repeat it.

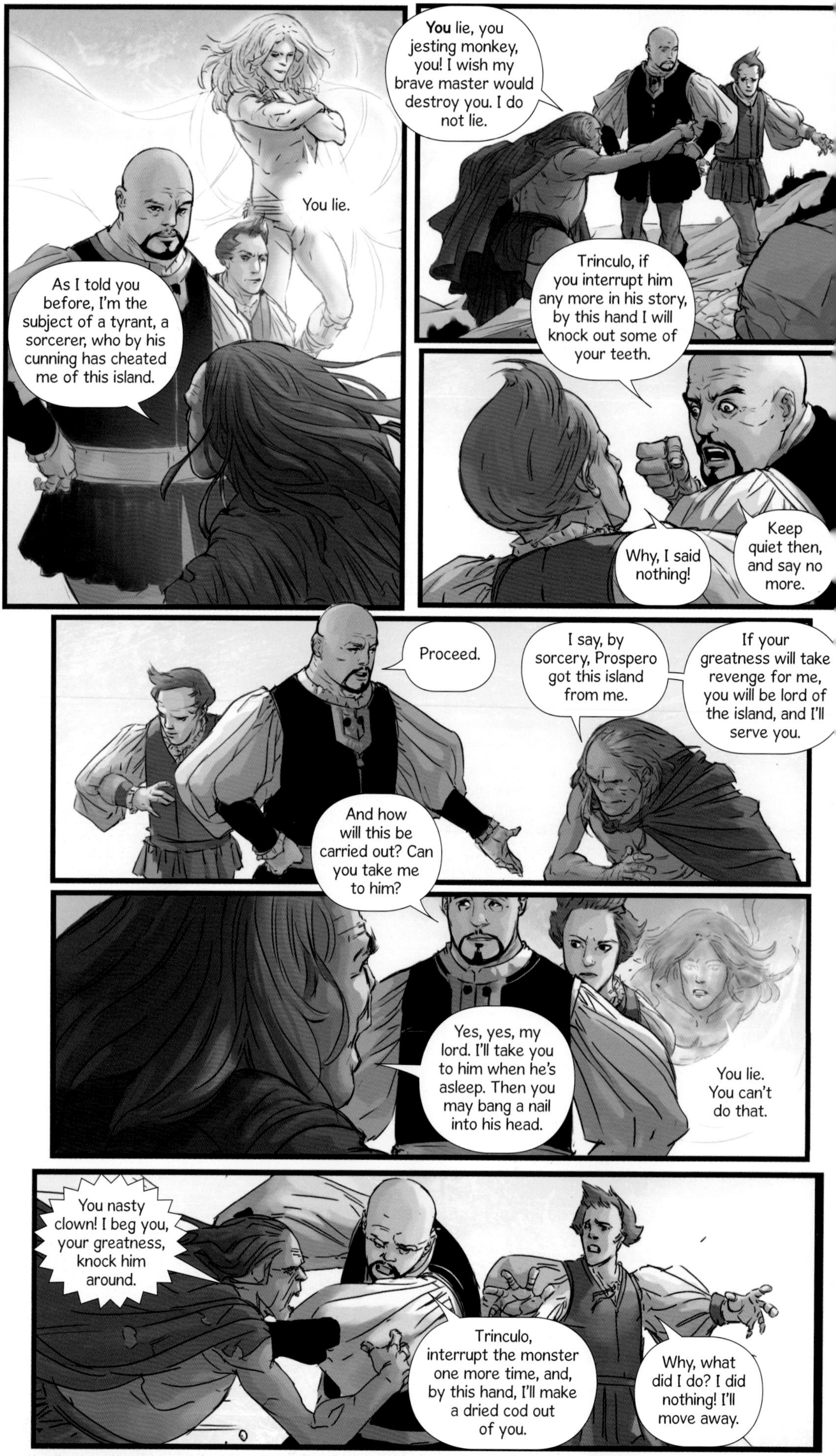
As I told you before, I'm the subject of a tyrant, a sorcerer, who by his cunning has cheated me of this island.
You lie.
You lie, you jesting monkey, you! I wish my brave master would destroy you. I do not lie.
Trinculo, if you interrupt him any more in his story, by this hand I will knock out some of your teeth.
Why, I said nothing!
Keep quiet then, and say no more.
Proceed.
I say, by sorcery, Prospero got this island from me.
If your greatness will take revenge for me, you will be lord of the island, and I'll serve you.
And how will this be carried out? Can you take me to him?
Yes, yes, my lord. I'll take you to him when he's asleep. Then you may bang a nail into his head.
You lie. You can't do that.
You nasty clown! I beg you, your greatness, knock him around.
Trinculo, interrupt the monster one more time, and, by this hand, I'll make a dried cod out of you.
Why, what did I do? I did nothing! I'll move away.

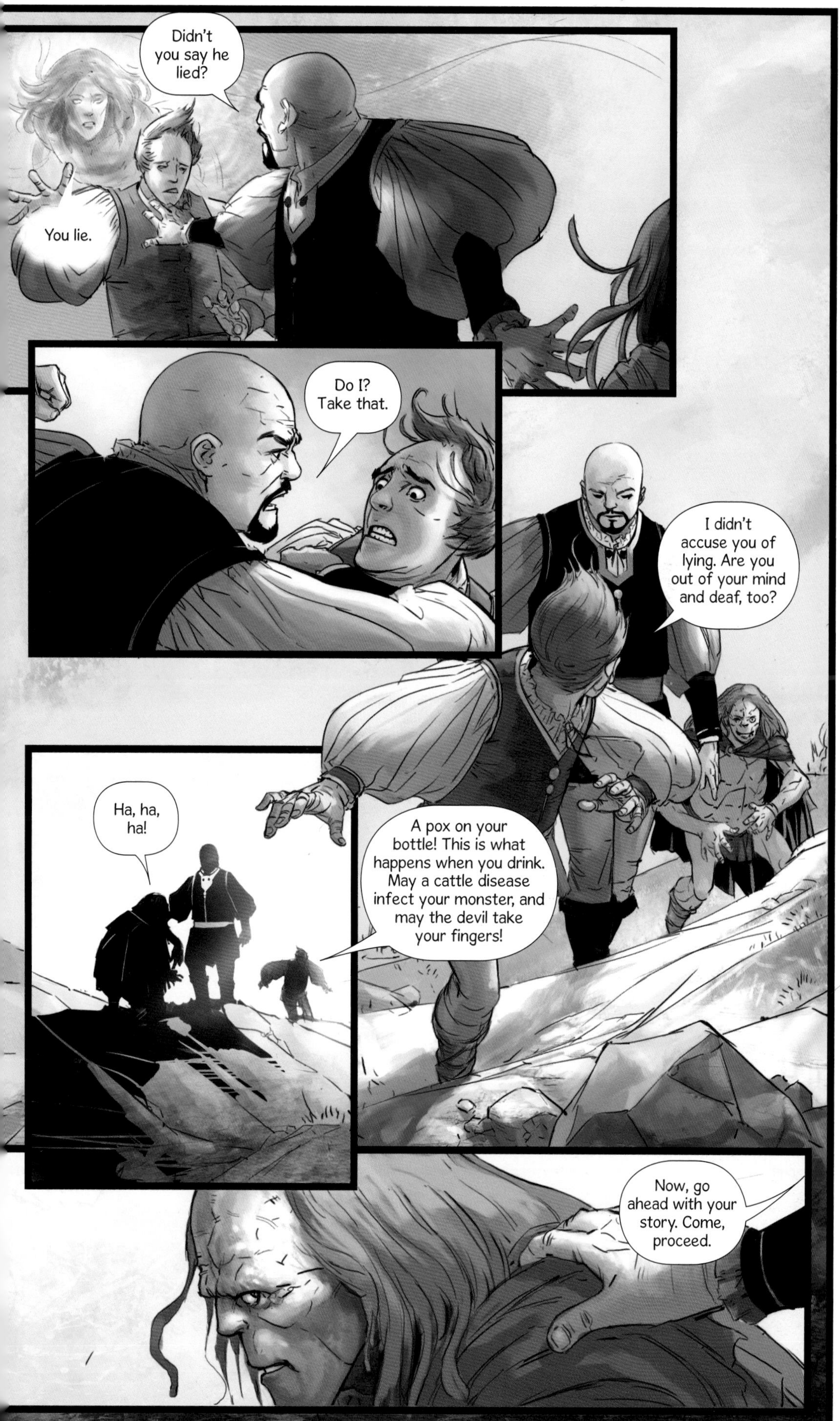
Didn't you say he lied?
You lie.
Do I? Take that.
I didn't accuse you of lying. Are you out of your mind and deaf, too?
Ha, ha, ha!
A pox on your bottle! This is what happens when you drink. May a cattle disease infect your monster, and may the devil take your fingers!
Now, go ahead with your story. Come, proceed.

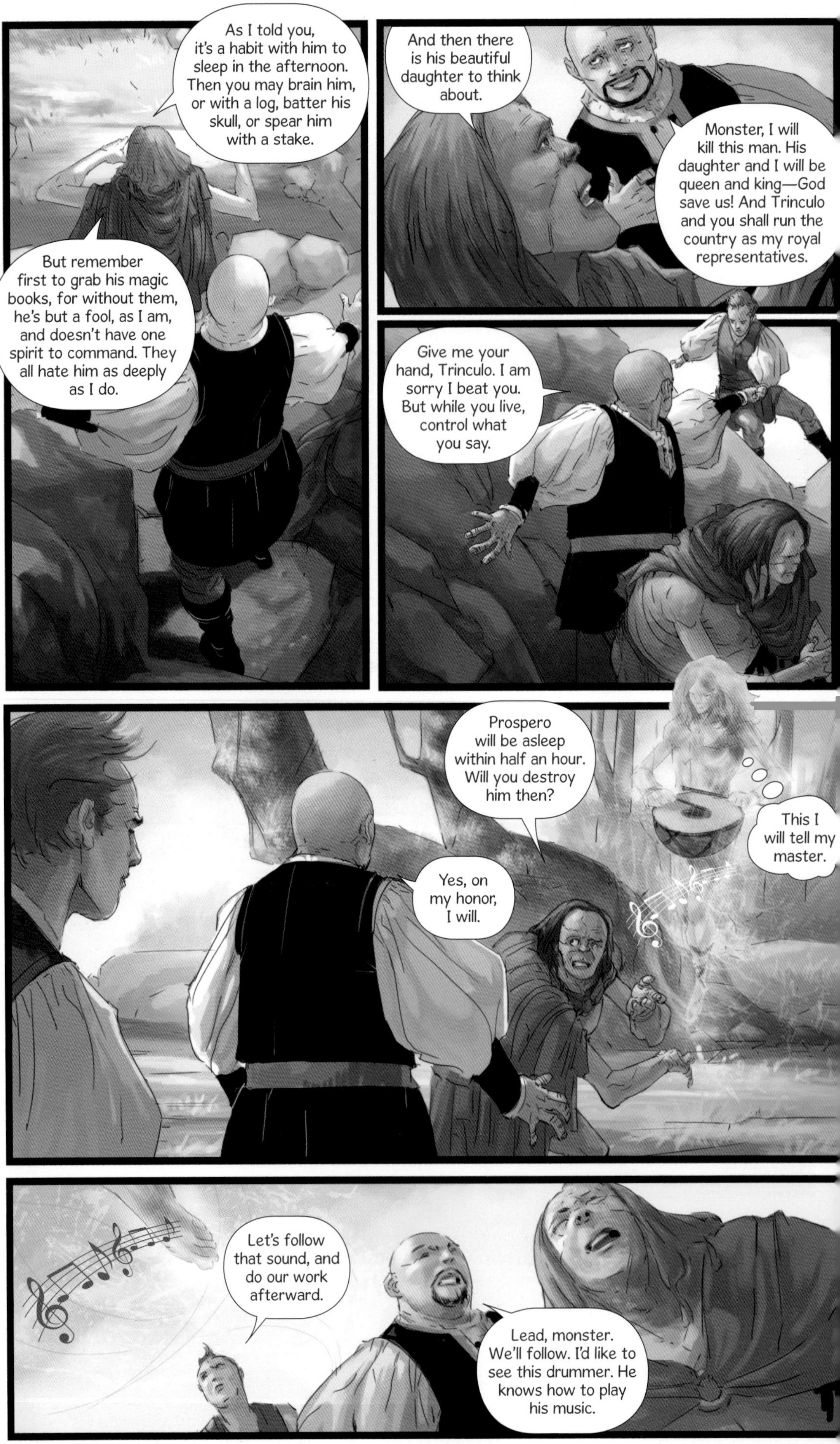
As I told you, it's a habit with him to sleep in the afternoon. Then you may brain him, or with a log, batter his skull, or spear him with a stake.
But remember first to grab his magic books, for without them, he's but a fool, as I am, and doesn't have one spirit to command. They all hate him as deeply as I do.
And then there is his beautiful daughter to think about.
Monster, I will kill this man. His daughter and I will be queen and king—God save us! And Trinculo and you shall run the country as my royal representatives.
Give me your hand, Trinculo. I am sorry I beat you. But while you live, control what you say.
Prospero will be asleep within half an hour. Will you destroy him then?
Yes, on my honor, I will.
This I will tell my master.
Let's follow that sound, and do our work afterward.
Lead, monster. We'll follow. I'd like to see this drummer. He knows how to play his music.

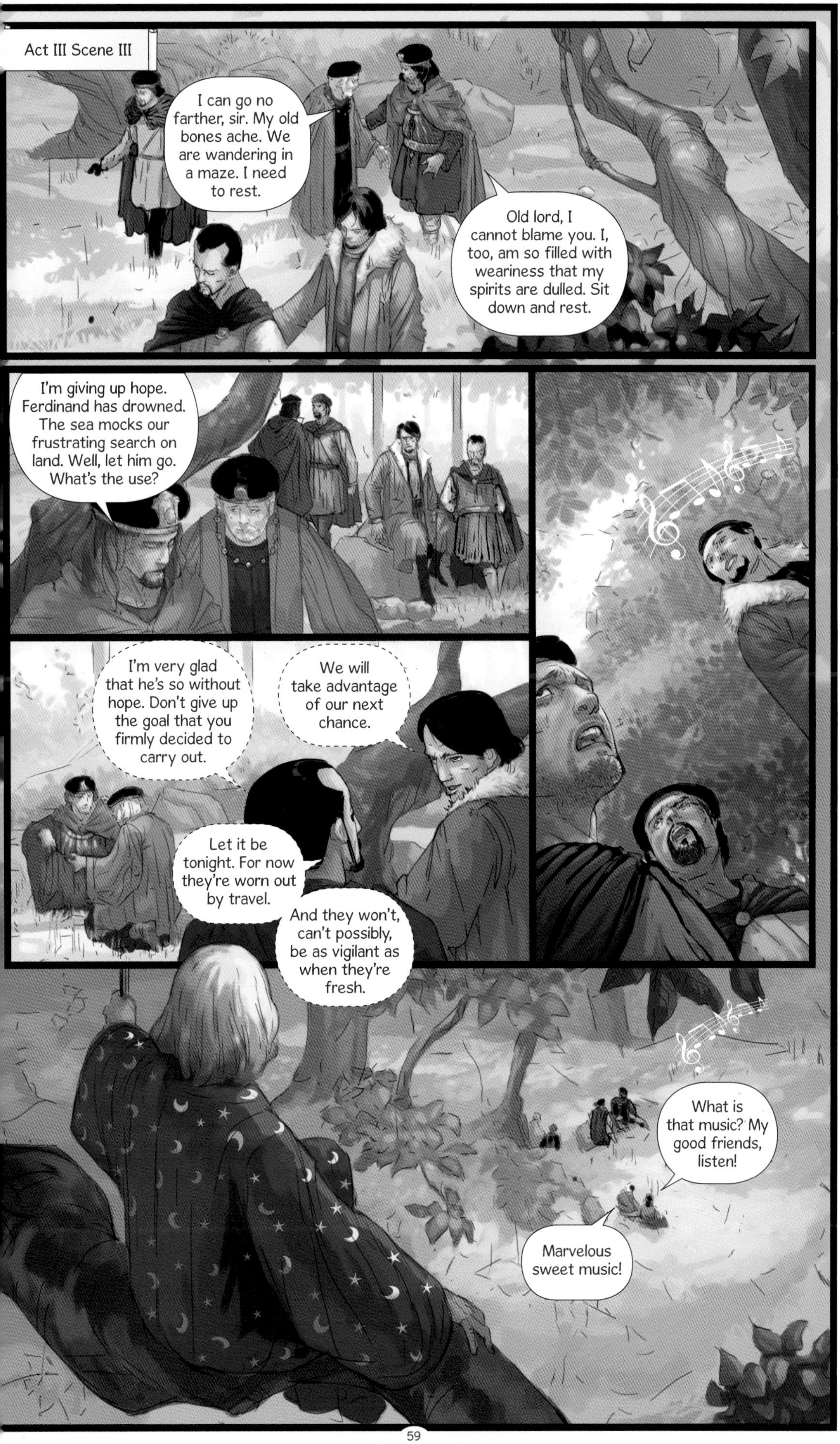
Act III Scene III
I can go no farther, sir. My old bones ache. We are wandering in a maze. I need to rest.
Old lord, I cannot blame you. I, too, am so filled with weariness that my spirits are dulled. Sit down and rest.
I'm giving up hope. Ferdinand has drowned. The sea mocks our frustrating search on land. Well, let him go. What's the use?
I'm very glad that he's so without hope. Don't give up the goal that you firmly decided to carry out.
We will take advantage of our next chance.
Let it be tonight. For now they're worn out by travel.
And they won't, can't possibly, be as vigilant as when they're fresh.
What is that music? My good friends, listen!
Marvelous sweet music!

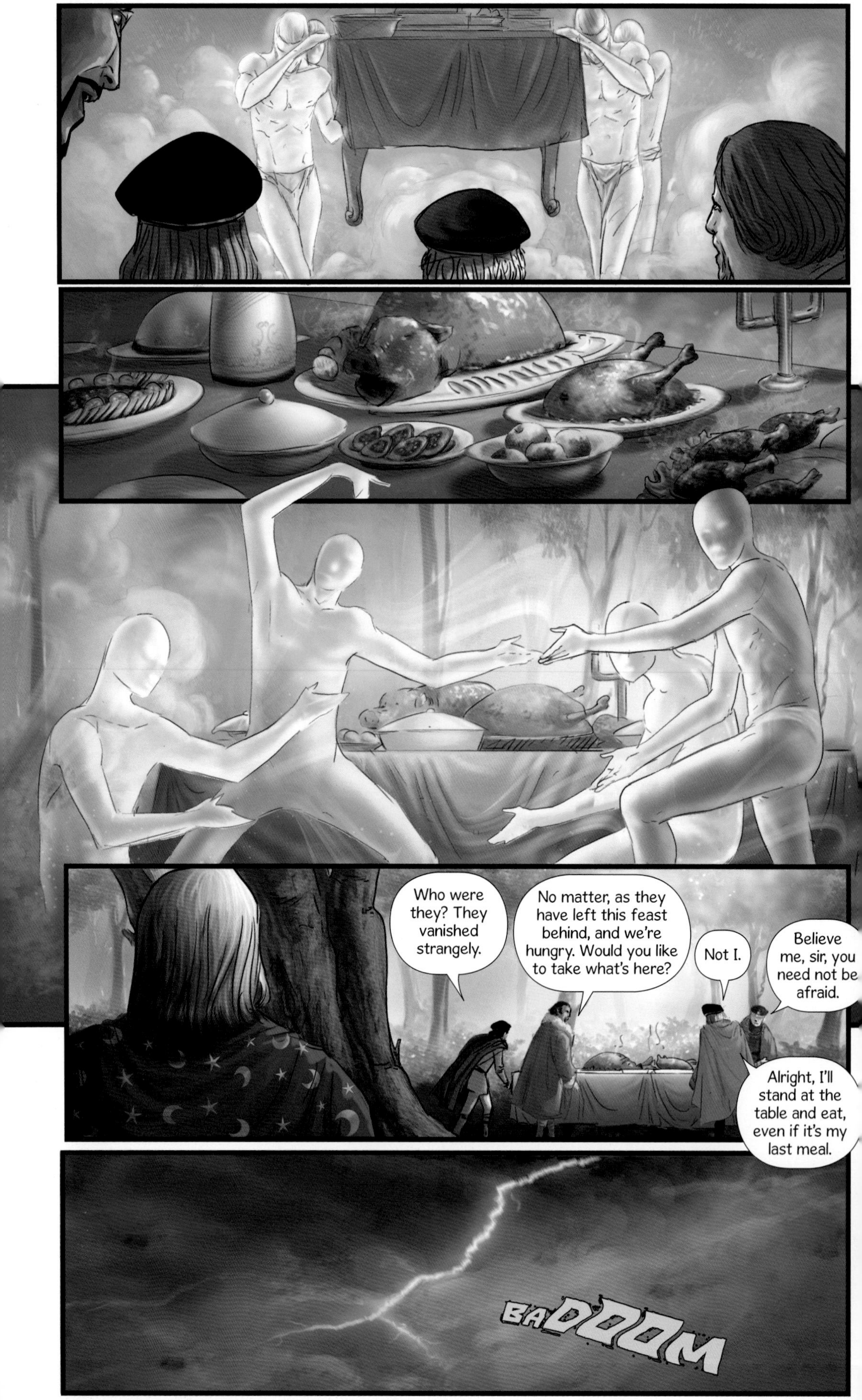
Who were they? They vanished strangely.
No matter, as they have left this feast behind, and we're hungry. Would you like to take what's here?
Not I.
Believe me, sir, you need not be afraid.
Alright, I'll stand at the table and eat, even if it's my last meal.
BADOOM

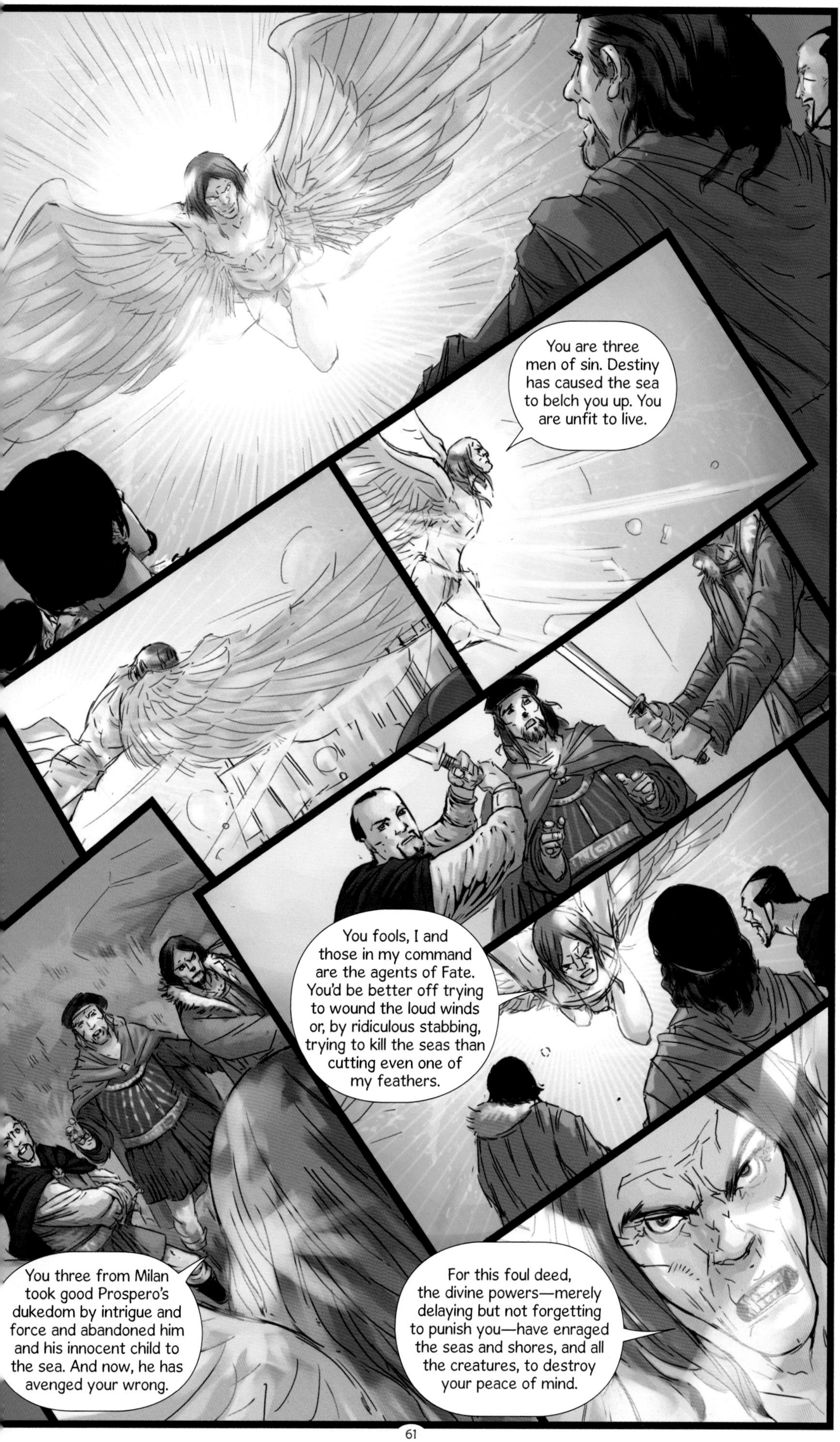

You are three men of sin. Destiny has caused the sea to belch you up. You are unfit to live.
You fools, I and those in my command are the agents of Fate. You'd be better off trying to wound the loud winds or, by ridiculous stabbing, trying to kill the seas than cutting even one of my feathers.
You three from Milan took good Prospero's dukedom by intrigue and force and abandoned him and his innocent child to the sea. And now, he has avenged your wrong.
For this foul deed, the divine powers—merely delaying but not forgetting to punish you—have enraged the seas and shores, and all the creatures, to destroy your peace of mind.

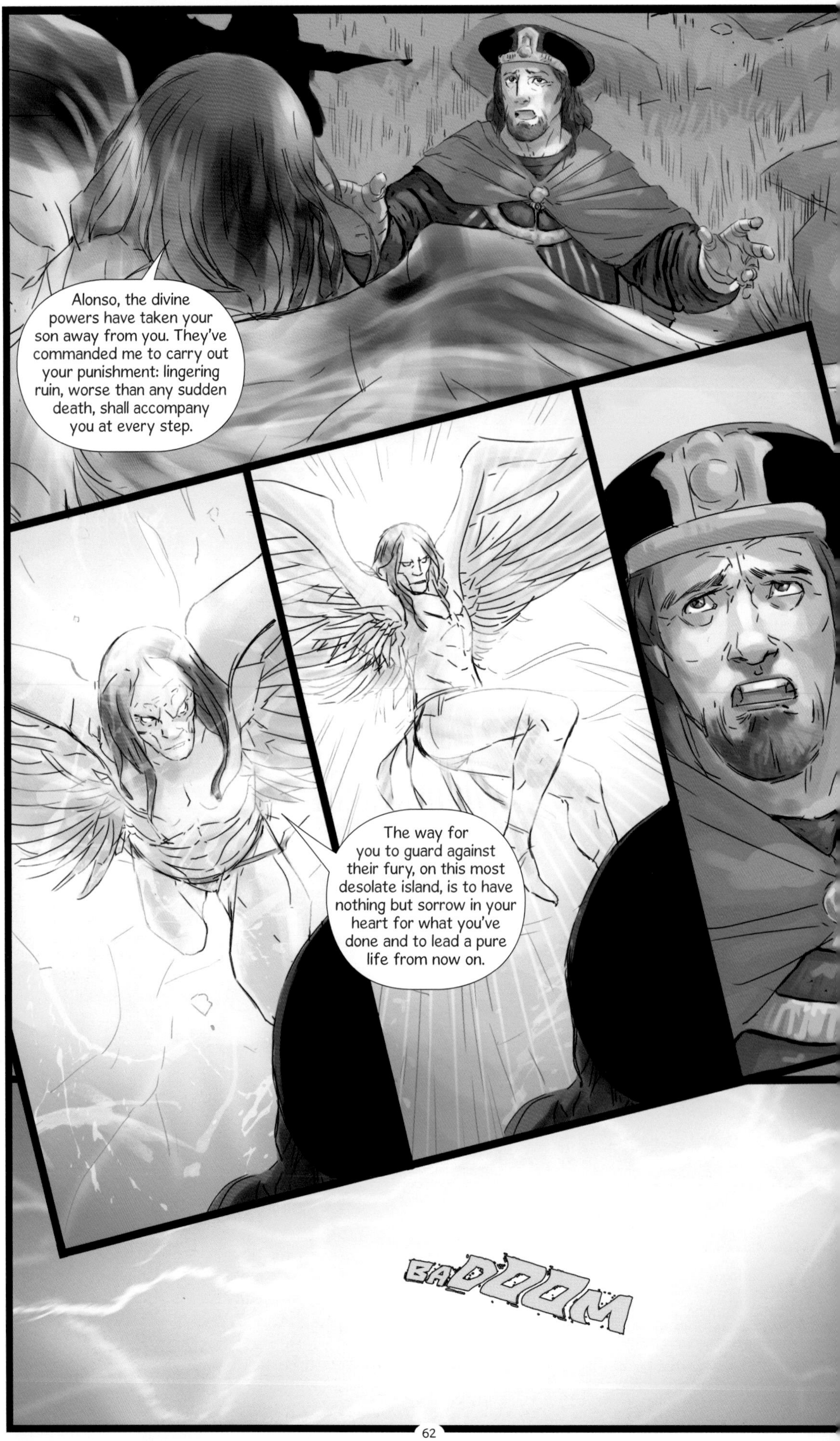
Alonso, the divine powers have taken your son away from you. They've commanded me to carry out your punishment: lingering ruin, worse than any sudden death, shall accompany you at every step.
The way for you to guard against their fury, on this most desolate island, is to have nothing but sorrow in your heart for what you've done and to lead a pure life from now on.
BADOOM

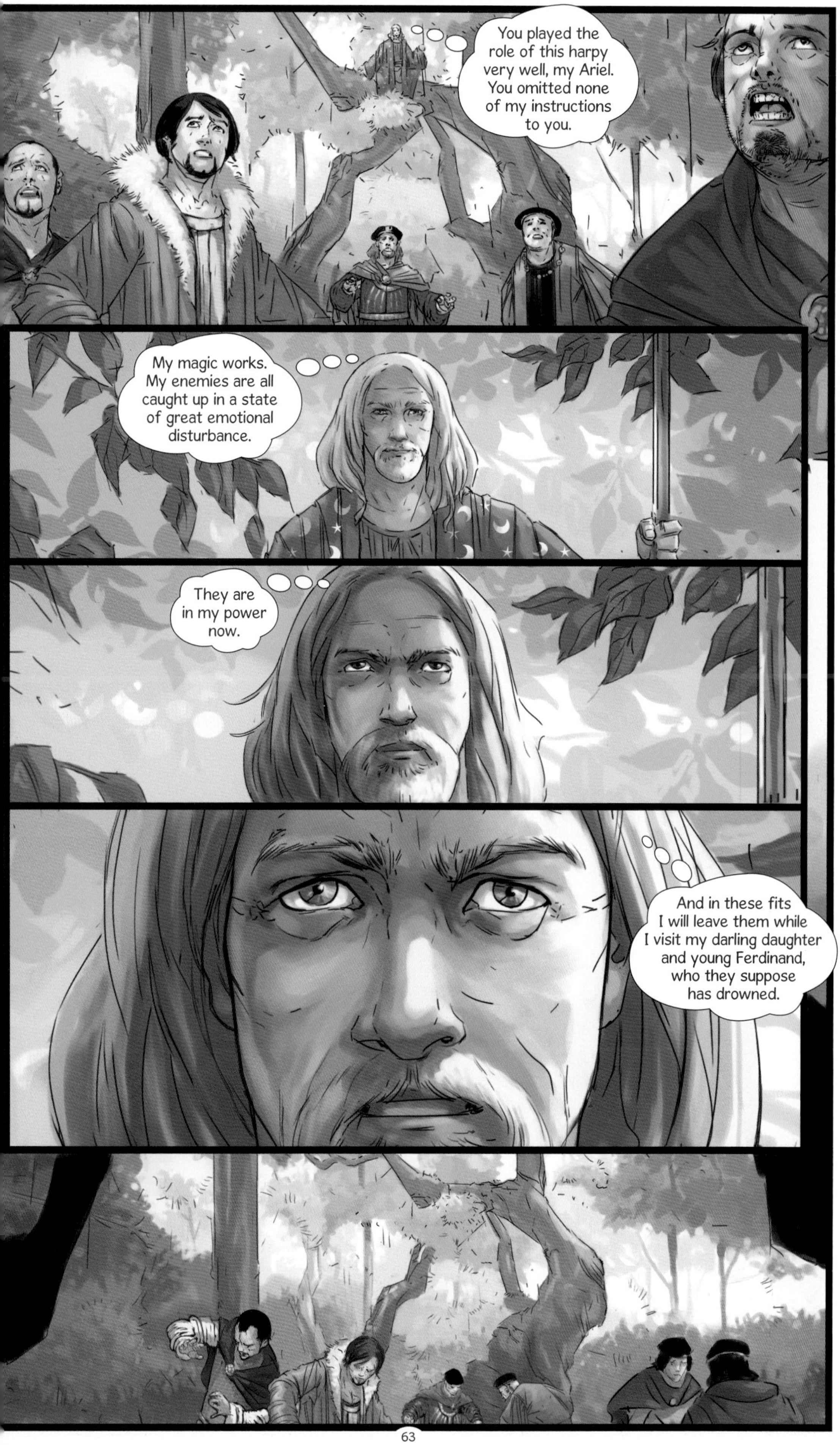
You played the role of this harpy very well, my Ariel. You omitted none of my instructions to you.
My magic works. My enemies are all caught up in a state of great emotional disturbance.
They are in my power now.
And in these fits I will leave them while I visit my darling daughter and young Ferdinand, who they suppose has drowned.

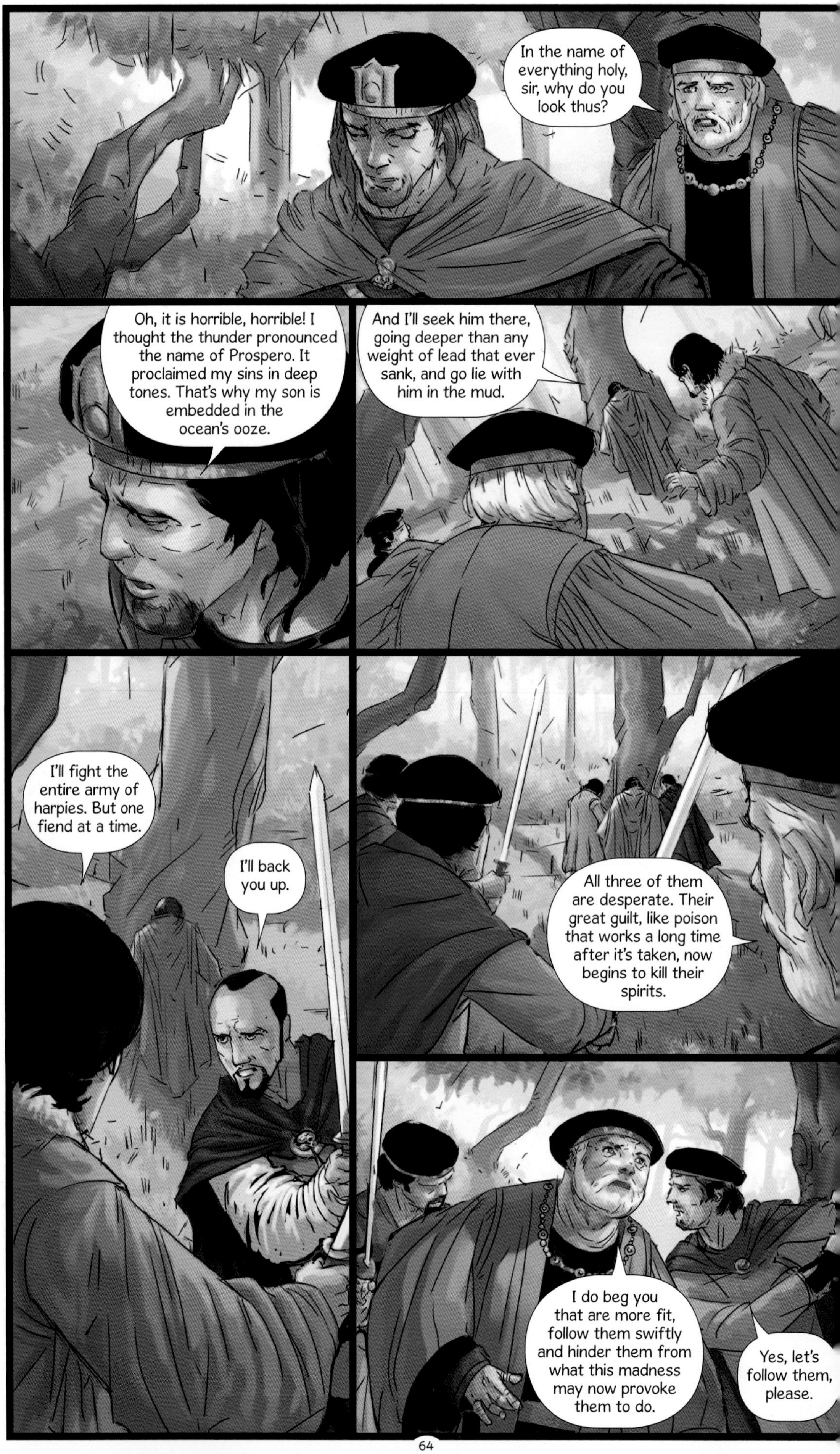
In the name of everything holy, sir, why do you look thus?
Oh, it is horrible, horrible! I thought the thunder pronounced the name of Prospero. It proclaimed my sins in deep tones. That's why my son is embedded in the ocean's ooze.
And I'll seek him there, going deeper than any weight of lead that ever sank, and go lie with him in the mud.
I'll fight the entire army of harpies. But one fiend at a time.
I'll back you up.
All three of them are desperate. Their great guilt, like poison that works a long time after it's taken, now begins to kill their spirits.
I do beg you that are more fit, follow them swiftly and hinder them from what this madness may now provoke them to do.
Yes, let's follow them, please.

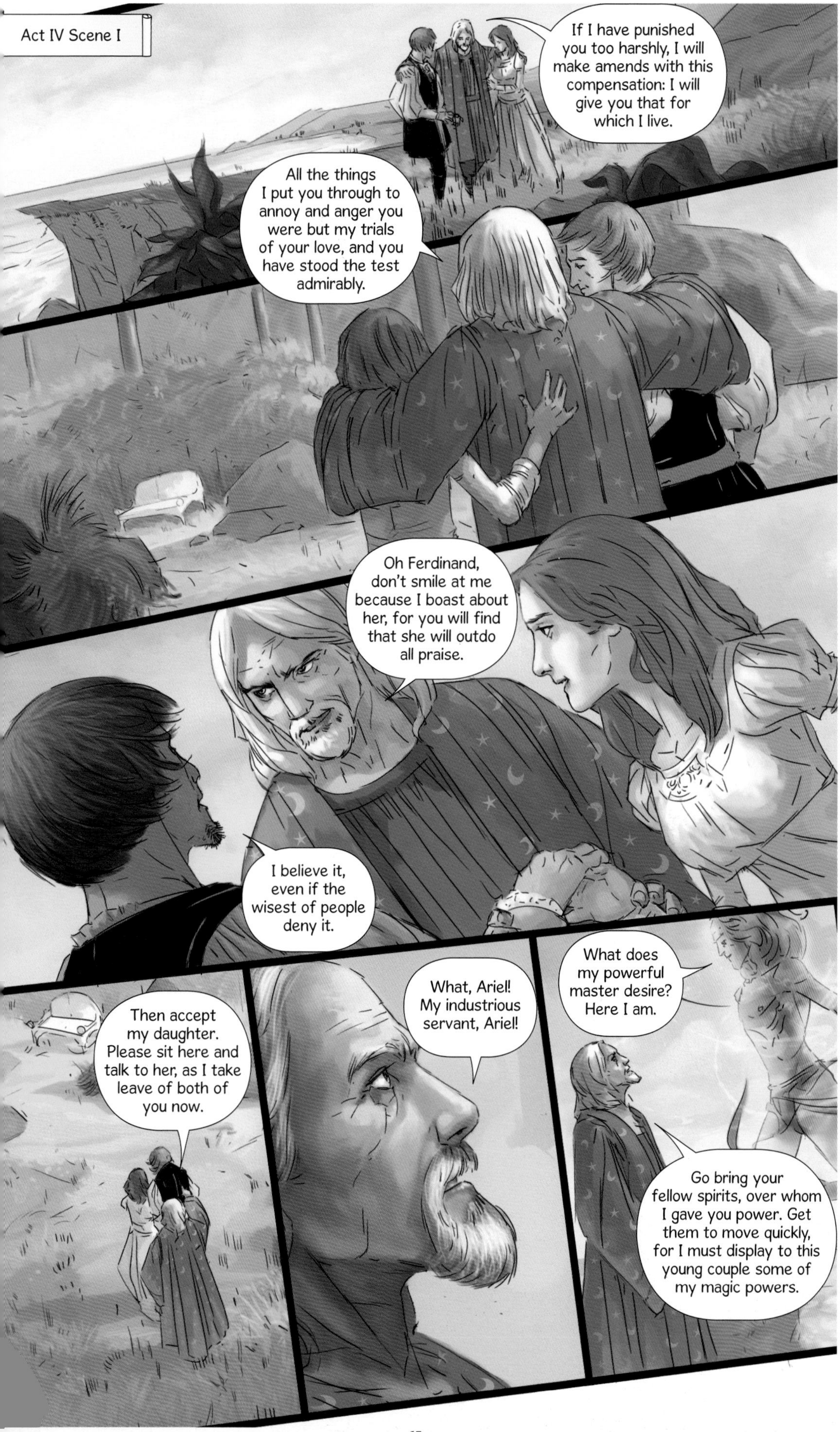
Act IV Scene I
If I have punished you too harshly, I will make amends with this compensation: I will give you that for which I live.
All the things I put you through to annoy and anger you were but my trials of your love, and you have stood the test admirably.
Oh Ferdinand, don't smile at me because I boast about her, for you will find that she will outdo all praise.
I believe it, even if the wisest of people deny it.
Then accept my daughter. Please sit here and talk to her, as I take leave of both of you now.
What, Ariel! My industrious servant, Ariel!
What does my powerful master desire? Here I am.
Go bring your fellow spirits, over whom I gave you power. Get them to move quickly, for I must display to this young couple some of my magic powers.

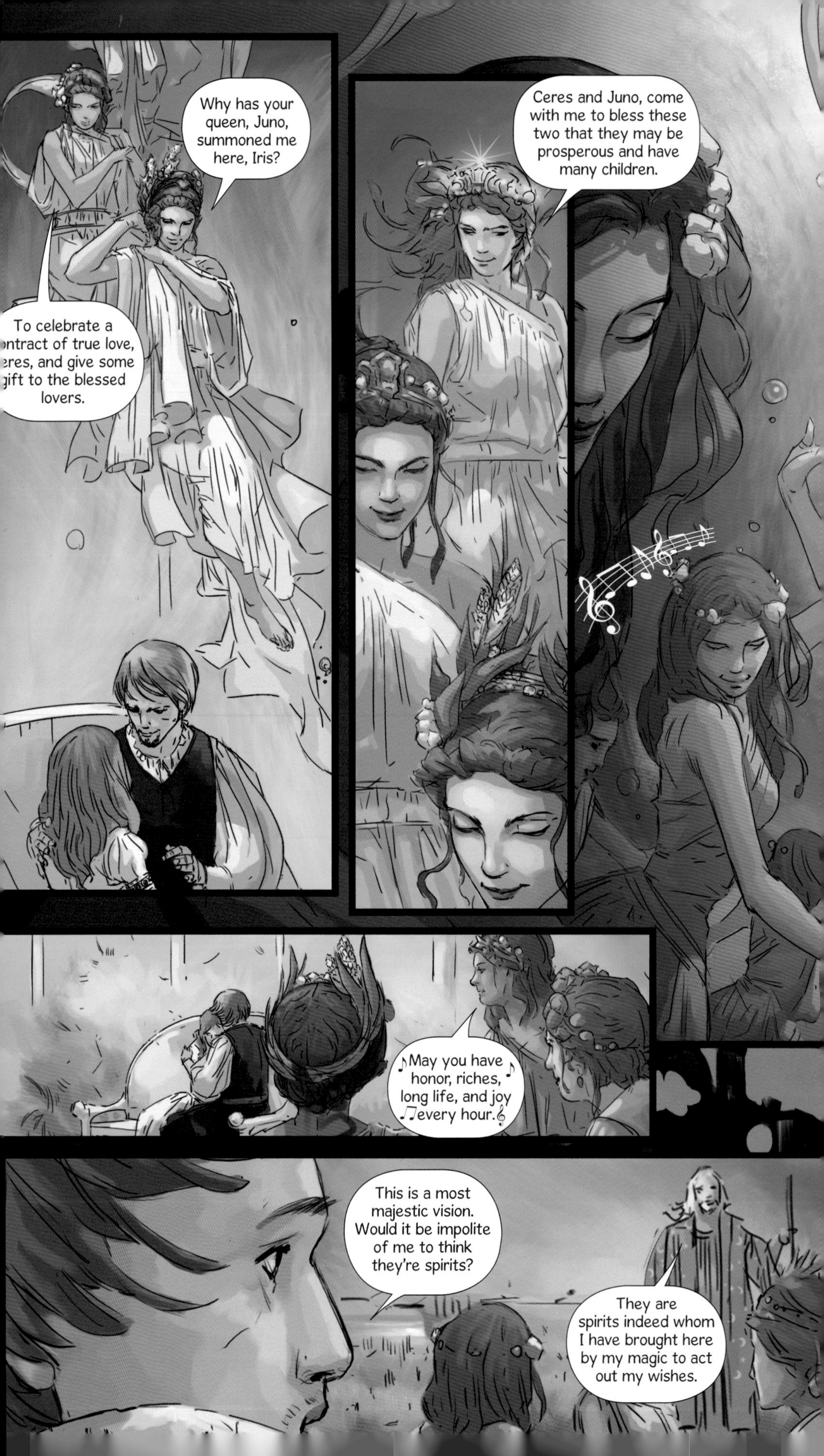

Why has your queen, Juno, summoned me here, Iris?
To celebrate a ontract of true love, eres, and give some gift to the blessed lovers.
Ceres and Juno, come with me to bless these two that they may be prosperous and have many children.
May you have honor, riches, long life, and joy every hour.
This is a most majestic vision. Would it be impolite of me to think they're spirits?
They are spirits indeed whom I have brought here by my magic to act out my wishes.

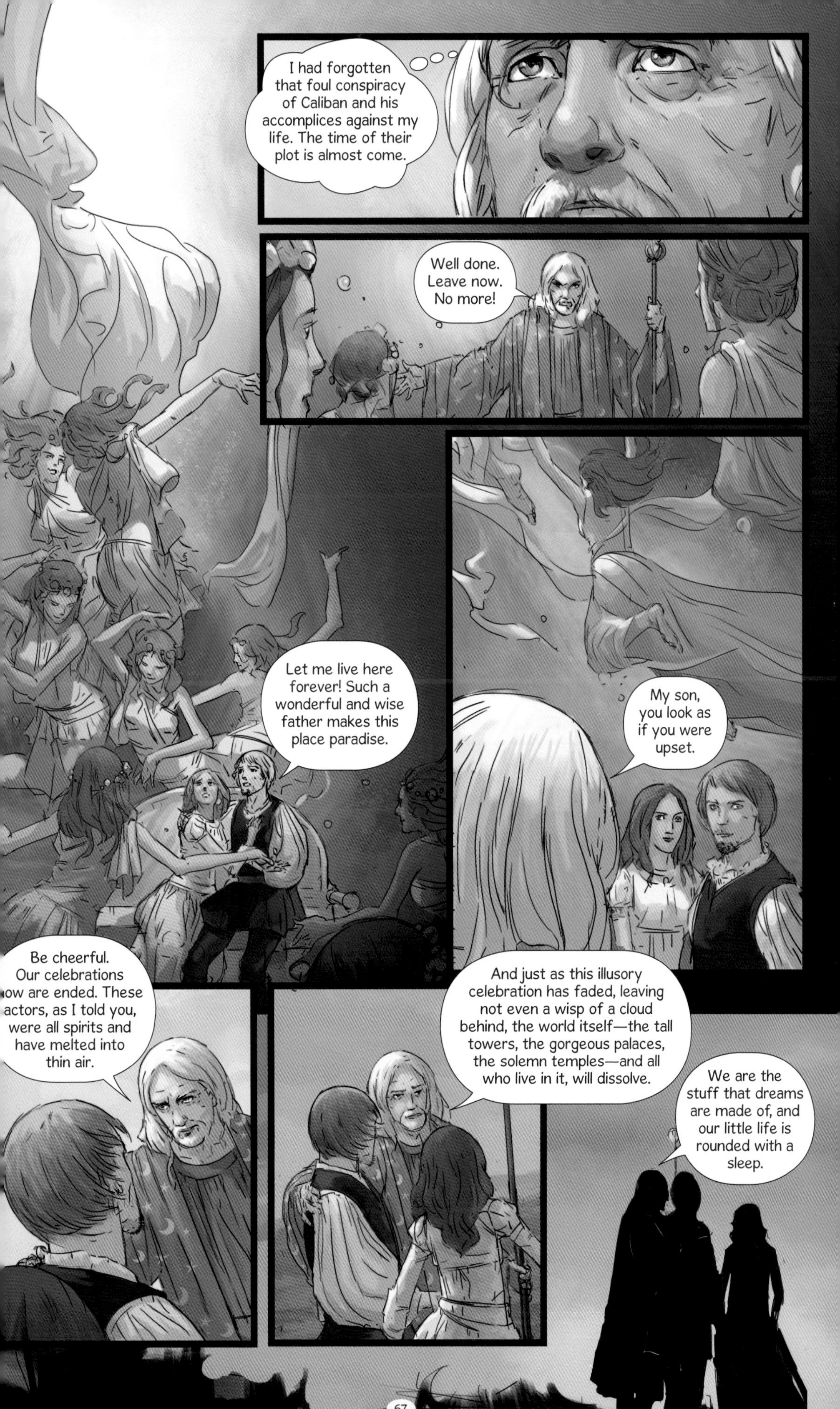
I had forgotten that foul conspiracy of Caliban and his accomplices against my life. The time of their plot is almost come.
Well done. Leave now. No more!
Let me live here forever! Such a wonderful and wise father makes this place paradise.
My son, you look as if you were upset.
Be cheerful. Our celebrations ow are ended. These actors, as I told you, were all spirits and have melted into thin air.
And just as this illusory celebration has faded, leaving not even a wisp of a cloud behind, the world itself—the tall towers, the gorgeous palaces, the solemn temples—and all who live in it, will dissolve.
We are the stuff that dreams are made of, and our little life is rounded with a sleep.

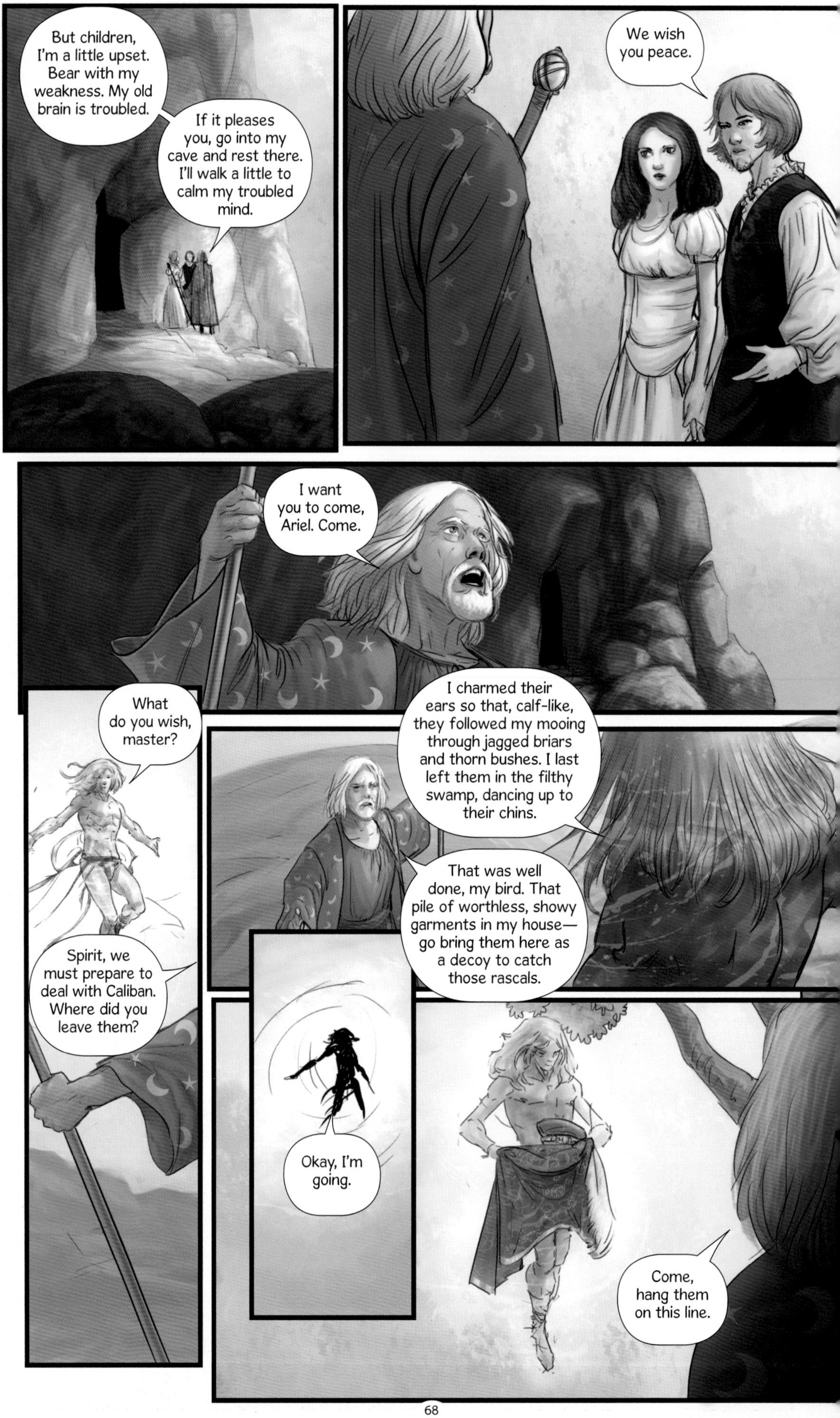
But children, I'm a little upset. Bear with my weakness. My old brain is troubled.
If it pleases you, go into my cave and rest there. I'll walk a little to calm my troubled mind.
We wish you peace.
I want you to come, Ariel. Come.
What do you wish, master?
Spirit, we must prepare to deal with Caliban. Where did you leave them?
I charmed their ears so that, calf-like, they followed my mooing through jagged briars and thorn bushes. I last left them in the filthy swamp, dancing up to their chins.
That was well done, my bird. That pile of worthless, showy garments in my house—go bring them here as a decoy to catch those rascals.
Okay, I'm going.
Come, hang them on this line.

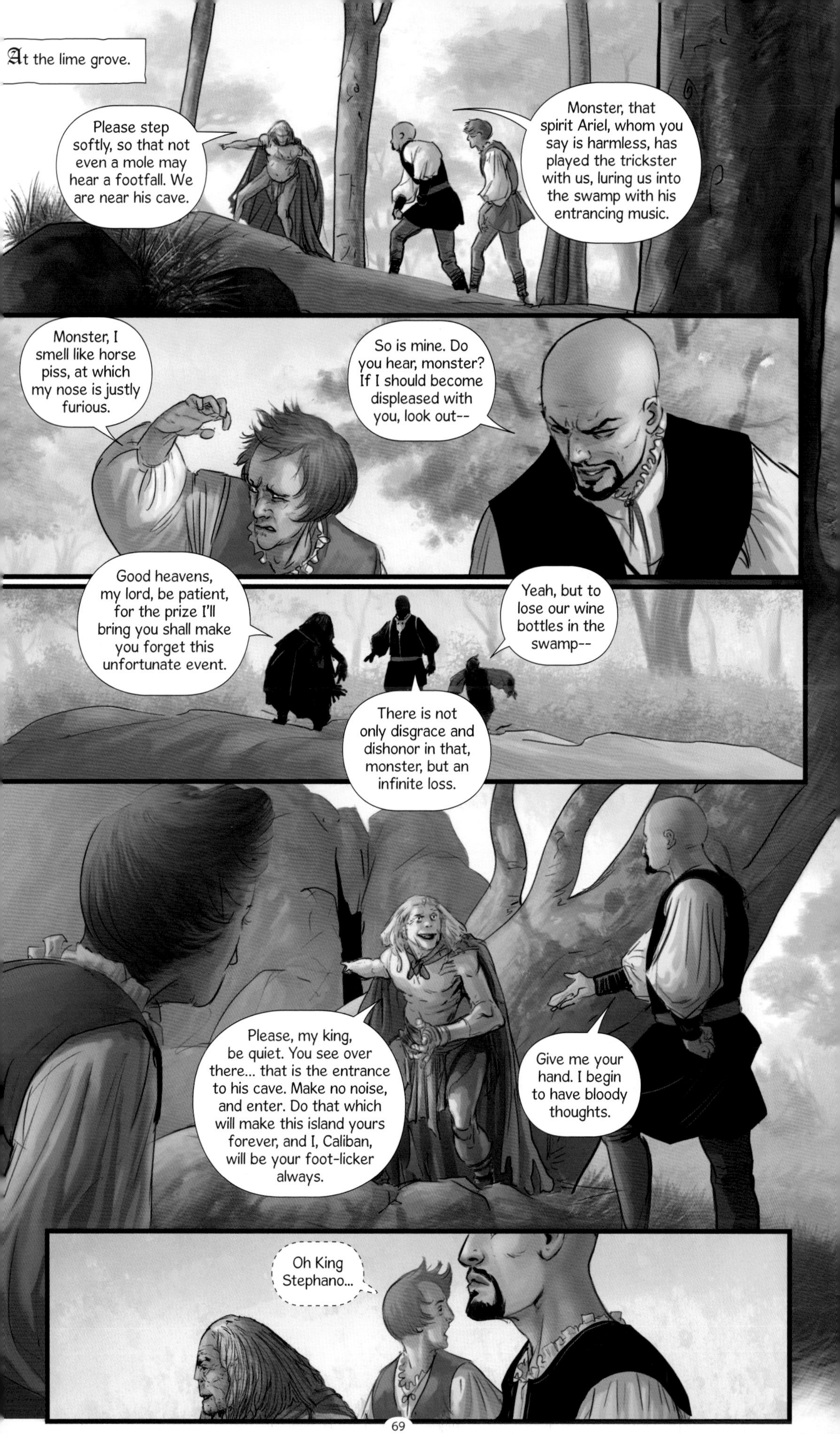
At the lime grove.
Please step softly, so that not even a mole may hear a footfall. We are near his cave.
Monster, that spirit Ariel, whom you say is harmless, has played the trickster with us, luring us into the swamp with his entrancing music.
Monster, I smell like horse piss, at which my nose is justly furious.
So is mine. Do you hear, monster? If I should become displeased with you, look out--
Good heavens, my lord, be patient, for the prize I'll bring you shall make you forget this unfortunate event.
Yeah, but to lose our wine bottles in the swamp--
There is not only disgrace and dishonor in that, monster, but an infinite loss.
Please, my king, be quiet. You see over there... that is the entrance to his cave. Make no noise, and enter. Do that which will make this island yours forever, and I, Caliban, will be your foot-licker always.
Give me your hand. I begin to have bloody thoughts.
Oh King Stephano...

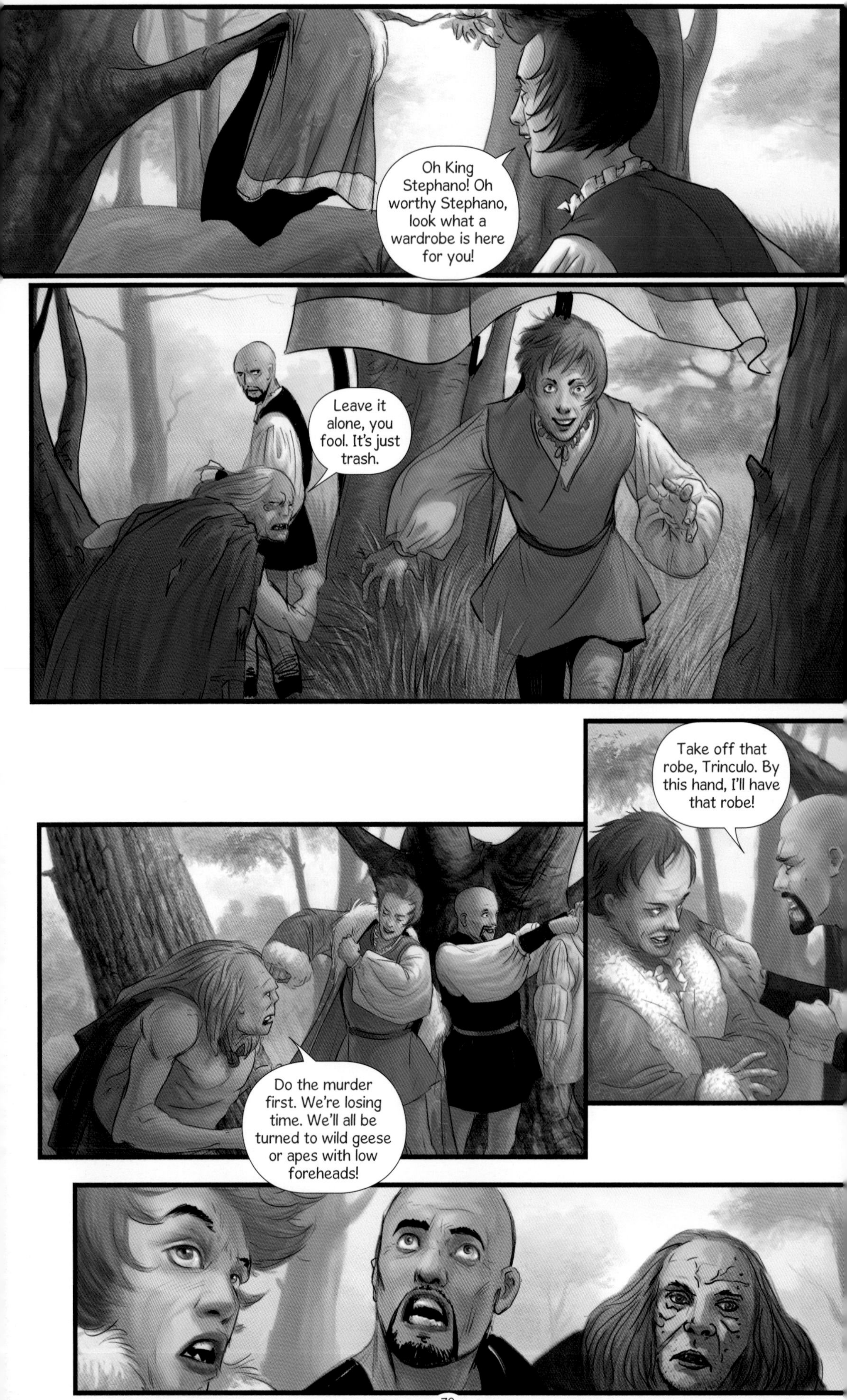
Oh King Stephano! Oh worthy Stephano, look what a wardrobe is here for you!
Leave it alone, you fool. It's just trash.
Take off that robe, Trinculo. By this hand, I'll have that robe!
Do the murder first. We're losing time. We'll all be turned to wild geese or apes with low foreheads!

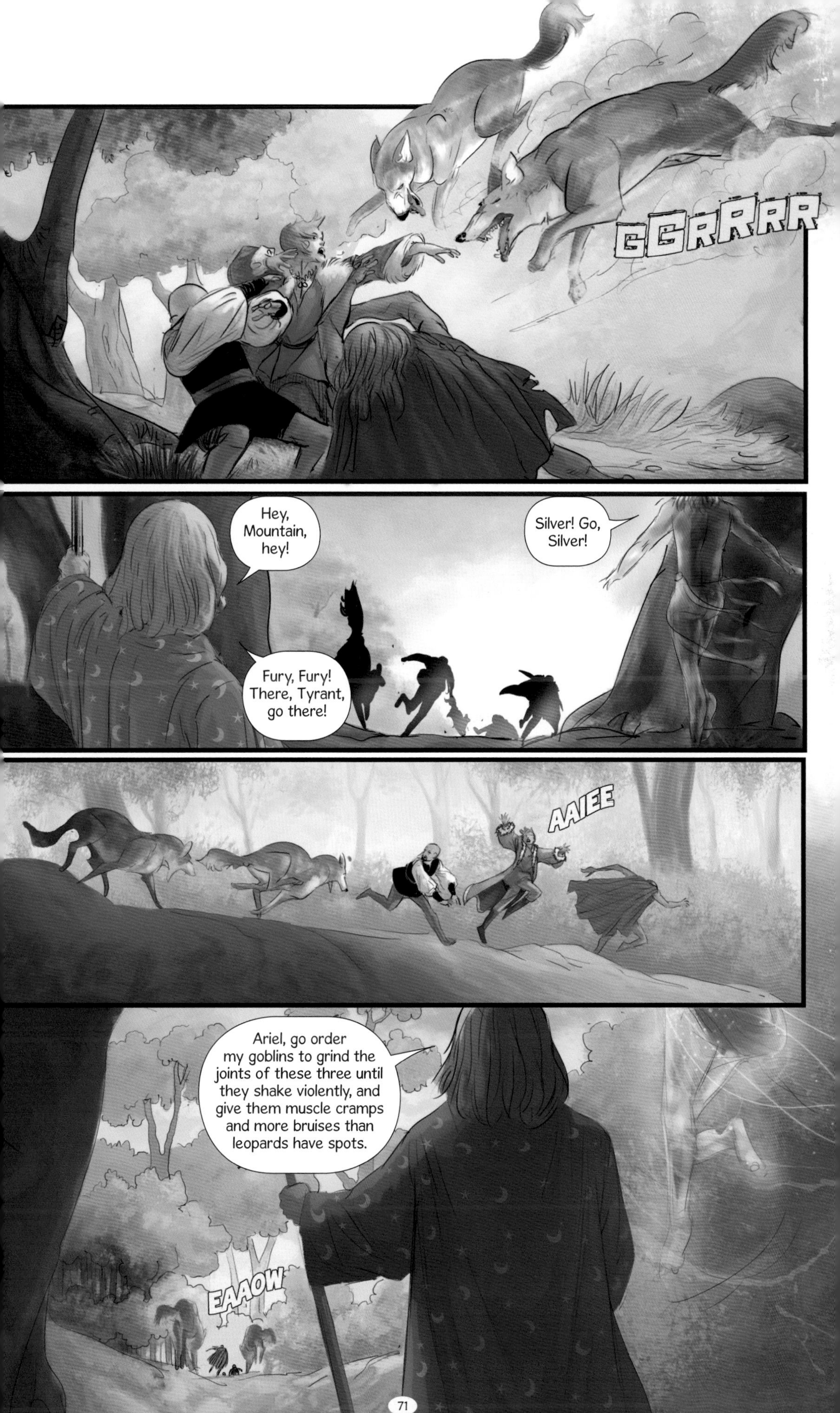
GGRRRR
Hey, Mountain, hey!
Silver! Go, Silver!
Fury, Fury! There, Tyrant, go there!
AAIEE
Ariel, go order my goblins to grind the joints of these three until they shake violently, and give them muscle cramps and more bruises than leopards have spots.
EAAOW

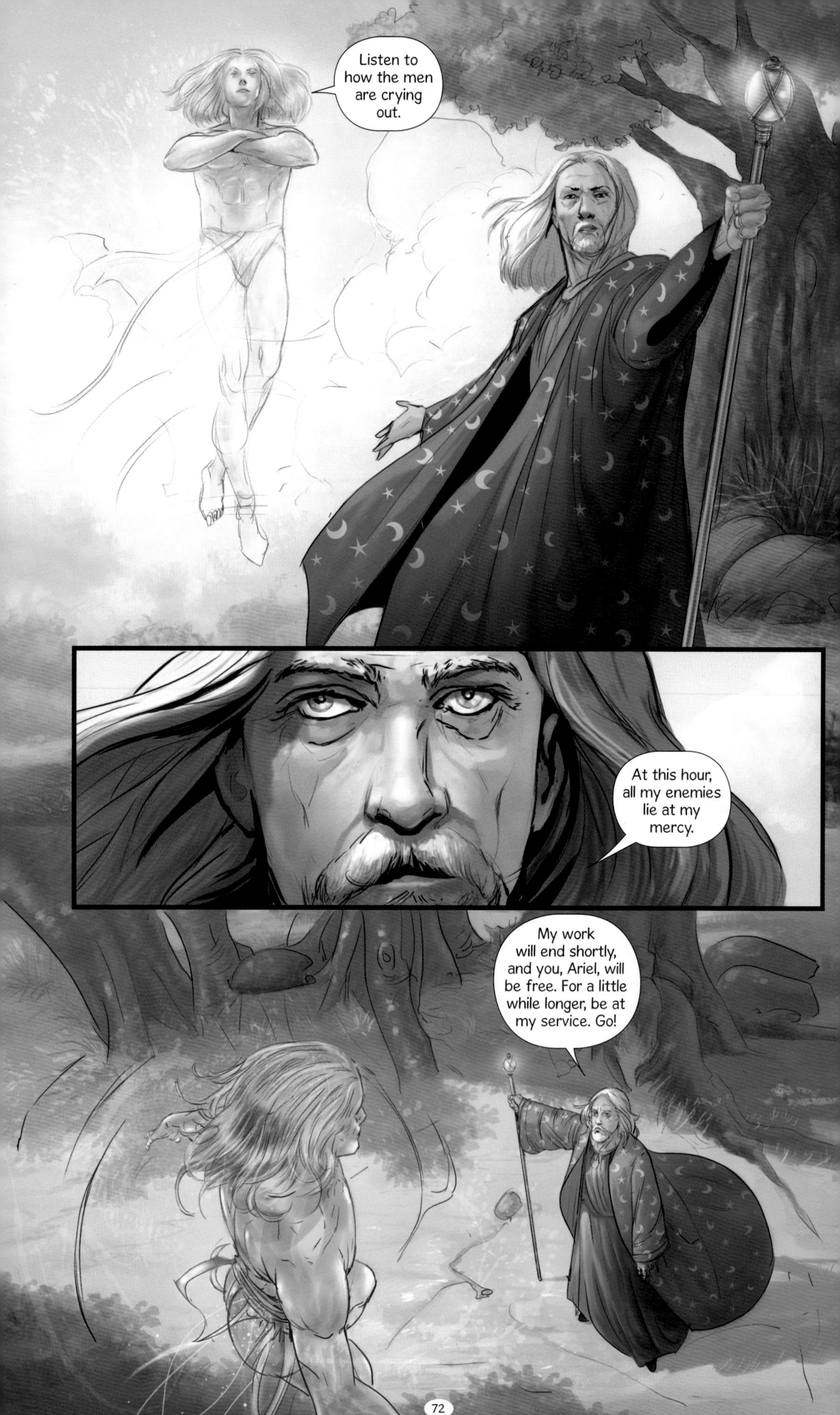
Listen to how the men are crying out.
At this hour, all my enemies lie at my mercy.
My work will end shortly, and you, Ariel, will be free. For a little while longer, be at my service. Go!

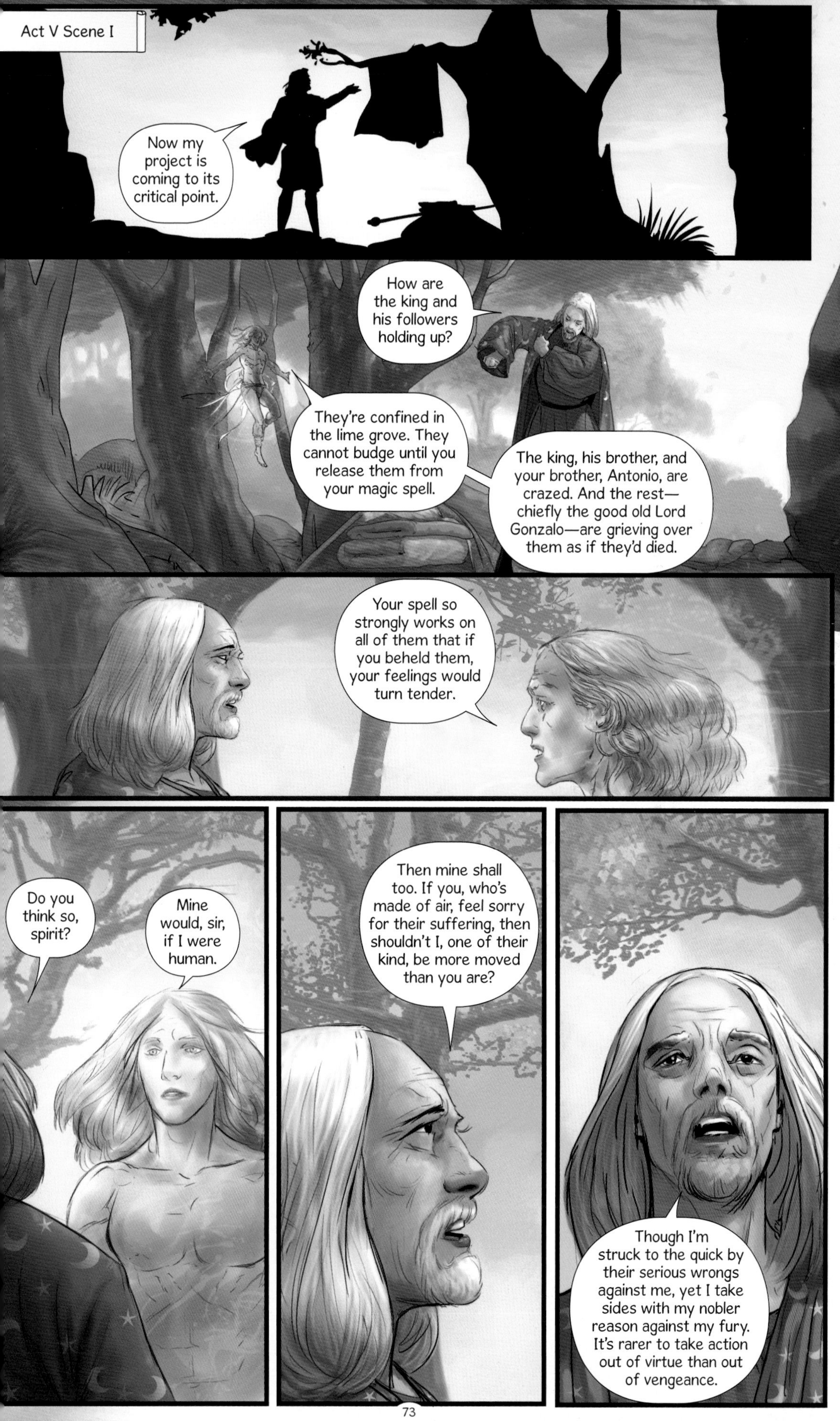
Act V Scene I
Now my project is coming to its critical point.
How are the king and his followers holding up?
They're confined in the lime grove. They cannot budge until you release them from your magic spell.
The king, his brother, and your brother, Antonio, are crazed. And the rest—chiefly the good old Lord Gonzalo—are grieving over them as if they'd died.
Your spell so strongly works on all of them that if you beheld them, your feelings would turn tender.
Do you think so, spirit?
Mine would, sir, if I were human.
Then mine shall too. If you, who's made of air, feel sorry for their suffering, then shouldn't I, one of their kind, be more moved than you are?
Though I'm struck to the quick by their serious wrongs against me, yet I take sides with my nobler reason against my fury. It's rarer to take action out of virtue than out of vengeance.

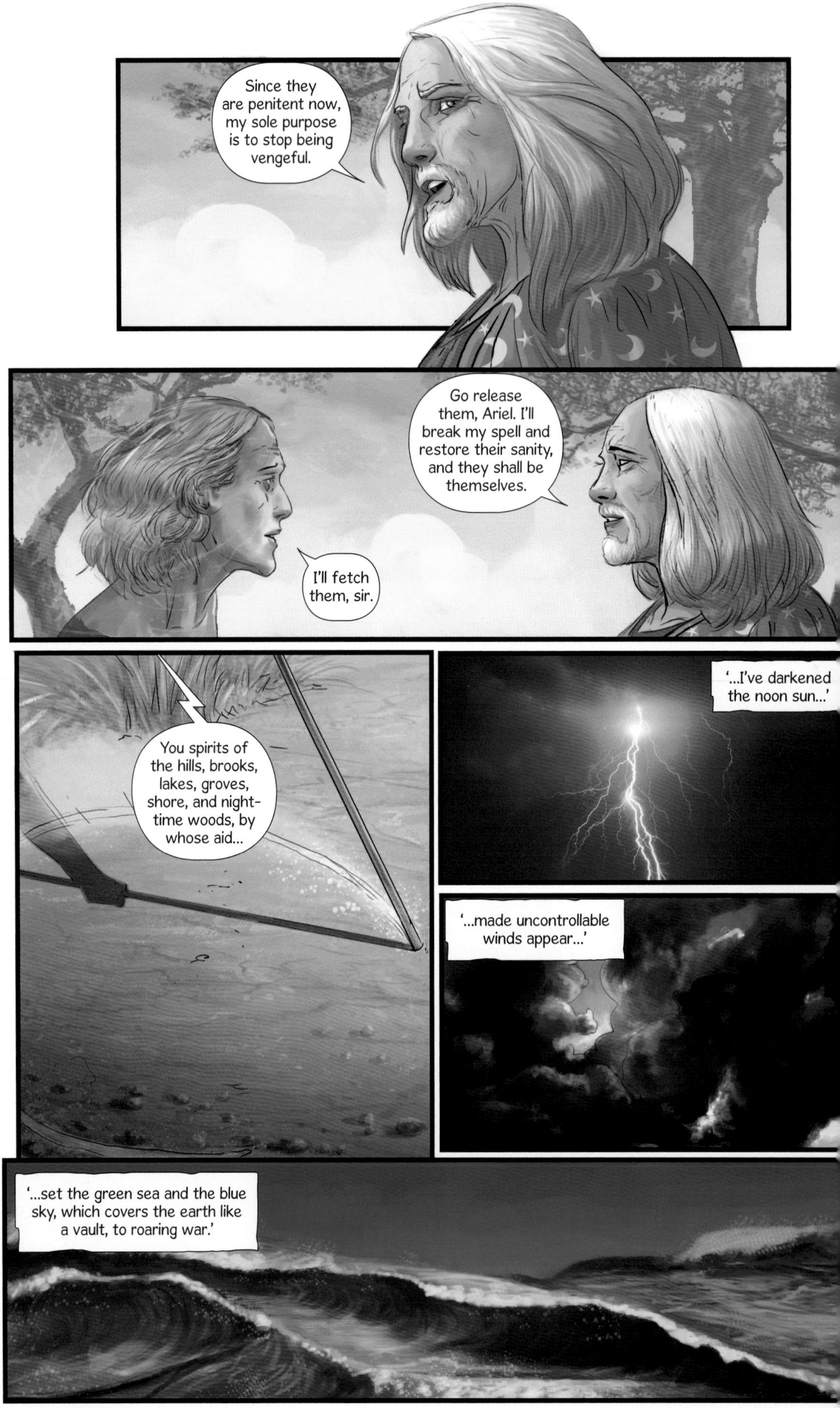

Since they are penitent now, my sole purpose is to stop being vengeful.
Go release them, Ariel. I'll break my spell and restore their sanity, and they shall be themselves.
I'll fetch them, sir.
You spirits of the hills, brooks, lakes, groves, shore, and night-time woods, by whose aid...
'...I've darkened the noon sun...'
'...made uncontrollable winds appear...'
'...set the green sea and the blue sky, which covers the earth like a vault, to roaring war.'

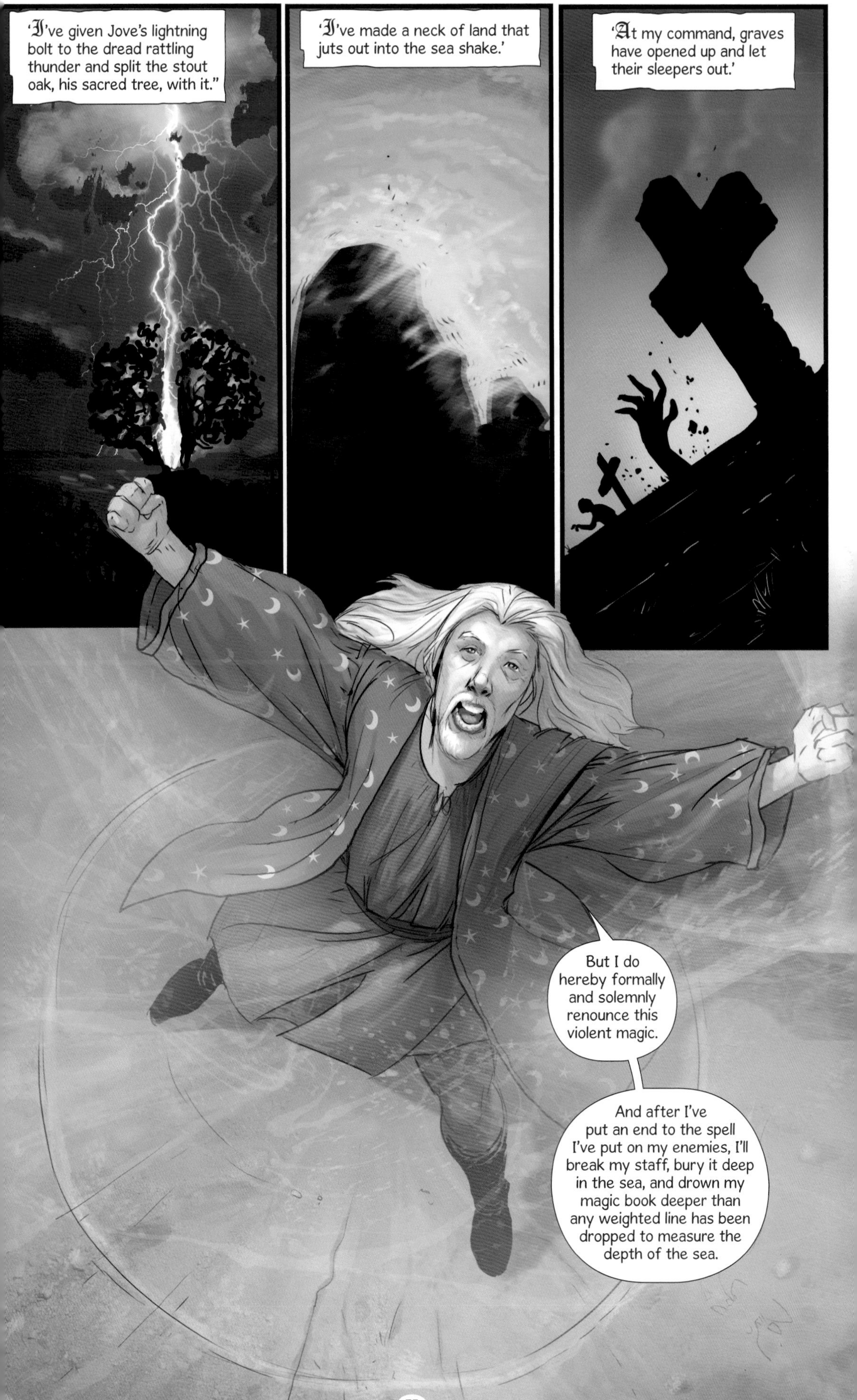
'I've given Jove's lightning bolt to the dread rattling thunder and split the stout oak, his sacred tree, with it."
'I've made a neck of land that juts out into the sea shake.'
'At my command, graves have opened up and let their sleepers out.'
But I do hereby formally and solemnly renounce this violent magic.
And after I've put an end to the spell I've put on my enemies, I'll break my staff, bury it deep in the sea, and drown my magic book deeper than any weighted line has been dropped to measure the depth of the sea.

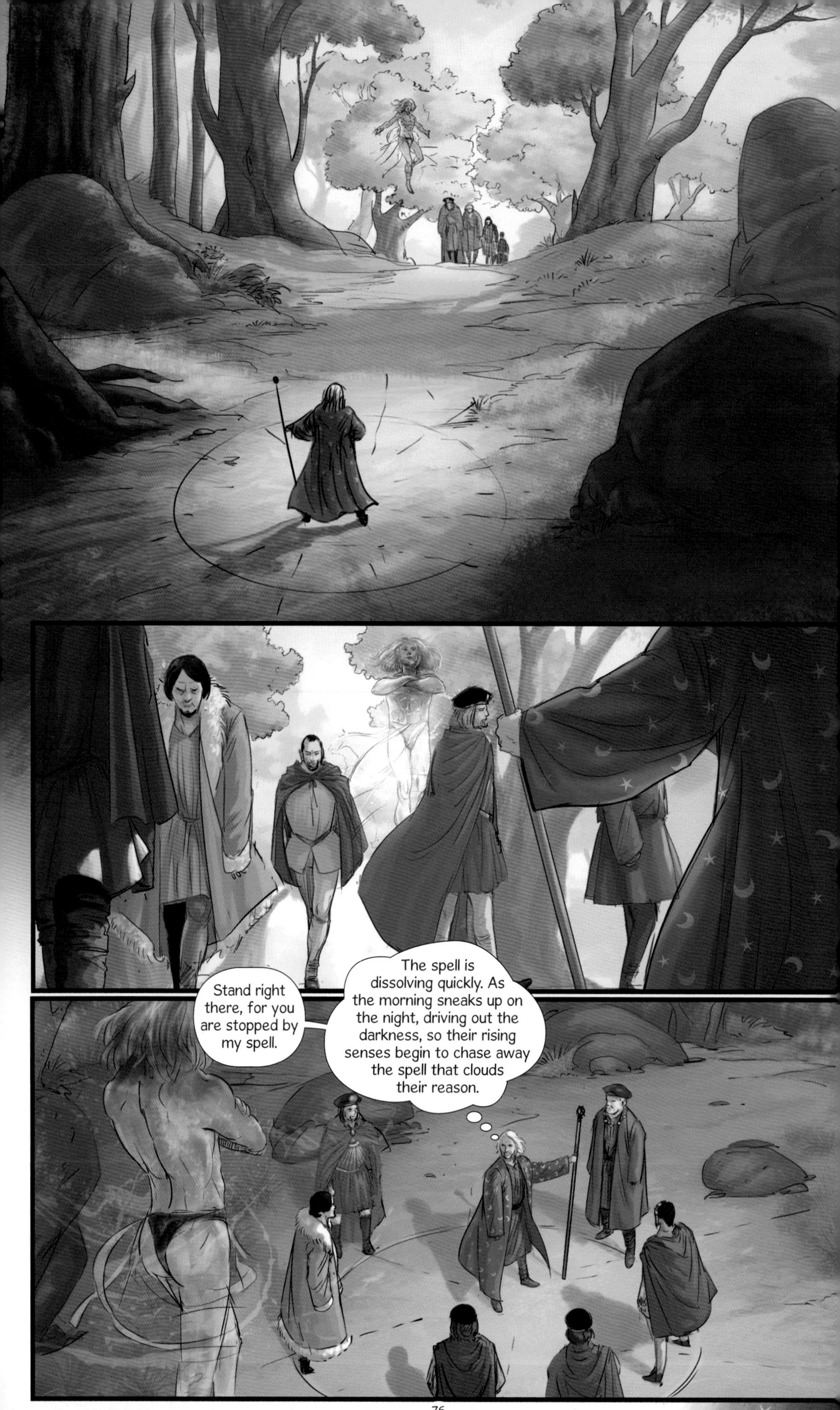
Stand right there, for you are stopped by my spell.
The spell is dissolving quickly. As the morning sneaks up on the night, driving out the darkness, so their rising senses begin to chase away the spell that clouds their reason.

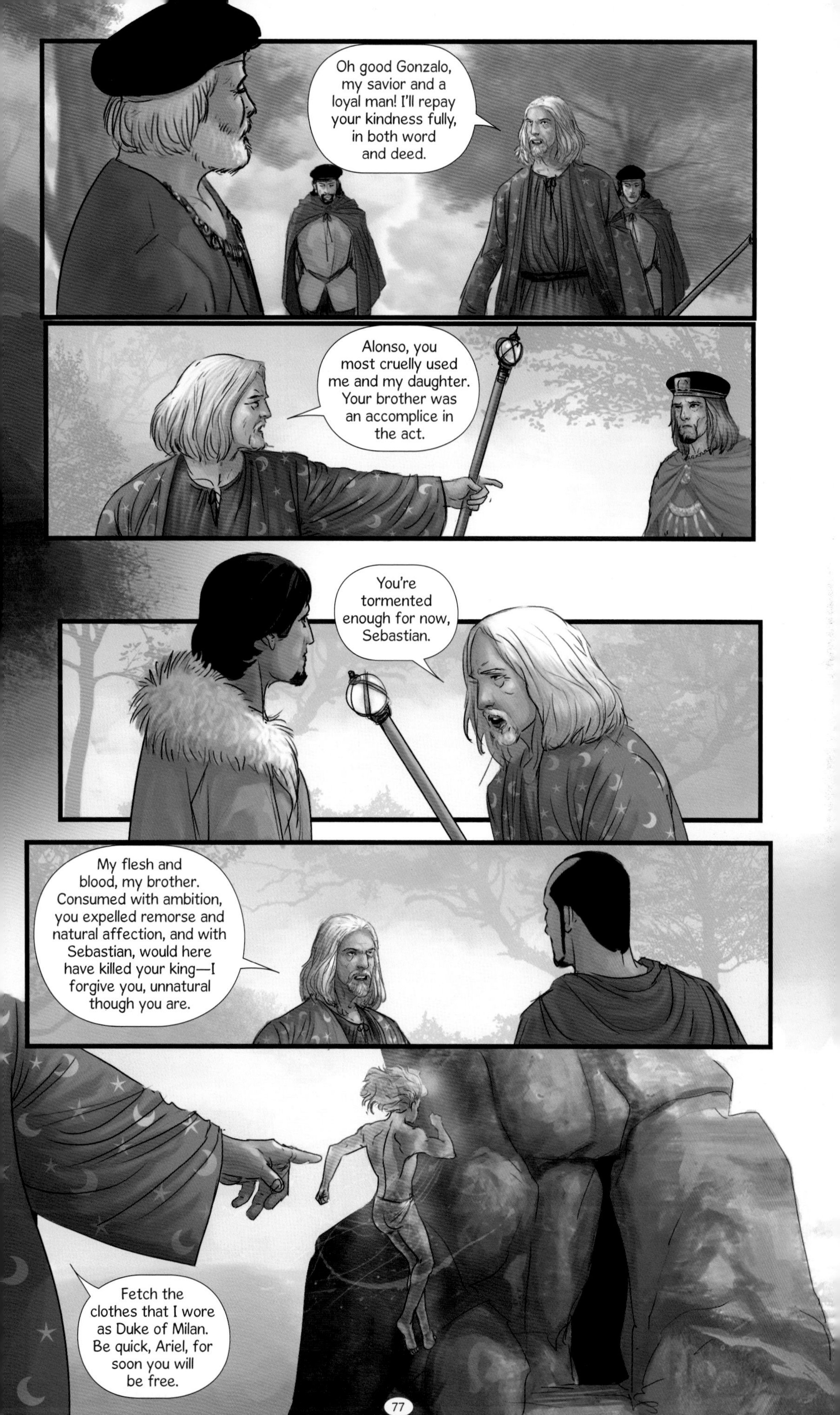
Oh good Gonzalo, my savior and a loyal man! I'll repay your kindness fully, in both word and deed.
Alonso, you most cruelly used me and my daughter. Your brother was an accomplice in the act.
You're tormented enough for now, Sebastian.
My flesh and blood, my brother. Consumed with ambition, you expelled remorse and natural affection, and with Sebastian, would here have killed your king—I forgive you, unnatural though you are.
Fetch the clothes that I wore as Duke of Milan. Be quick, Ariel, for soon you will be free.

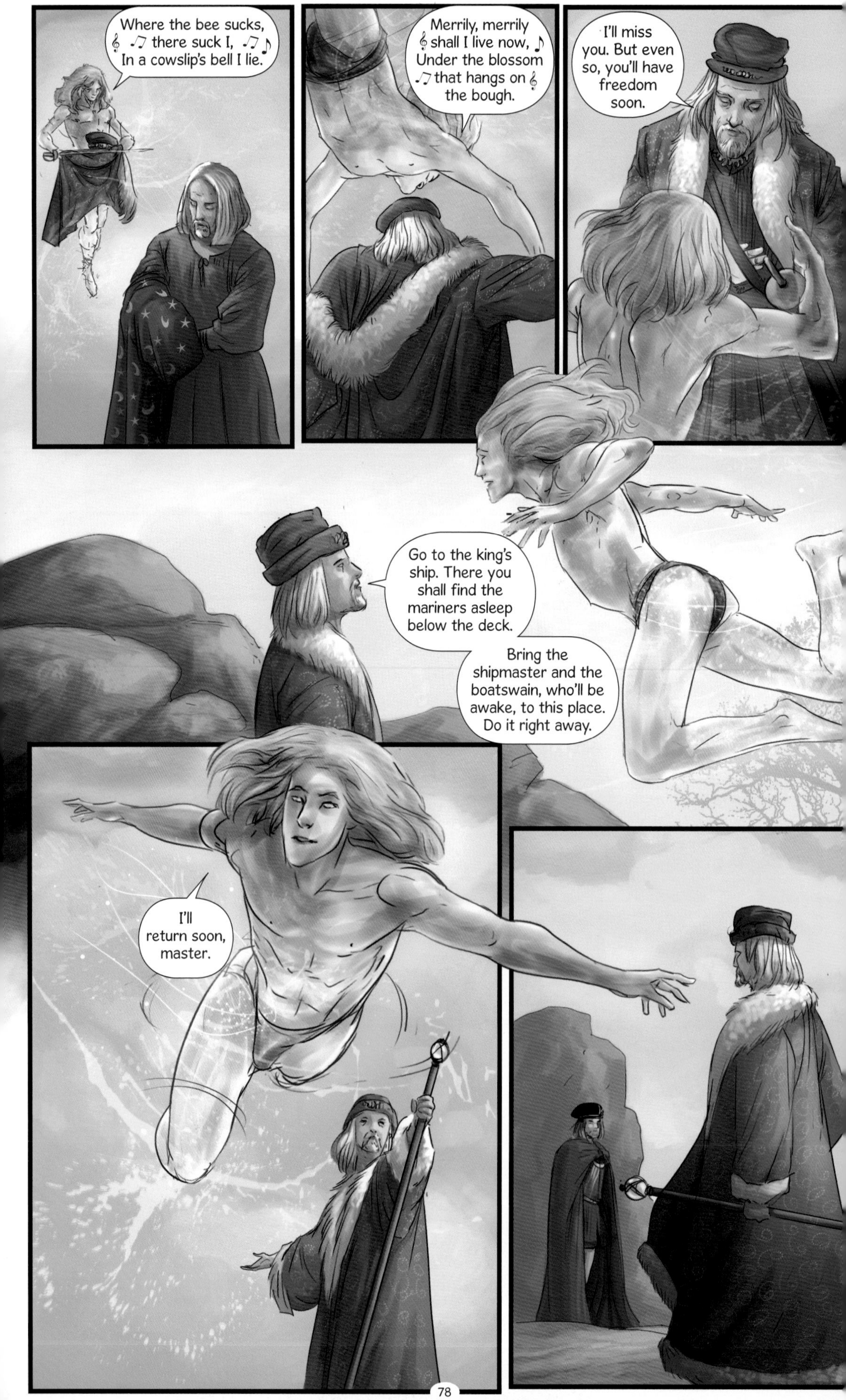
Where the bee sucks, ♫ there suck I, ♫ ♪ In a cowslip's bell I lie.
Merrily, merrily shall I live now, ♪ Under the blossom ♫ that hangs on the bough.
I'll miss you. But even so, you'll have freedom soon.
Go to the king's ship. There you shall find the mariners asleep below the deck.
Bring the shipmaster and the boatswain, who'll be awake, to this place. Do it right away.
I'll return soon, master.

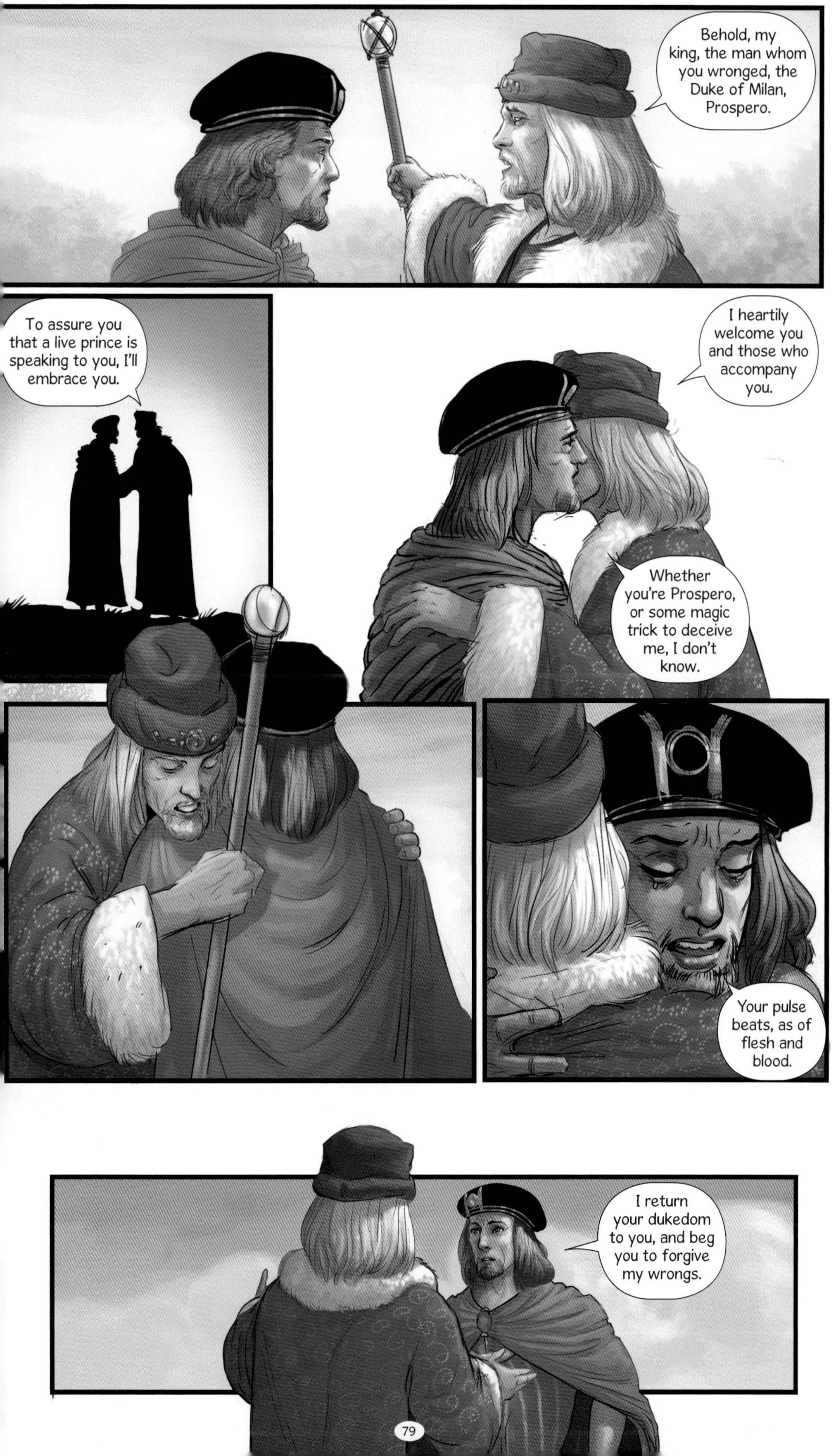
Behold, my king, the man whom you wronged, the Duke of Milan, Prospero.
To assure you that a live prince is speaking to you, I'll embrace you.
I heartily welcome you and those who accompany you.
Whether you're Prospero, or some magic trick to deceive me, I don't know.
Your pulse beats, as of flesh and blood.
I return your dukedom to you, and beg you to forgive my wrongs.

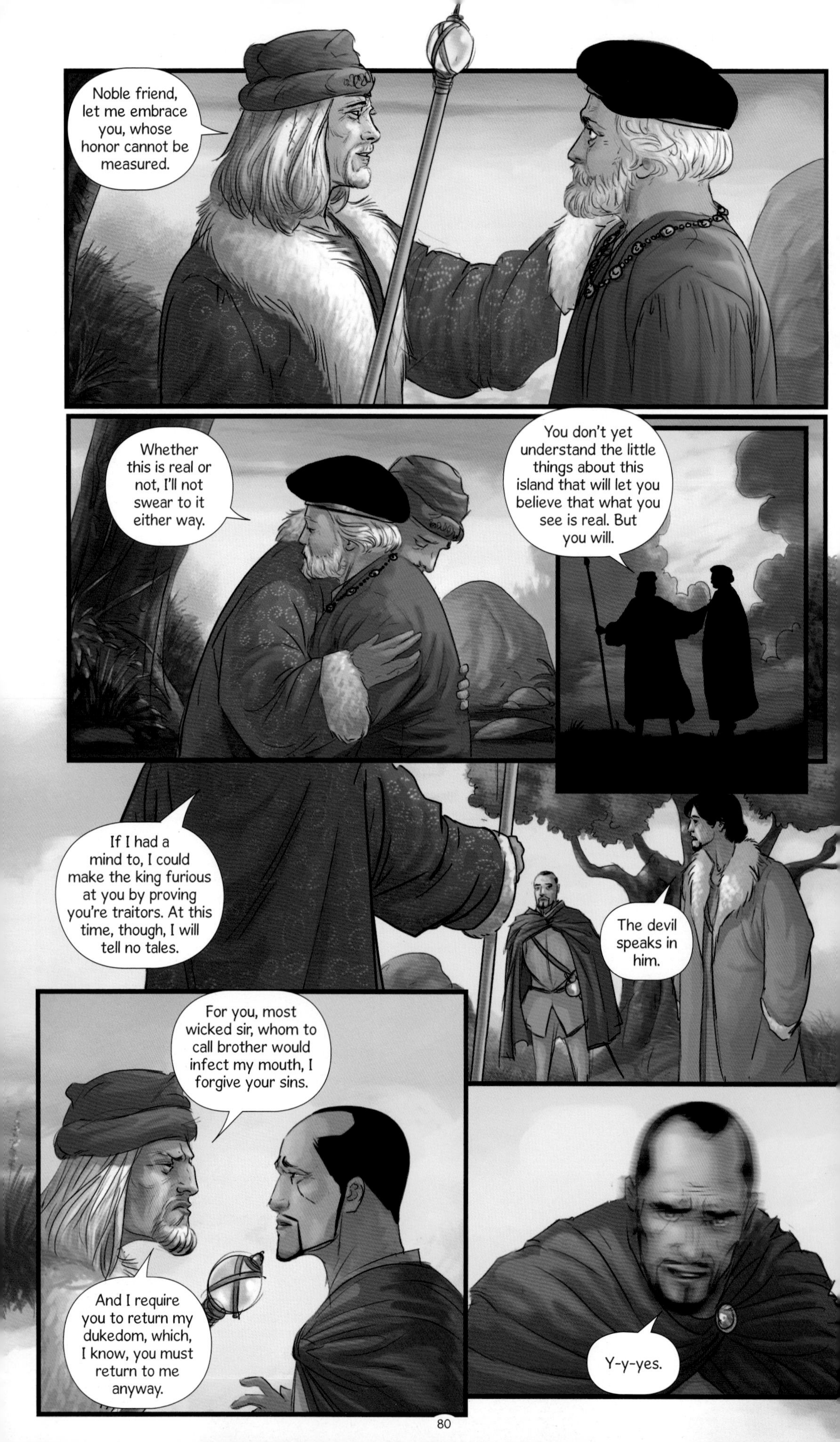
Noble friend, let me embrace you, whose honor cannot be measured.
Whether this is real or not, I'll not swear to it either way.
You don't yet understand the little things about this island that will let you believe that what you see is real. But you will.
If I had a mind to, I could make the king furious at you by proving you're traitors. At this time, though, I will tell no tales.
The devil speaks in him.
For you, most wicked sir, whom to call brother would infect my mouth, I forgive your sins.
And I require you to return my dukedom, which, I know, you must return to me anyway.
Y-y-yes.

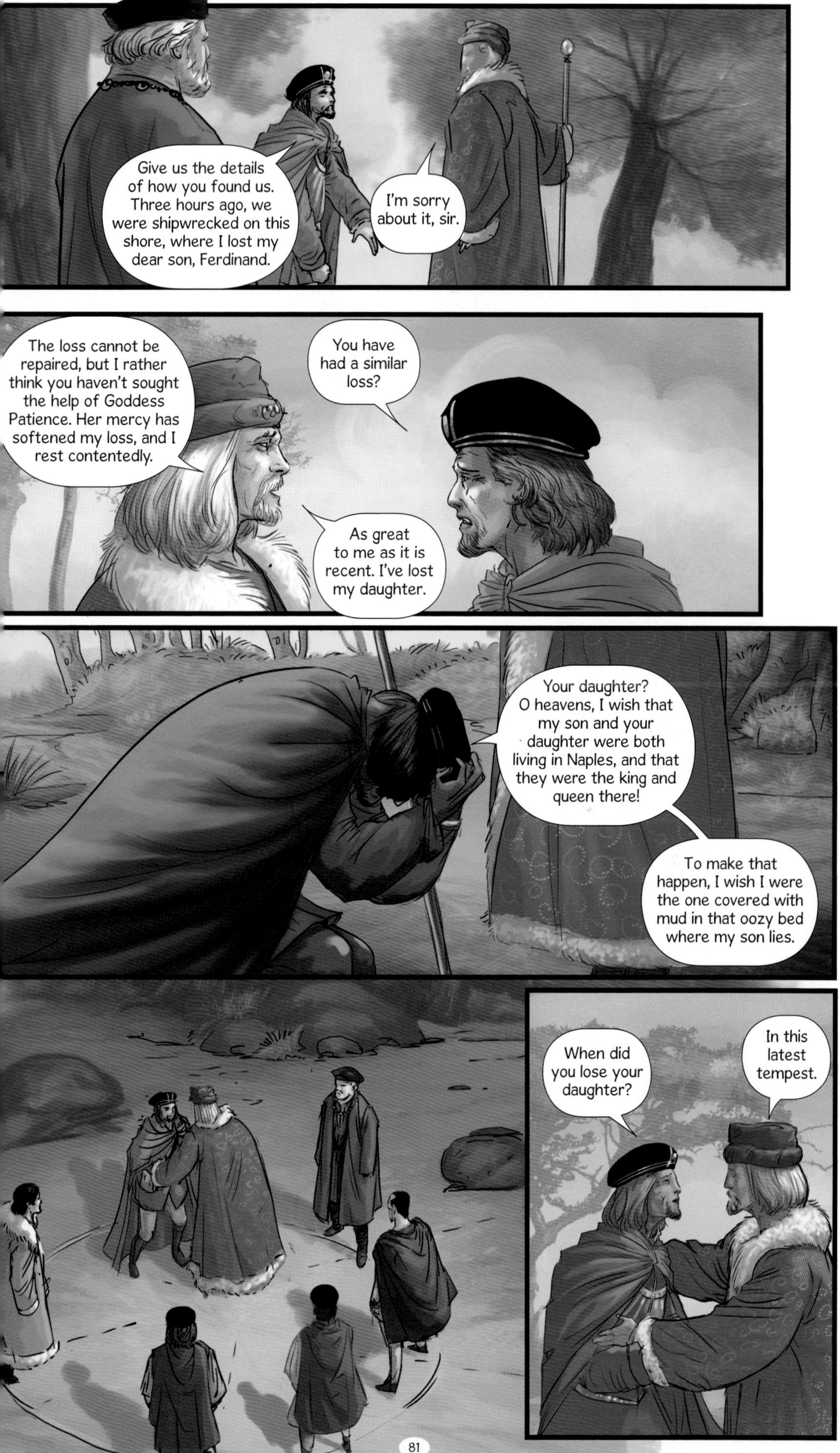
Give us the details of how you found us. Three hours ago, we were shipwrecked on this shore, where I lost my dear son, Ferdinand.
I'm sorry about it, sir.
The loss cannot be repaired, but I rather think you haven't sought the help of Goddess Patience. Her mercy has softened my loss, and I rest contentedly.
You have had a similar loss?
As great to me as it is recent. I've lost my daughter.
Your daughter? O heavens, I wish that my son and your daughter were both living in Naples, and that they were the king and queen there!
To make that happen, I wish I were the one covered with mud in that oozy bed where my son lies.
When did you lose your daughter?
In this latest tempest.

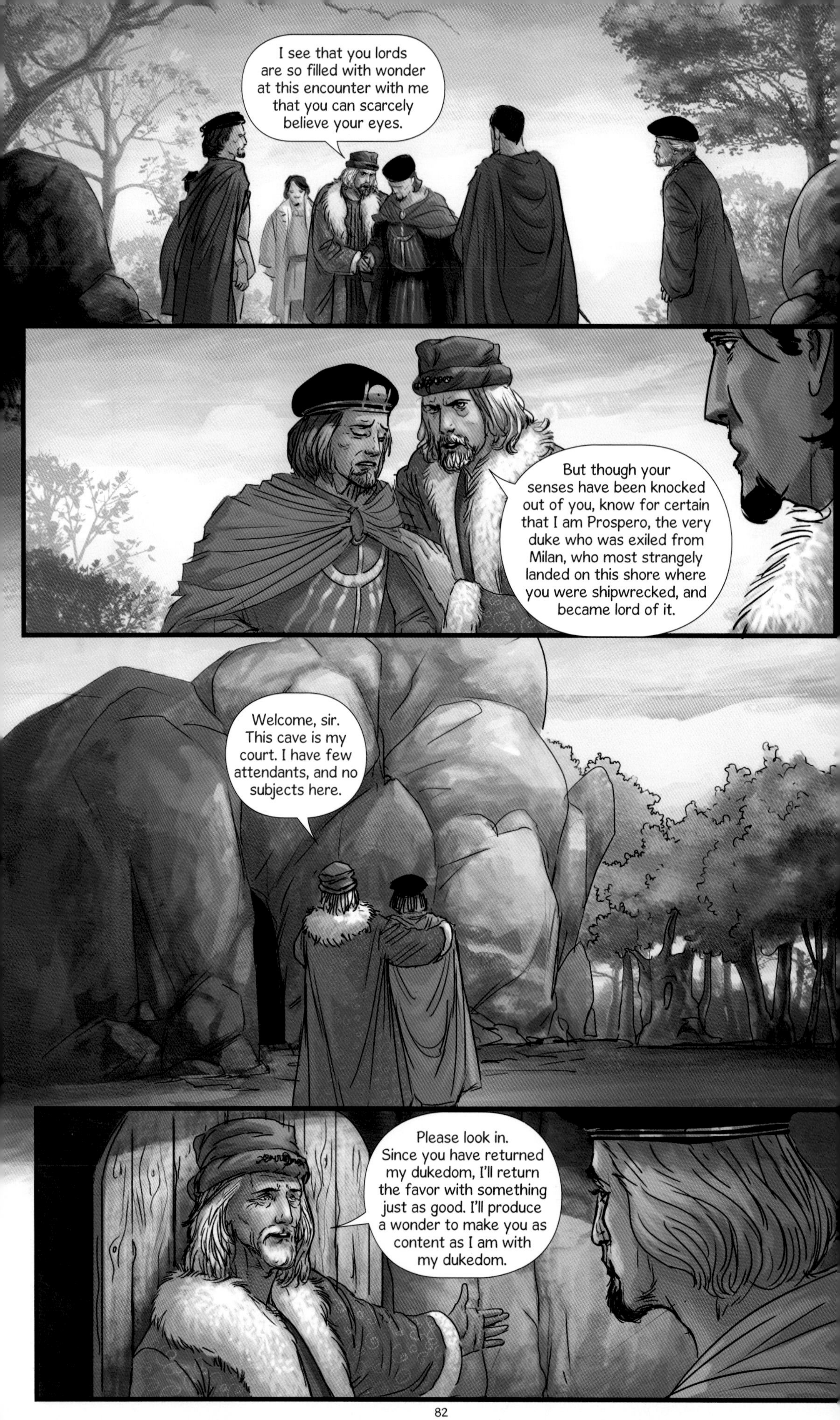
I see that you lords are so filled with wonder at this encounter with me that you can scarcely believe your eyes.
But though your senses have been knocked out of you, know for certain that I am Prospero, the very duke who was exiled from Milan, who most strangely landed on this shore where you were shipwrecked, and became lord of it.
Welcome, sir. This cave is my court. I have few attendants, and no subjects here.
Please look in. Since you have returned my dukedom, I'll return the favor with something just as good. I'll produce a wonder to make you as content as I am with my dukedom.

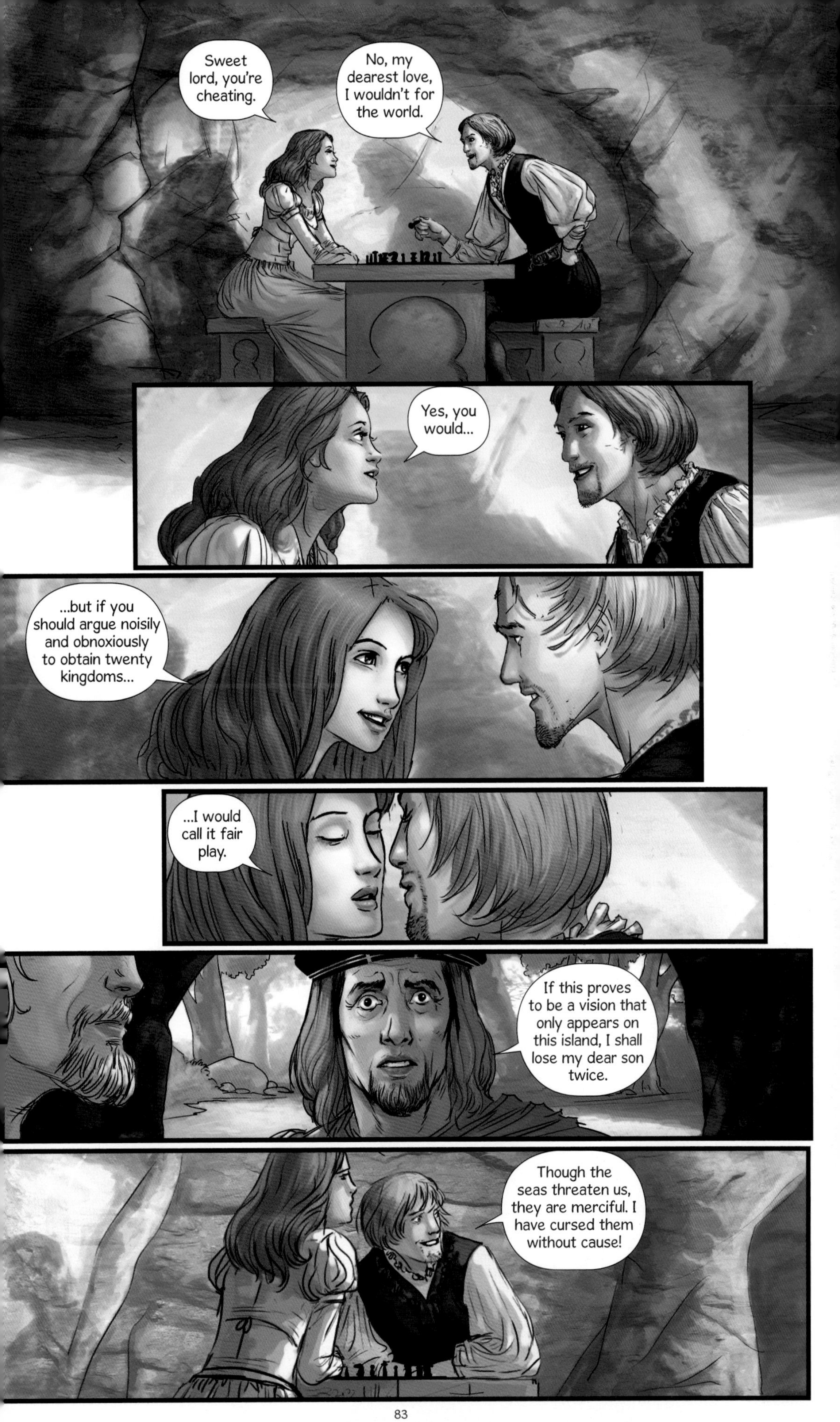
Sweet lord, you're cheating.
No, my dearest love, I wouldn't for the world.
Yes, you would...
...but if you should argue noisily and obnoxiously to obtain twenty kingdoms...
...I would call it fair play.
If this proves to be a vision that only appears on this island, I shall lose my dear son twice.
Though the seas threaten us, they are merciful. I have cursed them without cause!

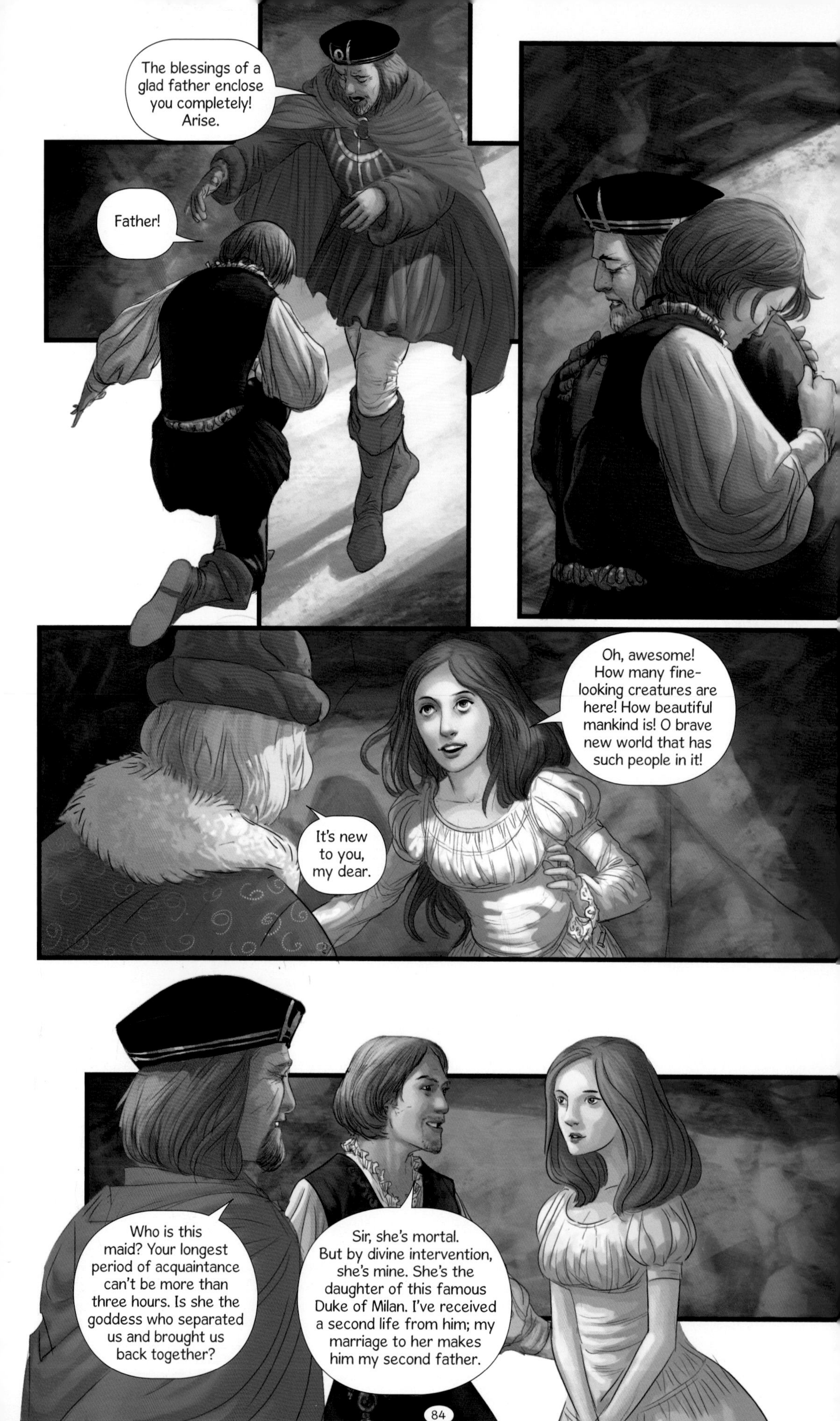

The blessings of a glad father enclose you completely! Arise.
Father!
Oh, awesome! How many fine-looking creatures are here! How beautiful mankind is! O brave new world that has such people in it!
It's new to you, my dear.
Who is this maid? Your longest period of acquaintance can't be more than three hours. Is she the goddess who separated us and brought us back together?
Sir, she's mortal. But by divine intervention, she's mine. She's the daughter of this famous Duke of Milan. I've received a second life from him; my marriage to her makes him my second father.

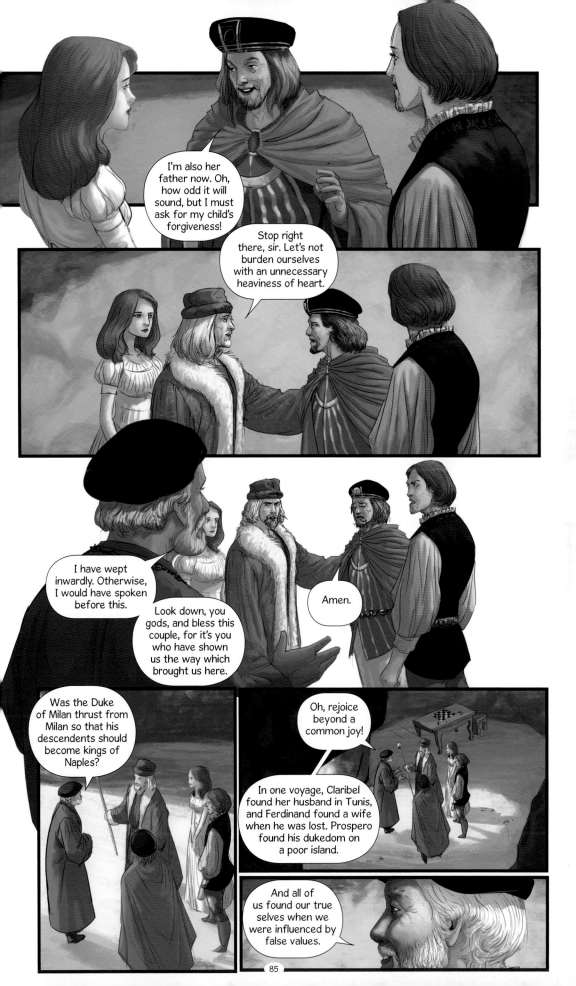

I'm also her father now. Oh, how odd it will sound, but I must ask for my child's forgiveness!

Stop right there, sir. Let's not burden ourselves with an unnecessary heaviness of heart.

I have wept inwardly. Otherwise, I would have spoken before this.

Look down, you gods, and bless this couple, for it's you who have shown us the way which brought us here.

Amen.

Was the Duke of Milan thrust from Milan so that his descendents should become kings of Naples?

Oh, rejoice beyond a common joy!

In one voyage, Claribel found her husband in Tunis, and Ferdinand found a wife when he was lost. Prospero found his dukedom on a poor island.

And all of us found our true selves when we were influenced by false values.

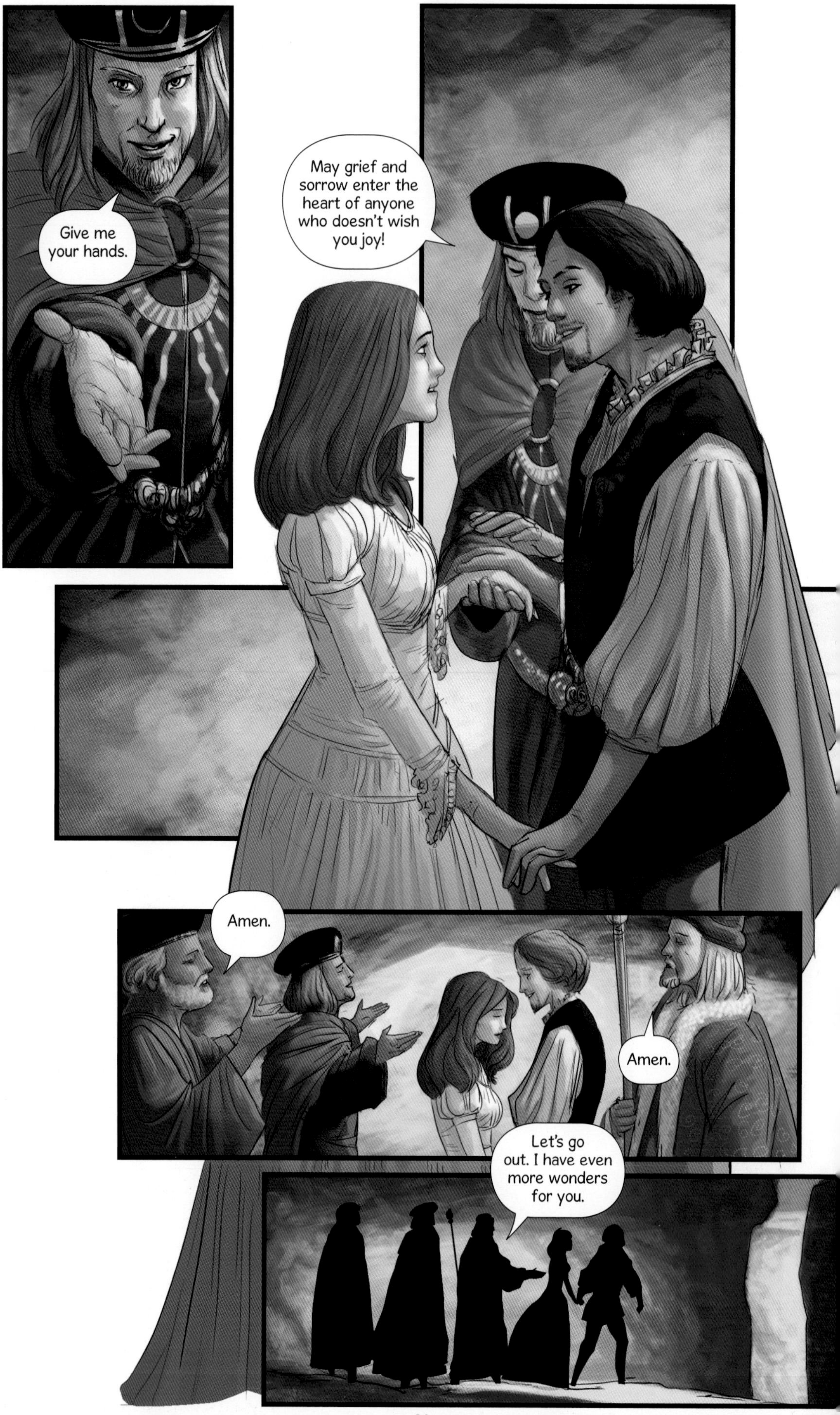
Give me your hands.
May grief and sorrow enter the heart of anyone who doesn't wish you joy!
Amen.
Amen.
Let's go out. I have even more wonders for you.

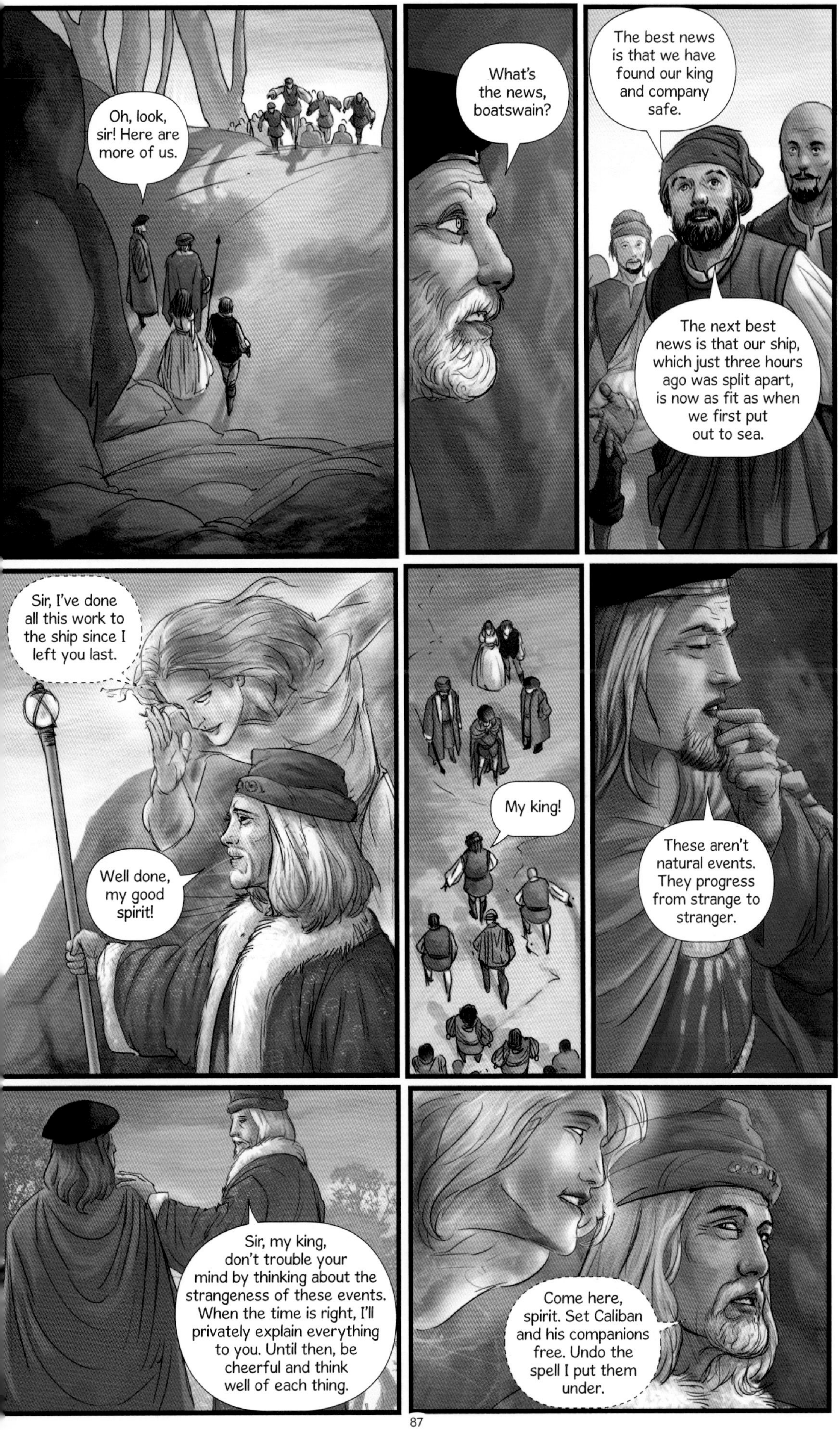

Oh, look, sir! Here are more of us.
What's the news, boatswain?
The best news is that we have found our king and company safe.
The next best news is that our ship, which just three hours ago was split apart, is now as fit as when we first put out to sea.
Sir, I've done all this work to the ship since I left you last.
Well done, my good spirit!
My king!
These aren't natural events. They progress from strange to stranger.
Sir, my king, don't trouble your mind by thinking about the strangeness of these events. When the time is right, I'll privately explain everything to you. Until then, be cheerful and think well of each thing.
Come here, spirit. Set Caliban and his companions free. Undo the spell I put them under.

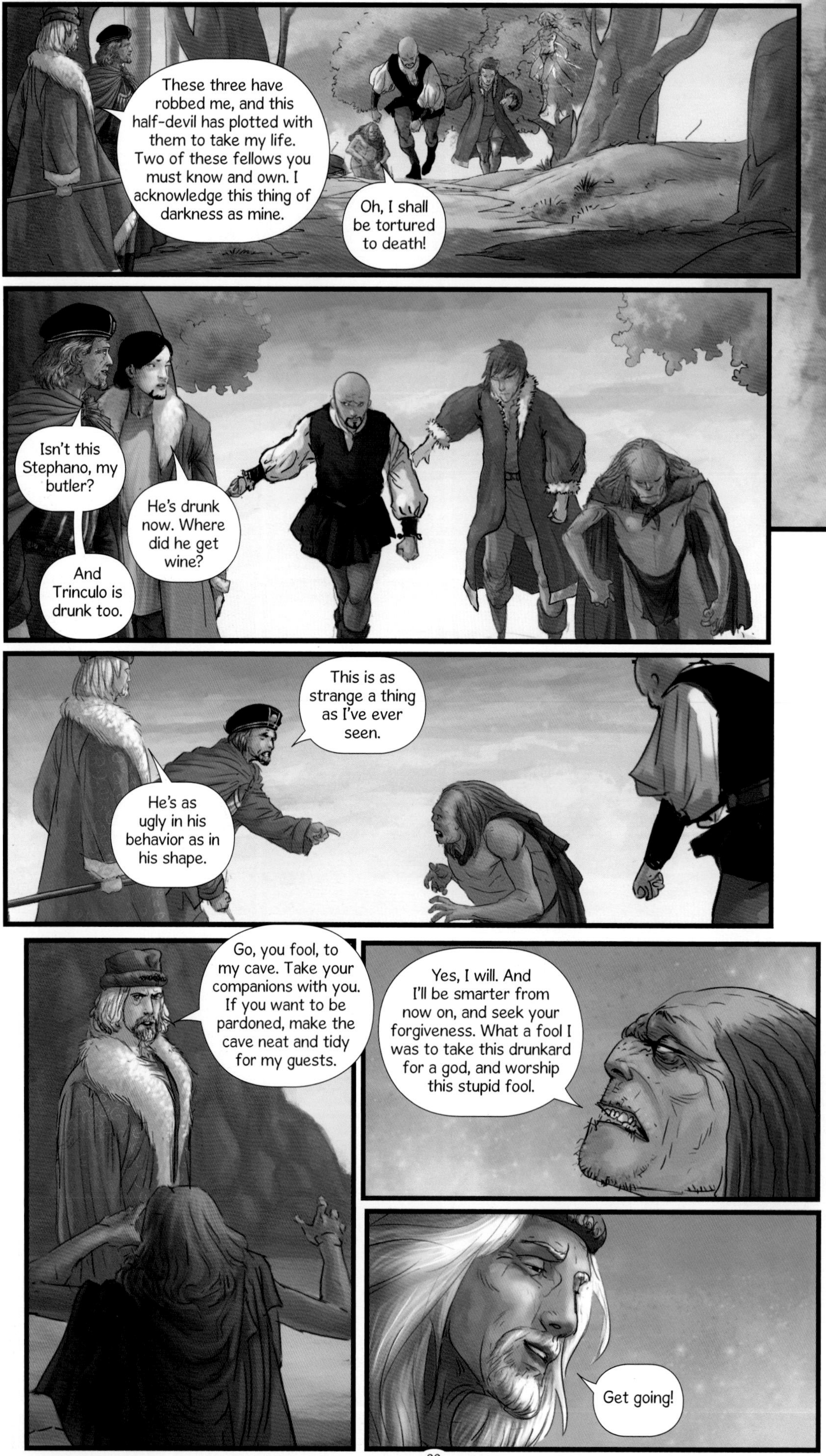
These three have robbed me, and this half-devil has plotted with them to take my life. Two of these fellows you must know and own. I acknowledge this thing of darkness as mine.
Oh, I shall be tortured to death!
Isn't this Stephano, my butler?
And Trinculo is drunk too.
He's drunk now. Where did he get wine?
He's as ugly in his behavior as in his shape.
This is as strange a thing as I've ever seen.
Go, you fool, to my cave. Take your companions with you. If you want to be pardoned, make the cave neat and tidy for my guests.
Yes, I will. And I'll be smarter from now on, and seek your forgiveness. What a fool I was to take this drunkard for a god, and worship this stupid fool.
Get going!

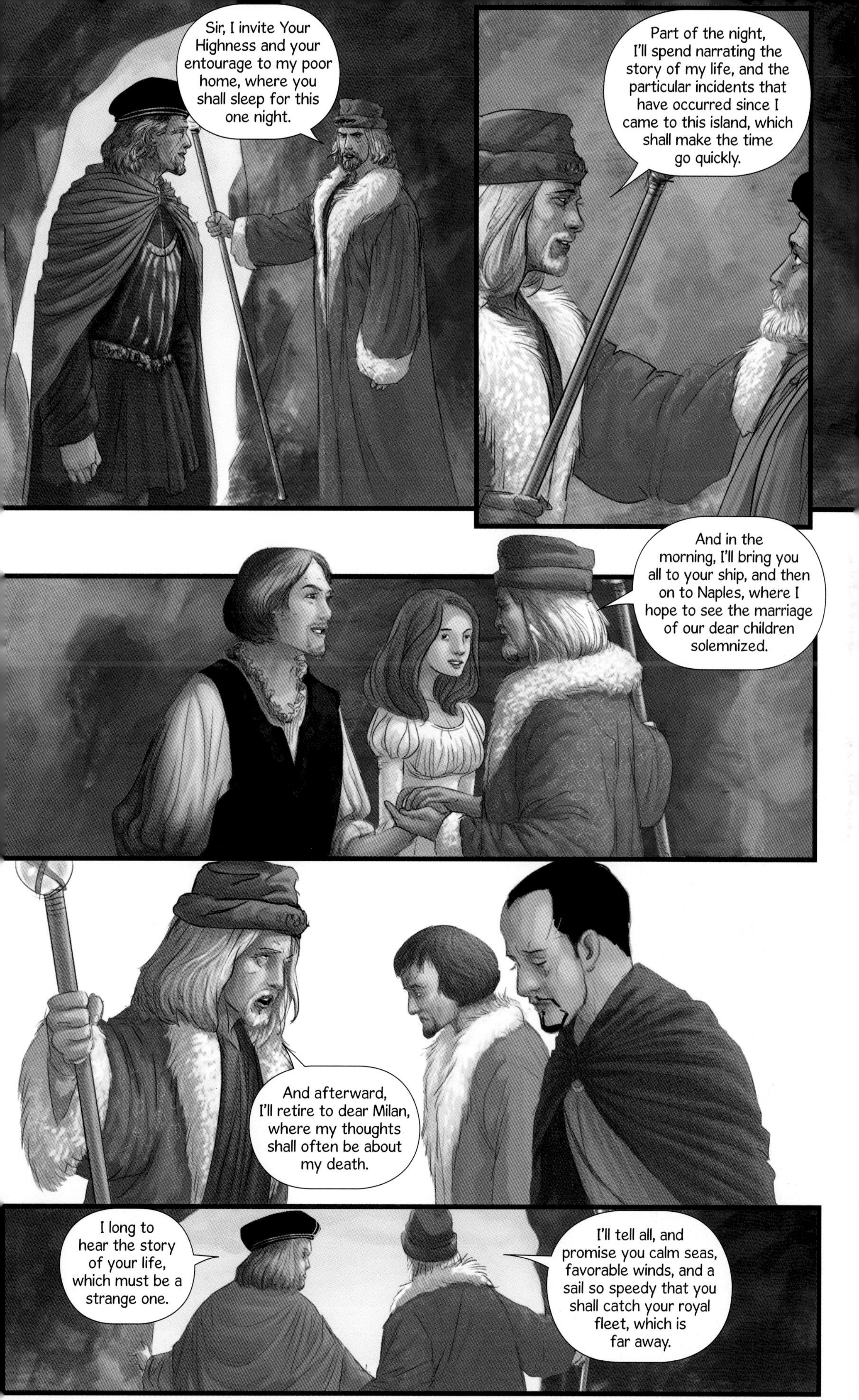
Sir, I invite Your Highness and your entourage to my poor home, where you shall sleep for this one night.
Part of the night, I'll spend narrating the story of my life, and the particular incidents that have occurred since I came to this island, which shall make the time go quickly.
And in the morning, I'll bring you all to your ship, and then on to Naples, where I hope to see the marriage of our dear children solemnized.
And afterward, I'll retire to dear Milan, where my thoughts shall often be about my death.
I long to hear the story of your life, which must be a strange one.
I'll tell all, and promise you calm seas, favorable winds, and a sail so speedy that you shall catch your royal fleet, which is far away.

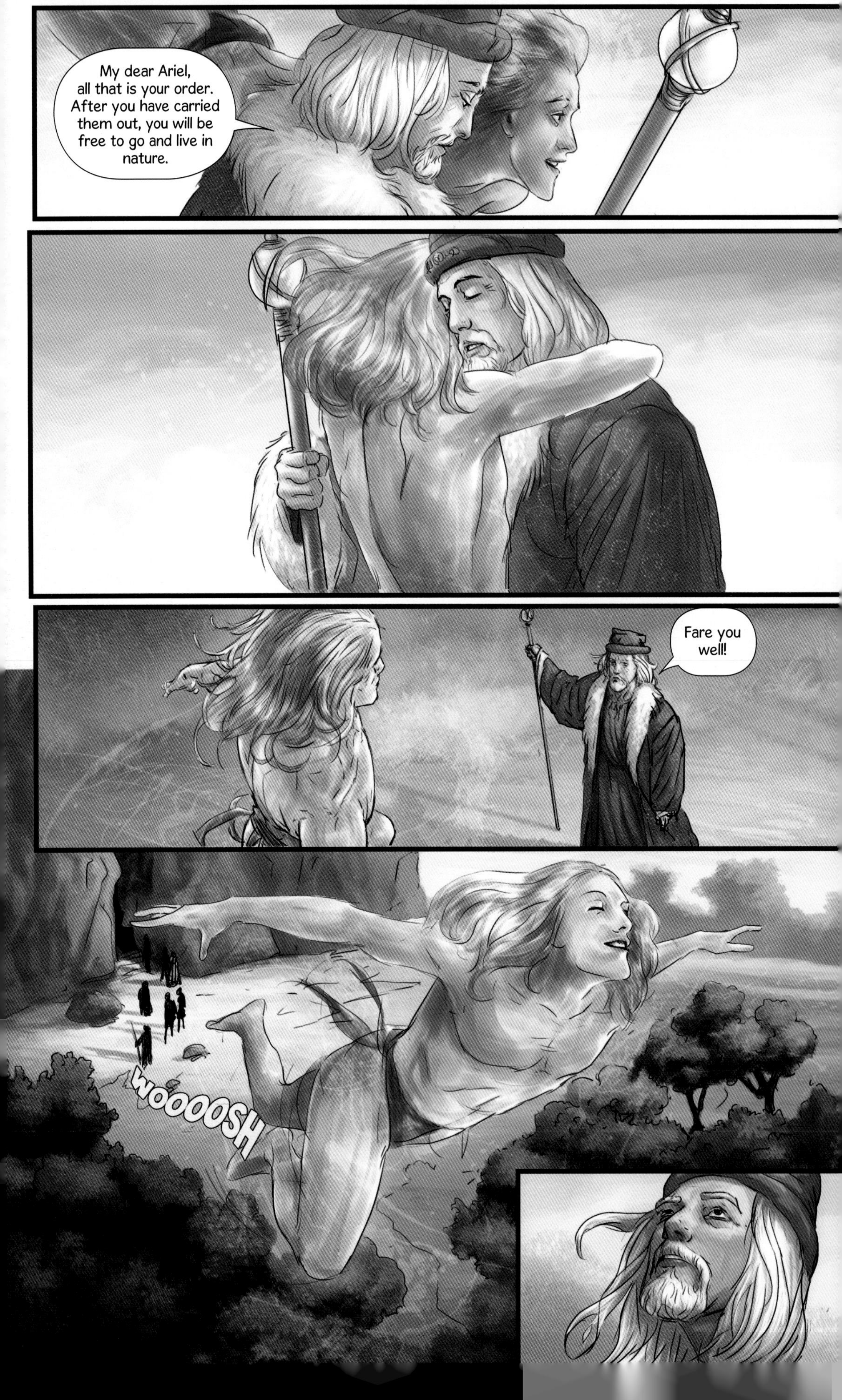
My dear Ariel, all that is your order. After you have carried them out, you will be free to go and live in nature.
Fare you well!
WOOOOSH

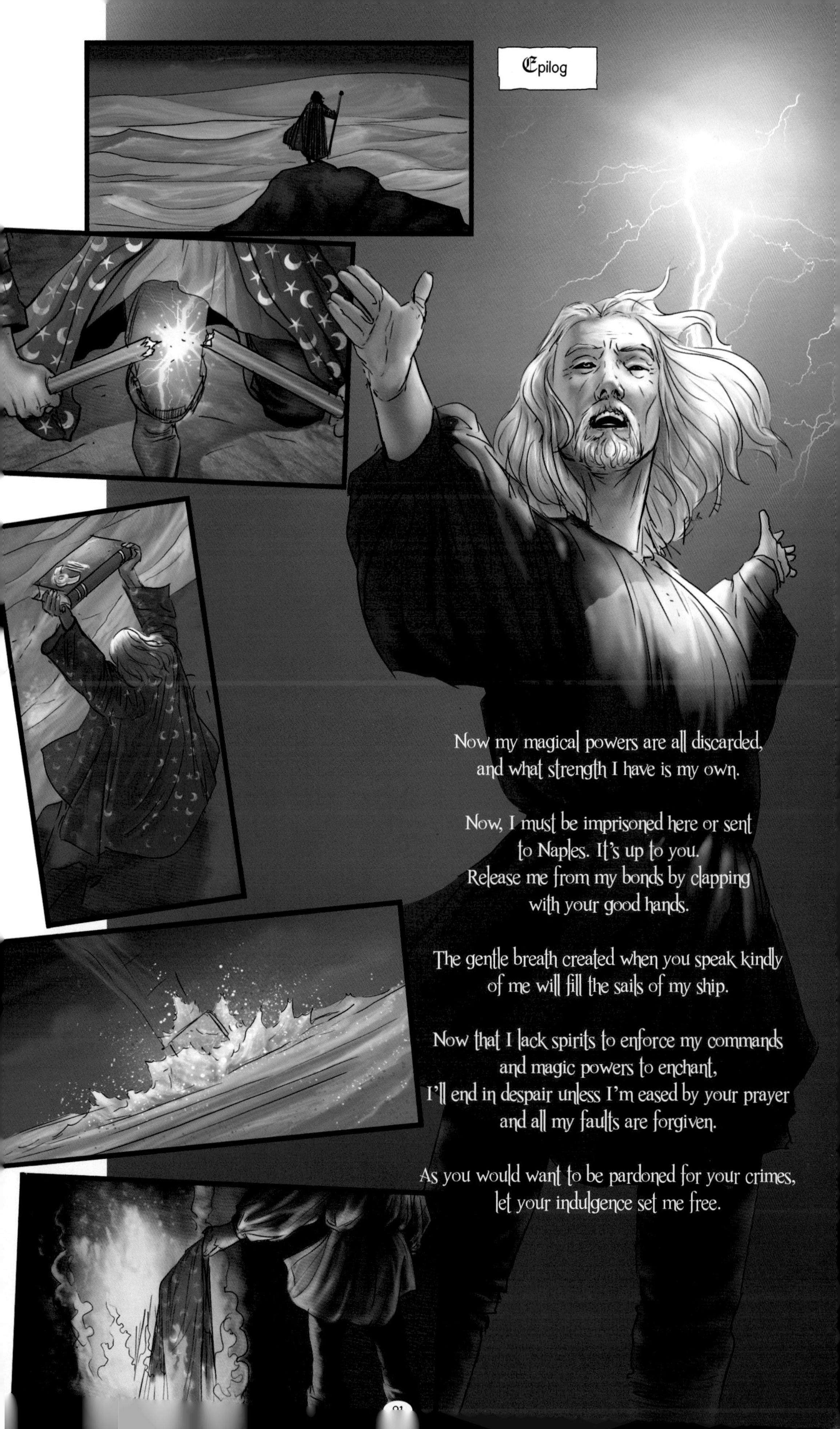
Epilog
Now my magical powers are all discarded,
and what strength I have is my own.
Now, I must be imprisoned here or sent
to Naples. It's up to you.
Release me from my bonds by clapping
with your good hands.
The gentle breath created when you speak kindly
of me will fill the sails of my ship.
Now that I lack spirits to enforce my commands
and magic powers to enchant,
I'll end in despair unless I'm eased by your prayer
and all my faults are forgiven.
As you would want to be pardoned for your crimes,
let your indulgence set me free.

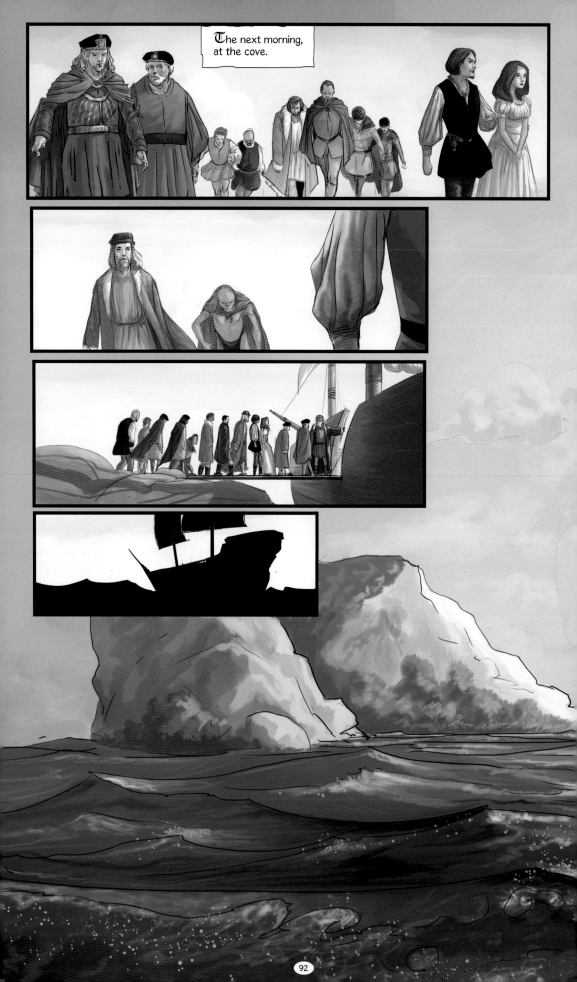

The next morning, at the cove.

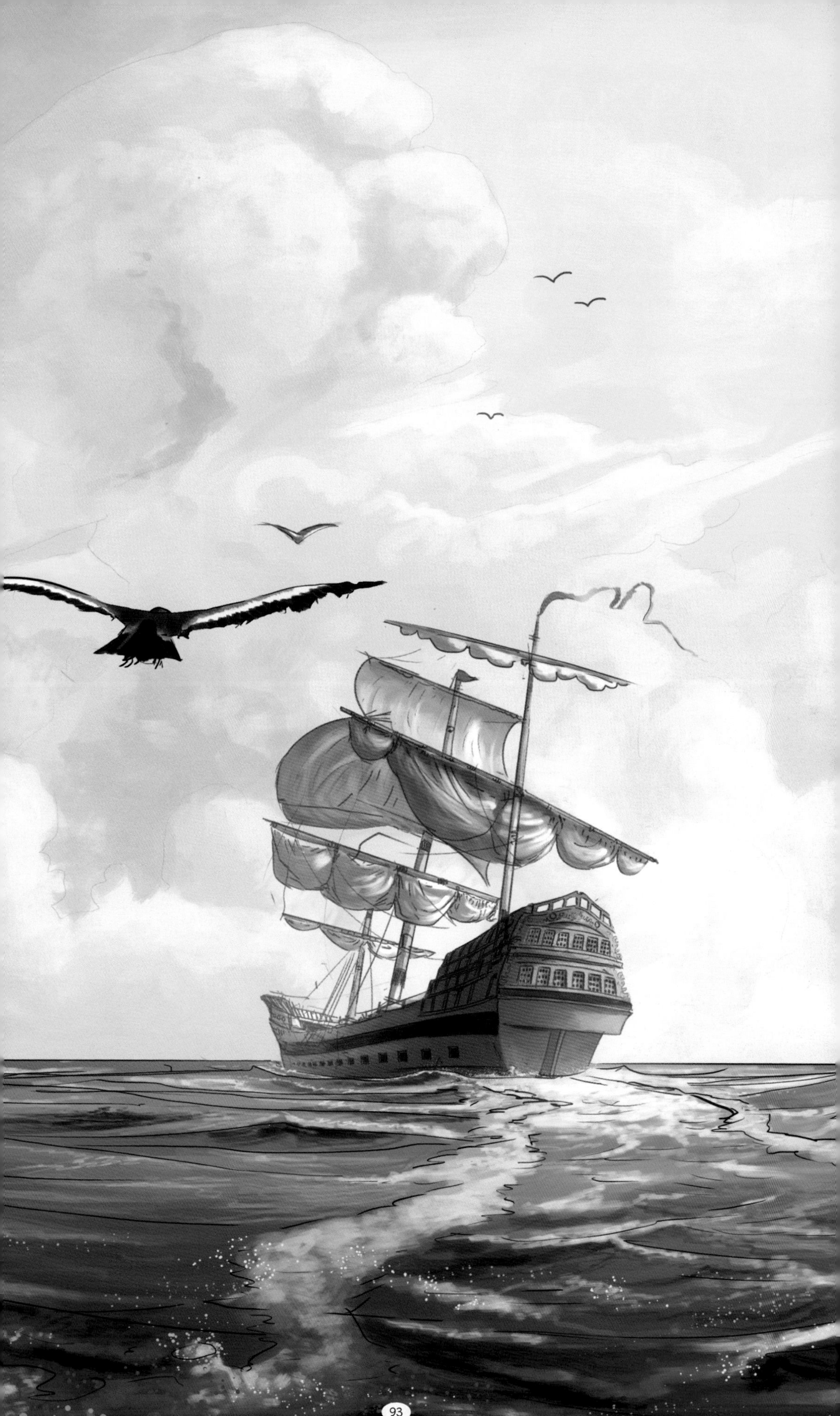

MAGIC AND THE SUPERNATURAL

The 16th century, the age in which Shakespeare lived, was one where magic and the supernatural seemed to be a part of everyday life. The world was a mysterious place to people who did not know the actual cause of diseases and other natural phenomena, and believed they had supernatural causes.

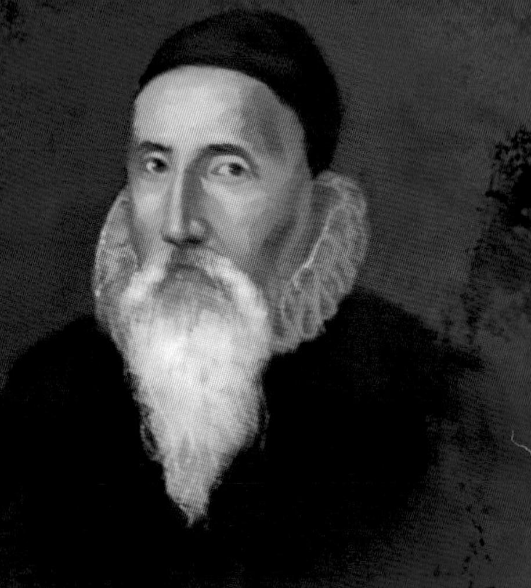

JOHN DEE

The character of Prospero was believed to have been modeled on the famous John Dee. Like Prospero, who was a learned man and practiced rational magic, John Dee was not just a magician, but a great scholar. John Dee was a great mathematician and astronomer, and his studies of navigation and maps helped Elizabethan explorers like Walter Raleigh and Francis Drake discover new lands. He was also a respected philosopher and astrologer, thus making him a trusted advisor to Queen Elizabeth I. He traveled all over Europe and collected so many books that he had the largest library in England. John Dee was deeply fascinated by the supernatural and divination. He experimented with crystal gazing and started working with occultist Edward Kelley, who became his medium to contact angels and spirits. Apparently, the angels and spirits revealed their secrets to them. John Dee became so obsessed with the occult that he spent most of his later life searching for its secrets.

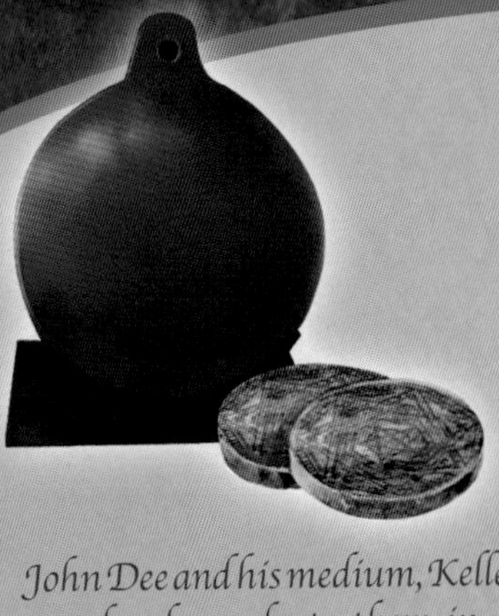

DID YOU KNOW?

You can find Dee's obsidian(volcanic glass)mirror that he used to conjure spirits, the small wax seals which supported the legs of his conjuring table, and a gold amulet engraved with one of Kelley's visions displayed at the British Museum today.

LANGUAGE OF THE ANGELS

John Dee and his medium, Kelley, claimed they conjured angels who spoke to them in a secret language which Dee decoded. Dee's journals described the language as 'Angelical' or 'Adamical' because, according to the angels, it was used by Adam to name all things in Paradise. It is also called 'Enochian language' as Dee declared that Enoch, the Biblical patriarch, had been the last human to know the language.

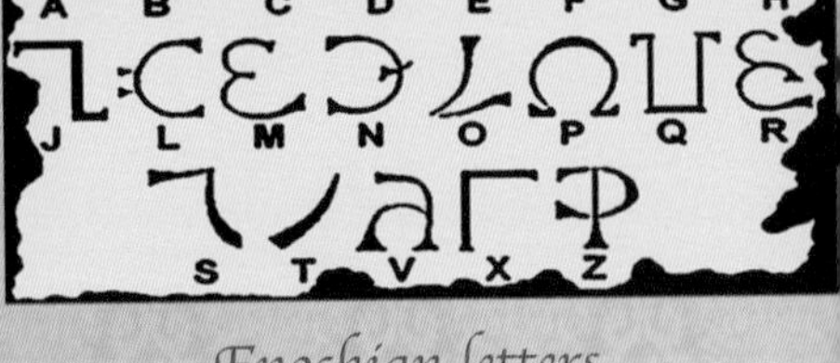
A B C D E F G H
J L M N O P Q R
S T V X Z

Enochian letters

Shakespeare's time was also an age of great expeditions. People certainly wanted to see more and know more. Just imagine the excitement when these adventurous men, bitten by the bug of wanderlust, would stock their ships with food and drinking water and sail across the seas toward unknown destinations. And all they would have were the stars and a compass, or maybe a not-so-authentic map to direct them. Slowly they started establishing new colonies in faraway lands. Scholars have found many parallels in *The Tempest* with the European colonization of newly discovered lands in the 16th and 17th century.

THE NEW WORLD

The New World was the two Americas which had been discovered around the 16th century. Explorers like Richard Hakluyt and Walter Raleigh came back with fantastical tales of exotic places, peoples, and animals. When the Europeans reached these lands, they claimed them as their own. The abundance of natural resources delighted them, and soon gold, tobacco, and fruits were all shipped home. They made the natives work for them as well—some even as slaves.

CALIBAN AND ARIEL AS NEW WORLD NATIVES

Caliban's relation with Prospero is much like the encounter of real-life natives of the New World with the Europeans. The natives lost their land to European colonizers much like Caliban who tells Prospero, 'This island is rightfully mine, because it belonged to Sycorax, my mother. You took it from me'. Caliban is also depicted as a 'savage', which is how most European travelers saw the natives. Similar to what the natives faced, Caliban, too, was made to work like a slave by Prospero. Ariel, who was saved by Prospero but enslaved by him again, is much like the colonized person who hoped to gain freedom by helping the colonizer.

Apart from taking away their lands and freedom, colonizers brought to the natives European diseases like smallpox and influenza, which killed many. They also introduced alcohol to cheat and capture the natives. Caliban's words to Prospero, 'You taught me language, and the benefit I got from it is I know how to curse' implies that what he learned hardly did him any good.

You may also like to read other titles from our

CLASSICS SERIES

William Shakespeare
The MERCHANT of VENICE
Adapted by John F. Mc Donald
Illustrated by Vinod Kumar

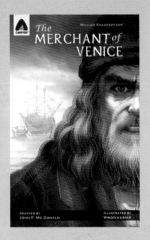

THE MERCHANT OF VENICE

A gamble on trading ships at sea, a penalty of a pound of flesh, a contest to win the hand of a rich heiress, and the final rescue in a court of law—*The Merchant of Venice* has everything to make it one of the most dramatic romantic comedies of Shakespeare. Antonio is the merchant of Venice who borrows money from Shylock, a shrewd moneylender, who devises a retribution unprecedented in the annals of law. Till a young lawyer defeats him in his own game. Who is this young lawyer? What is the clinching argument?

ROMEO AND JULIET

A story of ill-fated lovers whose untimely deaths unite two feuding families, *Romeo and Juliet* has become the archetype of young love destined to meet a tragic end. The hatred between the House of the Capulets and the House of the Montagues is well known in Verona. Yet love blossoms between Romeo and Juliet. A brawl between the kinsmen of the Houses leads to Romeo's exile, and from then on it is a series of misjudgments and chance—of time, place, and event that inexorably play out the lovers' doom.

Romeo & Juliet
William Shakespeare
Adapted by John F McDonald
Illustrated by Sachin Nagar

William Shakespeare
Macbeth
Adapted by Jyoti Bhansali
Illustrated by Naresh Kumar

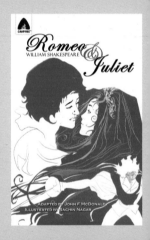

MACBETH

Fair is foul and foul is fair—so said three weird women in ghoulish glee, predicting a subversion of order in fair Scotland. In the reign of King Duncan, Scotland is a just and hospitable land, with loyal, warlike thanes guarding the best interests of people. Till the very best among them, Macbeth, gives in to a fatal temptation and commits regicide. But will the crown of Scotland sit easy on his head? Will justice be restored to Scotland? Or will Macbeth remain invincible?